WYRDE AND WILD

HOUSE OF WERTH: 3

CHARLOTTE E. ENGLISH

ONE

One could scarcely live all one's life as a member of the House of Werth without becoming an expert in the question of dead versus living persons.

As such, when Gussie entered her uncle's London house to find a recumbent person stretched upon the floor of the best parlour, it did not take her long to sum up the essence of the situation.

She reached for the bell.

It was Mrs. Gavell herself who came in answer to the summons, efficient and obliging as a housekeeper ought to be. Gussie wondered, distantly, what had become of the maid.

'Mrs. Gavell,' greeted Gussie. 'I don't know quite how it has come about, but we appear to have developed a corpse.'

'So we have, ma'am,' the housekeeper agreed. 'Most untidy. I shall have it cleared away directly.'

Gussie accepted this, and withdrew to the hall. She had but just come in from an errand, and handed her bonnet and pelisse to the maid — ah yes, that was what had become of the girl, the garment was six inches deep in dirt at the hem and required urgent care. Really, winter could be so tiresome.

A moment's reflection brought her back to the parlour. 'No, stay a moment,' she said. 'There ought to be some manner of enquiry, I suppose?'

'I don't see as how it could be necessary,' said the practical Mrs. Gavell, regarding the prone woman with an air of strong displeasure. 'She's dead as can be, and getting her nasty blood all over the master's good carpet, at that.'

'Indeed, a reasonable person could hardly expect us to sacrifice a good carpet in the name of justice and truth,' Gussie agreed. 'My aunt will be livid. It took her three hours to choose something just perfectly to match the curtains. Coroners, however (and, I daresay, relatives) are not known for possessing a great deal of common sense.'

'You think them interfering Runners will want a look at her,' sighed Mrs. Gavell.

'I think it just possible, yes.' In fact, Gussie was picturing Mr. Ballantine's enraged countenance if she permitted Mrs. Gavell to tidy away the inconvenient remains before he should have had a chance to examine them.

No, not rage; he was not a man of excitable temper. Exasperation, perhaps, and an air of patience strained to breaking-point.

She had caused the man trouble enough of late, she supposed. As amusing as it was to exasperate him — a lady must have something to occupy her, after all — she ought, perhaps, to consult him.

'Send a man out for Mr. Ballantine, please,' she said to Mrs. Gavell.

'Oh, but ma'am, can I not have her moved somewhere else? She won't do any harm in the cellar, however much blood should come out. There's a store-room standing empty just now which might have been made for the purpose.'

'It is a pity about the carpet,' Gussie agreed with regret. 'But I fear we shall have to disappoint my aunt, and leave her as she is. At least until the necessary persons have been informed.'

Mrs. Gavell bustled out, disapproving but resigned, leaving Gussie alone with the corpse.

The unfortunate slain was not a young woman, Gussie surmised, but nor was she of any very advanced age. Her garments were good enough: a decent silk lustring gown in a fashionable shade of red; the pelisse worn over it of good material; a bonnet, modestly trimmed, that looked new. Not a lady, in all likelihood.

Gussie had not an inkling as to who she might be, or, indeed, what she was doing in Lord Werth's parlour.

Her uncle and aunt were not home to ask, and neither was Theo. The latter was at his gentlemen's club, she supposed: Stebbington's, with that fellow Hargreve. The two got into a great deal of mischief together, leaving Gussie quite envious.

She went out of the parlour in search of a footman, and soon discovered one.

His name was Roger, she thought — was it? They were all new, hired a matter of weeks previously, when Lord and Lady Werth had taken up residence at their town-house following an unfortunate — and *entirely* accidental — fire at the Towers. Gussie had not had much to do with the hiring business, her aunt and Mrs. Gavell having arranged matters of staff and furniture between them.

'Roger,' she said, intercepting the young man as he was whisking his way towards the dining-parlour. 'Did you happen to admit a guest to this house anywhere this morning? A lady?'

The footman stood a little straighter in his pristine uniform, and made Gussie a slight bow. 'No, ma'am, I didn't.'

'Oh! I see. Very well then, on you go.'

The same question to the other footman — a nameless fellow, as far as Gussie's memory served — produced the same answer. After that she proceeded to question the maids, and finally Mrs. Gavell herself, and all with the same, curious result.

It appeared that nobody had admitted the woman into the house. There were staff enough to answer the door when somebody knocked, Gussie would have said; so why had nobody let her in? The sound could hardly have been missed; the door-knocker was a solid thing, and set up quite the ruckus when suitably applied.

Had the woman declined to knock? Perhaps she had crept into the house in secret, and wasn't that an appealing idea! Gussie immediately felt more interest in the case.

As she returned into the hall, a knock came upon the very door in question, nicely demonstrating Gussie's notions as to the impossibility of failing to hear it. In fairness, whoever it was *did* seem in something of a hurry, or perhaps displeased; the door shook with the force of the pounding blows upon it.

Gussie opened it, and smiled to find Mr. Ballantine upon the doorstep.

'What,' said he, in an awful voice, 'have you done now, Miss Werth?'

'I *do* like you in that waistcoat,' she replied. 'The red suits you admirably. I suppose that wasn't the entire reason for your becoming a Runner?'

'I didn't choose the profession because the uniform matches my complexion, though I am most gratified by your pointing it out. And now an answer to my question, if you please.'

Gussie stepped back, opening the door wide, and permitting him to stamp over the threshold. 'I haven't done anything, except one or two things I flatter myself you will find useful. For example, you'll be interested to know that none of the servants remembers admitting the woman to this house today, or ever at all. Is not that fascinating?'

'Which woman, where is she, and how came she to be a corpse?' Mr. Ballantine brushed past her, a trifle rudely, but Gussie plumed herself on her patience, and did not point it out.

'I do not have the first idea of her identity,' Gussie answered, shutting the door, and smiling down the perplexed footman who had appeared in order to answer it. 'I am sorry, Roger. I know it is eccentric of me to answer the door, and most likely improper, but I happened to be passing.'

An expression of mild disapproval crossed Roger's face, quickly suppressed, and he went away again.

Ballantine missed nothing of this. 'The poor fellows will soon grow used to you, I daresay, Miss Werth.'

'You don't believe that at all.'

'As a matter of fact, I don't. Take me to this unfortunate woman, please. I can only hope she knew what disaster was like to follow her entrance to this house.'

'Very likely not,' said Gussie cheerfully. 'She is this way. Now, I have, as I've told you, questioned the servants already, though you may perhaps have some enquiries of your own to make—' She stopped at the parlour-door, crestfallen, for besides an unfortunate quantity of drying blood upon the carpet, no sign remained of the deceased.

Mr. Ballantine, behind her, sighed. 'Some fresh calamity, I collect?'

Gussie advanced into the parlour, and conducted a search of the room. She did not really expect to find the slain woman hidden behind her aunt's favourite divan, or concealed behind the drapes, but one was obliged to make certain.

'No body,' observed Mr. Ballantine, pausing before the blood-stain, and frowning down at it.

'Not that it is much out of the ordinary for a corpse to think better of lying about, and take a turn about the room.'

'In this house I don't suppose it is. Still, were she in such a state as to permit of it, I don't imagine I would have been sent for.'

'No, I did not imagine it likely,' Gussie agreed. 'She did

appear to be very freshly dead, and was quite inert. And my uncle, you know, is not here this morning, so he cannot have had anything to do with it.' An idea occurred to her, and she rang the bell again. 'Mrs. Gavell was quite insistent on removing her,' she explained to Mr. Ballantine. 'I did give instructions otherwise, but the degree of her concern about the carpet was of such a nature that she might have—'

'About the *carpet*?' interrupted Mr. Ballantine.

'Yes. It is new, you see, and my aunt is so fond of it— ah,' she said to the maid just appearing at the door. 'Please enquire of Mrs. Gavell if she should happen to have removed the deceased person from in here after all. I shall quite understand if she has, and she is not to imagine herself in any trouble.'

The maid returned Gussie a wide-eyed stare, and with a wobbly curtsey went away.

'Do you have any trouble retaining servants as a rule, Miss Werth?' said Ballantine.

'I cannot at all imagine why we would,' said Gussie with some impatience. 'Really, one would think we were a troublesome family.'

'My mistake.'

Mrs. Gavell soon arrived, and, observing the unmistakeable absence of corpse, set her hands upon her hips. 'Well, I cannot say as I'm not glad of it,' she declared. '*Such* a mess as she was making! But no, ma'am, I did not ask for her to be taken out, and I'm certain none of the servants has done so.'

'Then there is nothing for it but to search the house,' Gussie decided. 'She cannot have gone very far, can she?'

In fact, she could, or so Gussie was forced to conclude.

'Not a single corpse in the whole building!' she said rather later, having participated in the search with great enthusiasm. Mr. Ballantine had not. He had confined himself to the parlour, where, he claimed, he would "examine the scene". But when Gussie returned to the room, out of breath and patience both, she found him seated calmly upon a chair by the window.

'Unfortunate,' said he, looking up at her. 'Either she has revived, then, in a fashion corpses are sometimes prone to do in these parts—'

'You refer, of course, to my uncle,' Gussie put in. 'And as I have said, he is not at home, so he cannot have interfered.'

'—or someone has removed her remains,' finished Mr. Ballantine. 'The same person, perhaps, who left her here in the first place.'

'The same person who killed her, you mean.'

'I don't know that yet.' He returned his gaze to the stained spot upon the floor. 'Did you happen to take note of how she died?'

'Oh, certainly! I should say she was savaged to death.'

'Savaged?'

Gussie nodded, smiling. 'There was, as you can see, a fair bit of blood, and her throat was entirely a ruin.'

'A ruin.'

'Quite.'

'If you would be so good as to try again, Miss Werth, in less dramatic language. How was it ruined? Slashed, say, with the blade of a knife? Crushed? What manner of weapon made the wound?'

Gussie smiled again, showing all her teeth. 'I would not say as it was any weapon at all, Mr. Ballantine, save those a person is born with.'

'She was bitten.'

'Yes, and untidily, too. Theo would be appalled.'

Mention of Theo's name brought Ballantine's keen gaze back to Gussie's face. 'Ah, yes. And where is Lord Bedgberry this morning?'

'At his club, I should imagine. He has been frequenting Stebbington's a great deal of late. He has scarcely come home all week.'

'Stebbington's,' sighed Mr. Ballantine. 'It would be that,

7

of course.'

Two

In point of fact, Theodore Werth — otherwise known as Lord Bedgberry, and (incidentally) the next heir to the Werth Earldom — was not at Stebbington's at that moment.

He was at the bottom of somebody's garden, with a shovel in his hands, hastily burying a certain corpse.

He couldn't have meant to kill the woman, of course – not that he remembered having done so, but that could not be said to matter. A few weeks' carousing had not, as yet, given him much of a head for liquor, and the events of the previous night – indeed, most nights — remained hazy. Nor had his head yet ceased to pound, and the sensation was distracting; every *whack* and *thud* of the shovel in the half-frozen earth prompted another sickening ache, and his temper was not in good order.

At this hour, he should be at home in bed, sleeping it off. Or still at the club, as Gussie had surmised.

He did not remember coming home, though he must have done so at some point. He *certainly* did not remember bringing a woman with him.

What had possessed him to snatch her? Had he carted her after him, like a sack of flour, and dumped her in the parlour? What on *earth* for?

It was as he had always feared, he supposed: the thirst had got the better of him, and in his addled and drunken state he had been unequal to resist the urge to slake it by any means available. The means in question must have been that unfortunate woman. Her limp form lay, like a silent reproach, on the frosted ground while he urgently prepared her impromptu tomb.

But that didn't make sense either. Theo's thoughts moved sluggishly and reluctantly, but even he had to conclude, after some little time, that he could not have been thirsty when he had come home from Stebbington's the night before. He had imbibed a great deal besides the liquor, and must have been happily sated.

And what could he have been doing in his mother's parlour – with, or without, a lifeless female? He never went in there, except when summoned to present himself.

He paused his digging, and took a moment to catch his breath. He stared, only half seeing, at the prone and insensate woman, and sighed. What a deal of nonsense.

Theo was rarely unhappy, and never self-reproaching, but that morning he was labouring under sensations of both. Either he had killed this unfortunate female in an uncontrollable lust for her blood, or – a better prospect, but not by much – he had interrupted the perfectly legitimate rest of a woman somebody else had partaken of, and now proposed to award her an ignominious grave next to somebody's prized rose-bushes.

Whose garden had he fetched up in? He glanced wildly about, struck all of a sudden by this thought, when it had not seemed to matter before.

Devil take it. He was still drunk, or – something. Fuddled.

'I suppose this won't do,' he informed the corpse. 'I shouldn't like to be slung into an unmarked grave by a shambling drunkard, and I don't suppose you are much enjoying it, either.'

He would have to take her back again, which was awfully inconvenient, for she was heavy, and Theo was tired.

Still, that was his own fault. Having passed the parlour door on his way in — and it having been standing open — he had caught sight of the woman's remains and… panicked, he supposed, like a small, startled animal. Not at all the thing. He could only hope that he could take her back again, quietly, and nobody would ever know that she'd been gone.

And after that, he would go to bed.

Which was what Theo did, supremely untroubled by the question of who *else* might have left a freshly-killed female lying on the floor of his mother's best parlour. Some freak of Lady Werth's, he supposed, and why shouldn't she keep a body or two about the place, if she liked it?

Lady Werth arrived home some few hours later, fresh from an engagement with the lavishly Wyrded Gouldings, and in high good humour.

This lasted until she entered her own, comfortable parlour, happily entertaining thoughts of a pot of tea, and discovered what had become of the room in her absence.

The bell was, once again, rung.

'Do please have this removed,' she requested of the harried maid, whose appalled stare at the spectacle of the corpse upon the carpet did not bode well for her career in the household. 'And pray ask Mrs. Gavell what she can manage by way of removing all that blood,' she added.

'It's back,' said the maid, incomprehensibly. 'Oh, sorry, my lady. I mean, *she's* back.'

Finding this babbling unintelligible, Lady Werth ignored it. 'Pray be a little quicker about it, my dear. I suppose it is too late to prevent any severe damage to the furnishings, but I should like to try. Oh! And while you are about it, please have Lord Bedgberry sent in.'

11

Really, it was careless of Theo to have left the remains of his meal in *here*, of all places. Careless of him all round, in fact, for he did not ordinarily kill when he dined, and it was most unlike him to make such a mess of it.

Lady Werth reposed herself in a chair far from the remains – they were not yet beginning to smell, thank goodness, but she preferred to avoid getting any blood on her gown as well as her carpets – and composed herself to wait.

It was neither Theo nor Mrs. Gavell who appeared first, however, but Gussie.

'The corpse is back!' she carolled as she swept in, her hands clasped together in delight. 'Famous!'

Dimly aware of some parallel between Gussie's pronouncement and the maid's, Lady Werth enquired.

'Oh, she was discovered in here earlier this morning,' said Gussie, striding over to the inert remains, and looming over them. 'Then she disappeared. Mr Ballantine was most displeased — he really gains nothing in liveliness or good humour, does he? — and went away in high dudgeon. But here she is again! I wonder how she came to get all this mud on her? She appears lifeless, as before, so I think it unlikely that she removed *herself* from the house. But perhaps it was only a temporary return to life and feeling, and she has gone off again.'

'Well, and I never!' said Mrs. Gavell, coming into the room all in a flurry. 'What with bodies appearing and disappearing, I hardly know whether I'm coming or going! I am sorry, my lady. I had Jane do her best with the carpet, but if people *will* keep disposing of their corpses in your ladyship's best parlour—'

Poor Mrs. Gavell was deeply aggrieved, as Lady Werth readily perceived. She was a dedicated and conscientious woman, and would not appreciate these attacks upon the spotlessness of her housekeeping. 'I quite understand, Mrs. Gavell,' she said. 'No blame can attach to you, I assure you. I shall, however, be *most* pleased if the unfortunate woman could be removed, once and for all.'

'You and me both, your ladyship,' said Mrs. Gavell grimly.

'Mr. Ballantine will be delighted by the news, I don't doubt,' put in Gussie. 'He was so disappointed to be deprived of a subject for his investigation.'

'Investigation?' echoed Lady Werth, aware of a feeling of foreboding. 'Mr. Ballantine has been called in, has he?'

'Yes! And now he will have to question all of us, which *will* be exciting for him. I'm so pleased.'

'Why…' began Lady Werth, but did not trouble to complete the sentence. People did tend to make rather a fuss about unexplained bodies; she had been a resident at Werth Towers, and the wife of Lord Werth, for so long as to forget this.

'Was it Theo?' she said instead, with weary resignation.

'I do not think Theo was home this morning,' Gussie said, this pronouncement reviving her aunt's flagging spirits a little. 'So I do not think it was he. Though I must own, he sneaks about so that I cannot keep up with his whereabouts at all. Perhaps it *was* him, after all. How disappointing. I should have liked to have someone else for the villain.'

'Your loyalty to your cousin is gratifying, if uncharacteristic.'

'Nothing of the kind,' said Gussie firmly. 'Theo has been the villain of the family for so long that there can be nothing left to interest me about it. Besides, if Theo has done it, then there is no mystery about the matter at all.'

'You would prefer a mystery, I collect?'

'Why, of course. If there is a culprit to be discovered, then I shall have to exercise my wits, shan't I? And when I present the answer to Mr. Ballantine, all neatly resolved, he can hardly continue to deny me a place at Bow Street.'

Lady Werth had enjoyed hopes that Gussie had divested herself of this latest of her mad ideas. She relinquished these hopes, faint though they had been, with a sigh.

Theo appeared at last, rumpled and displeased. 'What can be the matter now?' he demanded, hovering upon the threshold, and regarding the gathering in the parlour with misgiving. His gaze fell upon the corpse. 'Really, Mother, I would have thought you would have finished with that by now. Ordered it in for father's amusement, did you?'

'A fine idea,' said Gussie, in her tart way. 'My uncle has been a little low in spirits since the fire. A body or two would be just the thing to cheer him up.'

Lady Werth permitted this to pass without comment. 'Am I to understand that the presence of this unfortunate has nothing to do with you, Theo?' She watched his face closely as he answered, aware that he had never been much given to falsehood, even as a boy. He felt little shame, and therefore, could have no reason to lie.

'Nothing whatsoever,' he declared. 'That is, I did take the woman away for just a short while, but—'

'Why, Theo!' interrupted Gussie. 'How delightfully peculiar of you! I begin to take heart again.'

'Thought I might have done it, you see,' Theo explained. 'Better tidy up.'

'Hide the evidence, you mean,' Gussie surmised. 'For I cannot think you gave much thought to the fate of your mamma's comfortable arrangements.'

Lady Werth lifted a brow. 'Nor is it like you to hide your leavings. What could you have been thinking?'

'Drunk,' said Theo briefly.

Lady Werth permitted herself a small sigh.

'You become very nearly a rake, Theo,' Gussie said. 'Positively dissolute. I salute you. It just occurs to me to ask, however: *did* you kill the lady?'

'Can't have. I had enough blood last night to fill up a cow.'

'A delightful vision.'

'Perhaps two.'

'So,' said Gussie, walking a thoughtful circle around the

corpse. 'Let us attempt to reconstruct the events, as far as we know them. This woman died, by means and by villain unknown, and ended up in here, we know not how or why. But it most *definitely* wasn't Theo.' She directed an arch, shrewd look at her cousin as she spoke, a look many a man might have squirmed under, but not Theo. He merely nodded.

'Theo became aware of its presence somehow,' Gussie continued.'

'Wandered in,' Theo put in. 'Drunk, you know.'

'Theo was drunk and is therefore useless as a witness, even as to his own actions and motives,' said Gussie. 'But we would still like to hear where he took the body.'

Theo shrugged. 'I was going to bury it, but it's harder work than I thought.'

'You went grave-digging.'

'Only got a few inches into it.' Theo's tone was half apologetic. 'Ground's rather hard just at present.'

'Was this in a graveyard? I hardly dare ask.'

'No.' Theo waved his hand, vaguely. 'Garden somewhere.'

Gussie appeared to be in a state of no uncommon enjoyment. 'Lord Bedgberry attempted to give the woman a, shall we say, *decent* burial in some unsuspecting soul's garden, but finding the task a little too tiring he abandoned the project.'

'Brought her back here.' Theo seemed to be rapidly losing interest in the subject.

'And thus deposited the slain back onto his mother's freshly-cleaned carpet, before retiring, untroubled, to bed.'

'Yes, that's about it.'

'Thank you, Theo. That is most helpful.'

Theo accepted this, either unconscious of the irony or merely uninterested in it. 'Any chance of some chocolate?' he said to his mother. 'Might do something for this headache.'

'A night or two at home would do a great deal more for

it,' said Lady Werth. 'That man Hargreve dissipates you, Theo.'

'I can't tonight. Theatre.'

The arrival of the coroner put an end to this exchange before Lady Werth could remonstrate again with her son. He slipped away, and she did not attempt to prevent him. The blame for the night's events would likely fall on Theo's head, a fact that seemed, at present, to be escaping him. Let him sleep, while he could.

THREE

'You do not really imagine that Theo did it, do you?' said Gussie, a little later.

Mr. Ballantine had conducted a fresh examination of the scene, to little effect, as far as Gussie could tell. He had then been plied with refreshments by Lady Werth – her aunt felt more concern over the matter than might appear from her serene countenance, Gussie concluded – and now sat in the drawing-room, holding a delicate porcelain plate upon which reposed an untouched cake. A glass of wine sat, ignored, at his elbow.

The way to the Runner's good graces was not through food, it seemed.

Mr. Ballantine had been absorbed in thought, his gaze fixed on some indeterminate point beyond the winter-fogged window. Now he stirred, and glanced at Gussie. 'Your concern for your cousin is very natural, Miss Werth.'

'I am in no way concerned. The worst they could possibly do to him is hang him, and I imagine he would rather enjoy that than otherwise. I ask because, as an explanation, it is much too trite. There must be something else afoot.'

Her own wishes doubtless influenced her reason, and

she knew it. This might, perhaps, explain the extent of her delight when Mr. Ballantine said: 'You may be right.'

'Really!'

A brow quirked. 'I admit the case looks simple enough, on the face of it. Lord Bedgberry admits to having handled the corpse. A witness may easily be found to his having carried it through the streets of London, no doubt, for by his own admission, he was in no state to be circumspect. And a man who has done this much without hesitation or distaste may easily be capable of worse – of having, in short, killed the woman as well. But.'

'But!' said Gussie, when he paused. 'I am immensely encouraged to discover that there is a *but*.'

So was Lady Werth, by her demeanour of studied serenity. She sipped wine, and waited.

'But it is, as you said, rather trite. A man known for his unusual taste in sustenance is so dead to all possible consequence as to – *savage* a woman, as you put it, Miss Werth, and then abandon the body in his own parlour?'

'In fairness to Theo, he *could* be so dead to all possible consequence,' Gussie felt honour-bound to interject.

'Perhaps. I cannot claim a close acquaintance with Lord Bedgberry, but I have some passing familiarity with his ways. He has been a resident of the city for many weeks already, and has done nothing of the kind; nor did he have any taste for it at the Towers. It seems odd, therefore, that he should suddenly have taken to it now. And while he may be oblivious to convention – and occasionally, I might say, to law – he is by no means a foolish man. Even in a state of inebriation, I cannot imagine he would have been so careless as to dispose of the remains in this house.'

'Though that is exactly what he did do,' said Gussie. 'Having tried, first, to hide her, he then brought her back! Only Theo could behave so absurdly.'

'Gussie,' said Lady Werth, in a low tone.

'Yes, you do right to stop me,' Gussie allowed. 'I do not at all want Theo to be the villain of the piece, yet I am

18

arguing as though I do. Pray continue, Mr. Ballantine.'

'These do not seem the actions of a guilty man,' persevered the Runner. 'Attempting to hide her might be, but to bring her back again? No.'

'So Theo is exonerated.' Gussie beamed.

'In my mind, yes, but the case against him still looks very black,' Mr. Ballantine cautioned. 'I fear no one else would believe in his innocence.'

'We must find out who is guilty, then, and quickly.'

'Yes, we must. As yet I have no notion who the poor lady is, but I hope to rectify that soon. As to how, or why, she was abandoned in this house…' He hesitated. 'If it was not Lord Bedgberry, and we will take it as read, for a moment, that it was not either of you—' He paused, here, and looked at them both.

'You know it cannot have been my aunt,' said Gussie, casting a mischievous glance at Lady Werth. 'She would never have done anything that might damage the furniture.'

'Murder is one thing, but to ruin a carpet quite another?' said Mr. Ballantine.

'Indeed. As for me, I have never committed any murders at all. Not a single one. I hope you will not think the less of me for it.'

'I am sure you will get around to it in time, Miss Werth, if it should ever strike your fancy.'

'Which it very well might,' she mused. 'Like buying a new bonnet, or forming a new acquaintance. Very refreshing.'

Mr. Ballantine relented. 'In point of fact, I think your guess was correct, Miss Werth. The probable manner of the woman's demise lets the two of you out, for neither of you has the teeth for it. This is also true of Lord Werth, Miss Frostell, Lady Honoria, and all the servants. Therefore, whoever committed this deed is very likely not of this household. I must consider, therefore, two questions: how did they gain entry to the house in order to leave the body here? And, perhaps even more importantly: *why* did they do so?'

'You mean that we have an enemy!' Gussie crowed. 'Someone is trying to pin the blame on Theo! How wonderful.'

'I wonder if his lordship will find it so?'

'Theo exists now in such a stupor, he won't know anything about it.'

'You disapprove of his friendship with Mr. Hargreve.'

'Oh, no. I am thoroughly entertained by it.' She rose from her seat, downing the dregs of her own glass of wine. 'If you will excuse me, I seem to have a great deal to do.'

'For example?' said Mr. Ballantine, suspicious.

'First I must locate Great-Aunt Honoria. I would like to know if she was drifting about down here last night, as she very well may have been. If she was, you know, she might have observed how our new corpse came to arrive.'

'A good notion,' Ballantine allowed.

'And then a message must be sent to my uncle to present himself at—' She paused. 'Wherever it is unexplained bodies are taken in London.'

'What on earth for— oh, I see. You propose that she should be questioned.'

'Of course. If anybody knows anything about how she came to die, it must be the deceased herself. And after that I must compose a letter to General Sir Robert Epworth. Having so obligingly assisted him with Wyrding his soldiers, I intend that he should assist *me* with one or two things.'

This attracted Lady Werth's attention. She looked sharply at her niece, and said: 'Ah yes, *that* business.'

'I know you disapprove, Aunt, but it went off very well, I assure you. A fair number of fellows were Wyrded, but if they are to become a danger to the public, well, that is a problem for General Sir Robert Epworth.'

'And has he not already rewarded you for your participation?'

Gussie wrinkled her nose. 'He has promised that I and my Wyrde shall be suitably legitimised by the authorities, yes. And while I wait for that process to complete, I just have one or two other tasks for him. For one thing, I intend that he shall legitimise the rest of us, particularly Theo.'

'I suppose it must be done,' said Lady Werth.

'Except for Lady Margery. I am persuaded she would order me baked into a pie and served with a good dessert wine, were I to attempt it.'

Mr. Ballantine sat frowning. 'What precisely does it mean to be *suitably legitimised*, Miss Werth?'

'I am to be declared undangerous,' she smiled. 'A threat to nobody whatsoever, and free to go about my own business as I choose.'

Mr. Ballantine considered this. 'Has General Sir Robert Epworth met you at all?'

'No, he was not present for my visit to the camp.'

'That would account for his making such a colossal misjudgement, then.'

Gussie beamed at him. 'I own I am a little disappointed, but I quite see the practicality of it. It would be tiresome to be always an object of suspicion.'

'It would interfere with many an excellent scheme, no doubt.'

'Precisely. I wish you good day, Mr. Ballantine. Aunt.' She made her curtsey and withdrew, leaving Lady Werth and the Runner to entertain each other with their concerns, if they would.

Gussie swept up the stairs. Great-Aunt Honoria spent a great deal of her time out in the city, finding London endlessly absorbing ("So many people!" she had once explained. "And so busy! Like chickens, running and flapping about. Look! See how they squawk!". Nothing amused her so well as to manifest suddenly before some unsuspecting Cit on his way to his bank, or some fine lady strolling in the park, and get a little blood on them).

However, when she was at home she preferred to haunt a disused garret chamber. Gussie suspected she missed the cobwebs at the Towers.

Curiously, as she mounted the last of the attic stairs and strode down the passage, she heard voices coming from Lady Honoria's chamber. One certainly belonged to Honoria herself, but the second she did not recognise. It didn't sound like Great-Uncle Silvester's grinding tones, quite.

'Great-Aunt?' she called, and made sure to knock firmly upon the door.

'Come in!' carolled her aunt, with a ripple of laughter. 'Oh, Gussie! Lovely! *Do* come in. Ivo, permit me to introduce you to my niece: Augusta *Honoria* Werth. Do you see? She was named after me!'

Gussie stood, frozen with momentary surprise, only halfway through the door. Her aunt had, as usual, manifested only her head, and a little of her neck, the latter terminating in a ragged and bloodied stump. Apart from this, she was looking remarkably well: she appeared younger than the last time Gussie had seen her, by a full decade at least, and her eyes sparkled. Her white-bewigged hair, arranged in the fashion of the last century (when she had last been alive) was dressed higher than ever, and draped, not in cobwebs, but pearls.

Great-Aunt Honoria had, in short, conducted her toilet with unusual care.

And all for this Ivo, Gussie surmised, for her manner to him was positively *flirtatious.*

Well, Gussie was equal to anything. If she could accept the presence of *one* severed head about the place, she could easily accustom herself to a second.

'What a pleasure, Mr...?' she said, making her curtsey to the gentleman.

'It is Mr. Farthing, my dear,' said he, congenially. 'Though please call me Ivo.'

'Then you must address me as Gussie,' she said.

'Everyone else does.' Except for Mr. Ballantine, she recollected, who continued to call her "Miss Werth" with tiresome formality.

Mr. Farthing, or Ivo, seemed a youngish man, which might account for her great-aunt's partial transformation. He had been rotund in life, and still possessed a round-cheeked face and a double chin. His own neck had been more neatly severed than Lady Honoria's, and was free of blood. He was either more fastidious than she, then, or did not take the same ghoulish delight in terrifying those about him.

Gussie rather liked his smile, and he had friendly brown eyes.

'What a fine girl she is!' declared Ivo, smiling upon Lady Honoria. 'For a living woman, I mean.'

'Yes, no doubt death will improve me,' Gussie agreed. 'Those who take an interest in my well-being are hoping for the happy event any day now.'

'You will have a delightful funeral,' said Lady Honoria. 'Charming! I have made all the arrangements.'

This was news to Gussie, and not entirely welcome. 'Well, but tell me how the two of you came to be acquainted?' she said, without replying.

'Oh! The funniest thing!' Lady Honoria went off into another ripple of laughter, a melodic, flirtatious giggle that Gussie had never heard from her before. 'A stroll in the park, yesterday— no, stay, it was the day before—'

'It was yesterday,' interrupted Ivo. 'A fine day, my dear, if you recall, and the day before that it rained.'

'Oh yes, it rained *dreadfully* hard. You are quite right. Yesterday, then, in the park, and we chanced to manifest ourselves before the very same person — and at exactly the same moment! How she *screamed*.'

Ivo was chortling. Gussie revised her estimate as to his character. 'What a happy coincidence,' she agreed. 'I suppose the woman survived the encounter?'

'I am nearly sure she was still breathing when we left,'

said Great-Aunt Honoria.

'Well! You will find a warm welcome here, Ivo, I'm sure.' Gussie smiled upon him. 'Though I must ask you not to manifest at the breakfast-table, and get any blood upon the comestibles. It does upset my aunt.'

'Not at all, not at all,' beamed Ivo. 'I shall be snug up here with Lady Honoria. Shan't make a peep downstairs.'

If Mr. Farthing preferred skulking in the attic to making an appearance downstairs, Gussie would not be the person to gainsay him. 'I did actually come up to ask you a question, Aunt. Were you in residence overnight?'

'No, my dear, I was not.' She said this smiling, with a dreamy look in her eyes, and Gussie perceived her exchanging a conspiratorial glance with Ivo.

She did not choose to ask where her great-aunt had spent the night.

'Why, was I wanted?' said Lady Honoria after a moment.

'We have had something of an event, and I was hoping you might have some information about it. I am sorry to have interrupted you for nothing.'

'An event?'

'A corpse. Delivered, we must suppose, by some manner of fairy.'

Lady Honoria smiled, very widely. 'I admit, to my regret, that the fairy was not me. But how delicious! I will go and look, *at once*.'

'Oh, she is not there now—' Gussie began, but her great-aunt was already gone, with Ivo trailing behind her.

'So much for snug in the attic,' she muttered, and turned to retrace her steps downstairs.

FOUR

Theo did not surface from his repose until late in the afternoon, and only then with some reluctance. So thick-headed and sluggish did he feel, he almost felt that his mother might have been right to suggest a day or two away from the theatre, and the club. And he had been neglecting his books...

But a note arrived within half an hour, from Hargreve.

Do not fail tonight! (it said). *They say Mrs. Everleigh is returned, and will perform at Strangewayes. I depend upon you, Bedge.*

Which put paid to any thoughts of spending the night in the book-room. He hadn't a notion who Mrs. Everleigh might be, but perceived readily enough that she was quite the attraction.

When he ventured downstairs, he found Mr. Ballantine still present, and some manner of disturbance going on in the parlour. Hearing Lady Honoria's voice, and his mother's, he chose to avoid the room altogether, and slipped out of the house unnoticed. He did not object to Ballantine, ordinarily; a good fellow, the Runner, all things considered. But he did not perfectly like the way he had looked at Theo, earlier in the day. Not with any very great suspicion, but certainly with a *little*.

The woman in the parlour was a mighty inconvenience, Theo decided. The subject bored him excessively, and he would have nothing more to do with it. Gussie might be carried away with enthusiasm for detecting, if she chose; it would distract her from her nonsense over Ademar Wirt, and the infernal books, and that could only be a good thing. But she need not drag *him* into the middle of it.

This praiseworthy resolution having been made, he sauntered off to Stebbington's, where Hargreve would be waiting for him.

The Strangewayes Theatre was an old, old establishment, tucked away in a quiet street where it would avoid all casual notice. The place had been opened in the time of Queen Elizabeth, and but little altered since. Its boards had been trodden by the Wyrded and talented for many a long age, and, as something of an antiquarian, Theo enjoyed a frisson of appreciation for its heritage every time he stepped over its threshold. He could almost fancy himself a sixteenth-century courtier, bound to the theatre for an evening of Shakespeare, when it was fresh, still, and new.

The ladies and gentlemen he encountered upon going in soon shattered this illusion; not a ruff or a codpiece among them, and scant sign of any interesting Wyrde. Many among the audience at Strangewayes were not, themselves, Wyrded, or so Theo had heard it said. They attended out of curiosity, or fascination, for nowhere else in London could one expect to see the many peculiarities of the Wyrde put on such public display.

Something about this irritated Theo. He did not think of himself, or his family, as some kind of spectacle, to be gawked at by all and sundry. But Strangewayes managed the business tastefully enough, and besides, for those such as himself, there were – additional attractions. Private soirees, where one might meet the actors and actresses

26

who dazzled upon the stage. The unWyrded were rarely invited to those.

He looked forward to just such an evening, after tonight's performance. Hargreve's anticipation made the man effusive and jovial, and even Theo smiled as he took his seat in the Werth family box, and waited for the performance to begin.

The box had come as a surprise, not only to him but to his father. Upon Theo's first visit to the theatre, some weeks before, he'd been greeted by name and immediately asked: 'Shall you be wanting your box for this evening, my lord?'

'My box?' Theo had said, drawing a thorough blank.

'Secured by Lord Werth-as-was, sir,' came the answer. 'Your grandfather, I should think, and I can assure you we have kept it in excellent state.'

Theo had no notion at all what it cost to maintain a private box at a London theatre for several decades together, nor did he care. His father might.

But: 'Oh, do we still keep a box at Strangewayes?' Lord Werth had said, upon receipt of this news. 'Whatever for?'

He had almost immediately dismissed the matter from his mind, and since the subject of its possible expense had not seemed to trouble anybody, Theo had let it stand. And put it to frequent use ever since, to Hargreve's delight.

Hargreve had brought a lady with him for this evening's revelry, a Miss Manning. She was UnWyrded, and of ghoulish tastes, for she was thrilled to be in company with those who were. A man more observant, or interested, than Lord Bedgberry might have considered her disposed to admire him, for she greeted his every remark with a smiling enthusiasm and seemed preoccupied with the arrangements of her hair.

'Oh, shall it ever begin!' cried she, as they sat in the velvet splendour of Lord Werth's box, exchanging glances and salutations with passing attendees. 'I believe I shall die of suspense!'

'Pray do, if it would amuse you, Miss Manning,' said Theo. 'You find yourself in excellent company for such an experiment. If you are very lucky, there may be somebody about who could reverse the general effect, at least to a degree.'

'How you do tease,' said she, with a little laugh.

'Oh, he isn't teasing,' put in Hargreve, with an admonishing look at Theo. 'He is perfectly sincere, I'm sorry to say. But you should not like to become a revenant, Miss Manning, should you? It would ruin your complexion.'

Miss Manning only tittered, and seemed distressed for a reply.

'Not quite yet, no,' said Theo, his eyes upon the stage. 'Hargreve has the right of it. I believe most women prefer to wait until a later age.'

'And what of men?' said Miss Manning, rallying.

'I shouldn't like it at any age,' answered Theo.

'You see, Lord Bedgberry's vanity sets him against it.' Hargreve smiled at his guest. 'And so does mine, I confess.'

'But I hope neither of you gentlemen has any intention of *dying*,' declared Miss Manning. 'So young and handsome as you are!'

Theo gave a sigh, and checked his pocket-watch. 'Should not the play have begun by now?'

'There is some little delay, certainly,' said Hargreve. 'Doubtless it will begin in a moment.'

But it did not. Nearly half an hour passed before at last the curtains were hauled away, and the performance began. But something was amiss. The actors were not up to their usual standard, seeming distracted, reciting their parts by rote. A palpable tension turned their movements wooden and their faces stiff.

What's more, the actress playing the central part was the same lady Theo had seen some few times before. Mrs. Daughtry, he thought? A capable enough actress, but not the dazzling sensation Hargreve had described.

'Did not you say that there was a new leading lady for tonight?' Theo whispered to Hargreve, after a while.

Hargreve sat frowning, ill at ease. 'Not new, but new to *you*,' he answered. 'Mrs. Everleigh has been away from the stage some time, and was due to return to it tonight. The finest actress alive, not a doubt of it. I wonder what has become of her.'

'She is indisposed, no doubt,' said Theo, but Miss Manning interjected.

'Oh, but imagine if something very dreadful should have happened to her!' The prospect seemed to enchant her, for her eyes shone, and her mouth hung open in horrified delight.

Theo, about to utter a sharp set-down, paused. Something teased at the edges of his ideas, making his neck prickle.

Something very dreadful.

'What does this Mrs. Everleigh look like?' he inquired.

Hargreve thought. 'It is some time since I last saw her, but I should think she isn't a young woman anymore. Lightish hair?' Hargreve trailed off, his information exhausted.

Theo's premonition deepened. 'I begin to have a horrible feeling,' said he.

'Of what nature?'

'I've a notion your Mrs. Everleigh and I have already met.'

'What luck! Then perhaps you can tell us where she's like to be tonight.'

'Having conversation with my father, I should think.'

'Keeps a mistress, does he?' said Hargreve, nodding.

'That isn't at all what I meant.' Theo could occasionally feel impatient with Hargreve; the man wasn't so quick on the uptake as one might wish.

'Well then, where did you meet her?'

'What did she say to you, Lord Bedgberry?' put in Miss

Manning. 'Did she talk to you about the theatre?'

'Nothing of the sort,' answered Theo shortly. 'She said nothing at all, in fact, which is hardly surprising when you consider that I was digging her a grave at the time.'

This silenced Hargreve, but not Miss Manning. She gave a theatrical gasp, and declared herself ready to expire on the spot.

'Come on, old man,' said Hargreve, recovering himself, and attempting a laugh. 'This isn't at all amusing.'

'I should say it isn't, indeed.'

The mirth faded from Hargreve's face. 'You are not serious?'

'Perfectly. I shall go home, and see what my father has to say.'

'Perhaps it was some other female,' Hargreve tried. 'You don't absolutely *know* that it was Mrs. Everleigh you, er, met?'

'I don't know it for certain,' Theo admitted. 'But my cousin Gussie has involved herself in the business, Hargreve, and if there's one thing that's certain where Gussie is concerned, it's unmitigated disaster. I have only to imagine the worst possible outcome, and I can feel pretty sure it's that.'

When Theo entered his father's house he encountered Gussie almost at once, despite the lateness of the hour. 'Ohh, Theo!' she said, beaming, and advanced upon him across the hallway. 'You have missed a deal of excitement. Who do you think we had bleeding all over my aunt's parlour?'

'The finest actress alive,' answered Theo shortly. 'Or, she was.'

'Yes! Though how you should come to know of it I can't think— oh, but you have come from Strangeways, have you not? I congratulate you, cousin. You have leapt to conclusions as energetically as ever I could, and they are quite correct.'

30

'It's a pity about the play.'

'Yes, but my uncle has got her into much better state. I should imagine she will be well enough to perform tomorrow, or perhaps next week.'

Theo experienced a moment's discomfort. If his father had raised the woman, and she was in her senses again, would she remember his treatment of her? He had not been so careful with her inert form as he might have been, on account of her having been a corpse at the time. Might have knocked her about a bit, in his drunken state. Heavens, had he even *dropped* her at one point?

'She's been talking, has she?' he enquired, warily.

'A bit,' Gussie nodded. 'You shall speak to her yourself, if you want to, though to avoid disappointment I shall just tell you: her information as to the identity of her killer is not so specific as one could wish.'

'How can that be?'

'She appears to be suffering from a lapse in memory. She was at Strangewayes, she claims, in her dressing-room; and after that, she remembers nothing at all, until the moment my uncle revived her.'

Theo relaxed. 'How unfortunate,' he said, with more politeness than truth.

'Yes, but I should think it hardly surprising. People do sometimes forget shocking events, do they not, and what could be more shocking than one's own sudden death?'

A trill of laughter reached Theo's ears, coming from the parlour. 'Oh, no,' he sighed. 'You haven't let Honoria at her, have you?'

'She could hardly be prevented.' Gussie wore her secretive smile, slightly smug; she clearly knew something else, and had decided not to tell Theo, so as to preserve the unpleasant surprise.

Very well. Theo gathered his courage, and made for the parlour door.

A scene of high chaos met his appalled gaze. Far too many people were crowded into his mother's hitherto peaceful sanctuary. His mother and father sat together upon the divan; Miss Frostell had appeared from wherever she customarily hid herself — some chamber above stairs, he collected — and sat with her hands folded near the window; the corpse — no, the *actress*, for she was not quite a corpse now — stood in the centre of the room, commanding the attention of her audience, as actresses did. She looked rather good for the recently deceased. Most of the blood was gone from her flesh, if not from her garments, and she had fresh-arranged her hair. Someone had done a decent job of stitching up the ruin of her neck.

Mr. Ballantine was present, a little separate from the chaos. He had his back to the wall, and beheld the tableau with the air of a man regretting several of his more important life choices.

And no wonder, for above Mrs. Everleigh's head soared the earthly remains of Lady Honoria, trailing a little blood in her excitement.

She was not alone. Another, equally disembodied head had joined her, a fellow Theo had never seen before. There was Gussie's unpleasant surprise, then.

Theo quietly joined Mr. Ballantine. 'I'll warrant your life was a deal more peaceful, before you became a Werth.'

'I am a Werth, now, am I? Officially?' The Runner did not appear overpowered with delight.

'I'm afraid so. Once my family has accepted you as one of us, there can be no escape.'

Mr. Ballantine's gaze followed Gussie as she came back into the room after Theo. She regarded the unfolding imbroglio with an expression of high, and most unseemly, glee. 'I daresay I shall grow accustomed in time,' murmured Mr. Ballantine.

Theo could not help but laugh.

'Yes, I suppose that was an absurdity,' Ballantine agreed. 'Whatever horrors I may contrive to accept, there is bound to be some fresh atrocity awaiting my attention. I believe your cousin delights in producing them.'

Yes, Gussie has taken quite a shine to you.'

'Is that what it is? I shouldn't like to see what she does to those she dislikes.'

Theo clapped him on the shoulder. 'No chance of that now, I am sorry to say. What do you make of this business with Mrs. Everleigh?'

Mr. Ballantine made to reply, then shook his head. 'I hardly know, yet,' he said, and then raised his voice. 'Ladies, please. Gentlemen. I believe it will be best if Mrs. Everleigh is permitted to withdraw for the evening.'

Lord Werth rose from his seat. 'Quite right, Mr. Ballantine. Honoria, if you please? I believe there has been enough excitement for one day.'

Mrs. Everleigh appeared to be enjoying herself, judging from the shine to her freshly-dead eyes. But she bowed her head to Lord Werth, and said: 'Very well, I am quite ready to return home. Only I do feel some small concern. Do you think I shall be safe?'

She had a vibrant, deep voice, perfect for the stage. Theo's regret for the lost performance deepened.

'Perhaps you had better stay here,' Gussie offered. She said this graciously, but something in her face told Theo she was not acting out of charity. She was up to something.

'Will that answer?' Theo said quickly. 'Somebody got in here with Mrs. Everleigh's corpse, after all.'

This won him the actress's attention, for the first time. She regarded him with a green gaze: a look of speculation, and distaste. 'My corpse,' she echoed. 'Yes, I suppose it was that, was it not?'

'Do not mind Lord Bedgberry, ma'am,' Gussie put in. 'He never was capable of any subtlety.'

'He has the right of it,' said Mr. Ballantine. 'We do not yet know who entered this house with Mrs. Everleigh's remains, or how, or why. However, I can hardly imagine what further harm they might expect to do to you, ma'am.'

The lady appeared arrested by this thought. 'How true. I shall never have to fear death again. Most invigorating! I ought to have perished years ago.'

'Furthermore,' said Ballantine, bearing admirably with this unorthodox sentiment, 'nowhere in the city is so well-provided with the vicious, the ruthless and the remorseless as the Werth residence. You shan't lack for protectors.'

'Yes, do please accept our hospitality,' said Lady Werth, accepting this questionable tribute without a blink.

'I shall be honoured,' Mrs. Everleigh smiled.

'Hurrah!' sang Lady Honoria from somewhere above. 'A fresh corpse to play with! You see, Ivo, I *told* you how it would be.'

'Charming,' said the other severed head, beaming upon the gathered company. 'Delightful.'

Mr. Ballantine drew nearer to Theo. 'The question of *who* accessed this house and left Mrs. Everleigh here,' he murmured. 'It is a fair one, my lord. Your own erratic behaviour rules you out, I believe, but otherwise, I don't at all know who to suspect. One thing only seems clear, and that is: whoever it was had a key. Either that, or they had the assistance of someone inside who could open the door for them.'

'Are you certain?' Theo frowned.

'Fairly. The windows are bolted shut from the inside, and there are no signs anywhere in the house that someone forced or battered their way in. They can only have entered through one of the doors. And since they effected this errand without being detected, it must have been accomplished quickly and simply. This parlour is at the front of the house. Could they have come in at the back, and made their way through most of the ground floor before depositing their burden, and escaping unnoticed? Perhaps, but it isn't likely. It is my belief they entered by the front door, and with help.'

This disquieted Theo. He understood the gist of Ballantine's argument: while the killer may well have been a stranger, he or she had the help of someone presently under Lord Werth's roof. Ballantine's lowered voice and secretive manner told him the rest: while it may have been a servant who had done it — they were most of them new hires, after all — it might also have been a member of the family. Ballantine had not ruled out this possibility, nor could he.

'I see what you mean,' he said, rather heavily.

'Perhaps you will keep your eyes open for anything… unusual that might occur.'

'I shan't spy on my own family, Mr. Ballantine,' said Theo. '*Your* family also, as I've just been saying.'

'I don't expect it shall come to that.'

A thought occurred to Theo, and produced a smile. 'Does Gussie know that she is under suspicion of duplicity and treachery?'

'I haven't judged it advisable to inform her of it.'

'That's a pity. She would be so pleased.'

FIVE

'Frosty,' said Gussie, upon the following morning. 'You are the perfect person to assist with this important investigation, this is true. But *not* by cleaning my aunt's carpets, if you please.'

'Oh, but it is such a great pity!' said Miss Frostell, pausing her vigorous labours to gesture at the ruin of the floor. The carpet was a pale blue, more's the pity, for the brownish stain upon it stood out starkly against the airy colour. 'I am persuaded your dear aunt is more unhappy about it than she has let on.'

'That may be true, but there are servants enough about to scrub floors, Frosty. Moreover, I do not think anything *can* be done about this now. It will have to be replaced, and my aunt is, in all likelihood, already making the arrangements.'

Gussie had wandered in after breakfast to do a little investigating of her own, now that the room was finally deserted. But the sight that met her eyes was not of a serene, empty room ripe for a little detecting work, but of poor Miss Frostell on her knees before the hearth, a bucket of water at her elbow and a scrubbing-brush clutched in her thin hands.

'I daresay you are right, my dear,' conceded Miss Frostell with a sigh. She dropped her scrubbing-brush into the bucket, and accepted Gussie's assistance in rising to her feet. She was no longer young, Miss Frostell, and her joints sometimes failed her. 'It *is* such a pity,' she said again.

'I applaud you. Your concern for the carpet far outweighs your concern for the poor woman who bled all over it. I knew we would make a Werth of you at last.'

'Well, but the poor lady does not seem so terribly cast down by it?' offered Miss Frostell. 'In fact, she seemed rather pleased, in the end.'

'So she did, but we mustn't forget that a horrible crime has been committed,' said Gussie firmly. 'People should not go about making corpses of other people without their consent, however desirable the ultimate effect may prove to be.'

'No, my dear, you are quite right.'

'And that puts me in mind of what I wanted to say to you, Frosty. I do need your help.'

'Then you shall have it, my dear.'

Miss Frostell's serene acceptance of whatever her erstwhile protégé might ask touched Gussie's heart, a little to her chagrin. 'Are you sure you should agree so promptly?' she said, half laughing. 'You know that I have no shame, and might ask all manner of dreadful deeds of you.'

Miss Frostell only smiled. 'And I hope I shall perform them to your satisfaction.'

Impulsively, Gussie hugged her dauntless governess, a gesture Miss Frostell accepted with some surprise. 'You are far better than I deserve, Frosty, and I shall take all possible advantage of the fact. How should you like to do a little interrogating?'

Miss Frostell engaged in a moment's thought. 'I don't know as I should like to interrogate anybody very alarming,' she decided. 'And if the thumb-screws are to be applied, then I do not think I shall be equal to it.'

'No indeed. If anyone is to be applying thumb-screws then I hope it will be me. No, I only want you to be your own, gentle self, and make friends with my aunt's new servants. I believe we can exonerate Mrs. Gavell from suspicion; she has been here such an age, I can't imagine she could have any possible motive for sabotage. And besides, she and my aunt are thick as thieves. But there are so many strangers in the household, and any one of them could have let the murderer in, and helped to ruin the carpet.'

This last fact weighed with Miss Frostell; she took on an expression of determination, and straightened with purpose. 'Yes. What a horrid thing to do! You may rely on me, my dear. I have already had some little speech with Gabriel — the new footman, you know — and Mabel, the upper housemaid. And last time I had occasion to go down into the kitchens, I found the scullery maid quite conversable. I shall ask them if they've had anything to do with this unpleasant business.'

'Perfect, Frosty, I knew I could rely on you. I wouldn't ask them outright, though; they are hardly like to baldly admit to treachery, even to you. No, what I'd like you to discover is whether any of them seem to have... unsupportive ideas about the Wyrde. The victim is a Wyrded actress, after all, and she was left in the most Wyrded house in London.'

Miss Frostell was not, herself, Wyrded; Gussie hoped this might make her an acceptable confidant for such a person, aside from her unassuming manners and congenial nature.

'I shall begin directly,' Miss Frostell decided. Casting one last, sad look at the immovable bloodstain upon the floor, she took up her bucket and went out.

'Perfect,' said Gussie again, to herself. 'Now, what shall I do?'

This question was not so easily answered. The parlour

furnished nothing by way of further clues, though she had not really expected to find any. Mr. Ballantine had already investigated it, and she had no cause to doubt his thoroughness. Nobody had come in by the window, that much was clear; therefore, whoever had left Mrs. Everleigh must have come in by the door, and thus passed through the hall.

Gussie was as capable as Mr. Ballantine of following the same line of logic. She knew that the intruder must have enjoyed a certain assistance from within. And while she was not quite so quick as he to imagine a member of the family capable of it, she was perfectly aware that it wasn't impossible.

Great-Aunt Honoria had not, she thought, done it; her delighted surprise at the news of the corpse's arrival had seemed too genuine.

Her new beau, however, was a different matter entirely. It might have been a coincidence that such a person had joined the household at the same time as the corpse, and secretly at that. On the other hand, it might not be.

Gussie decided to make Ivo Farthing's better acquaintance, and soon.

Apart from that, there was Mrs. Everleigh herself. She claimed to have lost all memory of the event that had robbed her of life and breath, and perhaps she had. Gussie could think of no immediate reason for her to dissemble on such a point.

But this occurrence had got her into the Werth residence, and on sympathetic terms. Gussie had not idly invited her to remain, nor had she done so out of compassion. No, she was curious about their serene murder victim. The woman had not even pretended to be downcast, nor did she seem troubled by the question of who had savaged her to death.

This did not seem so very odd to Gussie as it might to another person. However, something about the situation gave Gussie pause, and raised questions. Now that she had achieved an introduction to the household, what might Mrs. Everleigh choose to do with it?

Gussie resolved upon making Mrs. Everleigh's better acquaintance, as well.

The actress had not presented herself at the breakfast-table. This came as no surprise to Lord Werth; when their guest's absence was remarked upon by his wife, he had only said: 'I have yet to encounter the corpse that requires sustenance, my dear.'

'Neither fear of death or harm, nor need for food and water!' Gussie had said. 'Why, I begin to feel my great-aunt has the right of it. I ought to enrol myself in the annals of the dead at once. How freeing it would be.'

'Yes,' came Honoria's voice, unexpectedly, as she materialised above the toast-rack. 'You begin to see the benefits, my dear! How glad I am. And I shall myself teach you to decorporate.'

Decorporating, Gussie supposed, referred to her great-aunt's capacity to manifest a corporeal form for herself as she chose, and fade away to nothing when she did not. That idea, too, held some small appeal for Gussie. 'A generous offer, Aunt,' said she. 'What a formidable spy I should make.'

She had spoken in jest, but the idea had lingered. Not that she had any real intention of hurling herself from a window, or drowning herself in the Thames; she felt the claims of life and youth powerfully enough, after all. But Honoria, already on the other side of the threshold between life and death, might make a wonderful recruit in the pursuit of espionage, provided she could contain her taste for mischief.

But she could not be expected to spy on her new companion, of course, being far too enamoured with the amiable Mr. Farthing.

Gussie climbed the stairs to the upper garrets with alternative ideas turning in her mind. She found her aunt and that lady's paramour both in residence, and entered the room with some attempt at stealth, closing the door behind her.

'I am here in secret,' she told them, in a half-whisper. 'I must ask you to divulge my visit to nobody.'

As she had hoped, this display of clandestine intent strongly appealed to her great-aunt. 'Oh, but there is important business on hand!' agreed Lady Honoria. 'You may rely upon me, my dear!'

'I knew that I might,' Gussie said, warmly. 'Mr. Farthing?'

'Soul of discretion,' said he, smiling. 'Excellent at secrets.'

Gussie's smile widened. She could not yet trust Mr. Farthing, but for this particular errand she was undisturbed by his presence. 'I have come to ask for your help,' she went on. 'It's to do with this *decorporating* that you are both so talented at. Can you manage to be entirely invisible, and yet remain in possession of your senses?'

'Oh, but yes!' declared Lady Honoria. 'We do it all the time!'

Gussie wondered, in passing, just how much of the family's household business had been secretly observed by Lady Honoria, and let the thought go. There was nothing to be done about that *now*. 'Capital,' said she. 'Then I must ask for your aid in the matter of Mrs. Everleigh.'

'The mysterious actress!' said Ivo.

'The corpse!' said Lady Honoria.

'Yes. You see, the circumstances surrounding her death strike me as unusual in the extreme. Would not you agree?'

'I do not know that I would,' mused Lady Honoria. 'Many a fine lady or gentlemen has enjoyed a good brutalising, you know, and expired from it with perfect grace. I've seen it happen, many a time.'

'Quite right,' put in Ivo, his floating head nodding. 'Seen it myself, a time or two.'

'I don't mean that. I mean her being placed *here*, of all

41

possible locations to dump the lifeless remains of a celebrated actress, and her knowing nothing about the event afterwards. Or so she claims. I encouraged her to remain here because I want her watched, and the two of you are the perfect people to do it.'

And if Ivo turned out to have something to do with it, Gussie thought, he might be reassured by her seeming to suspect only Mrs. Everleigh, and let down his guard. The scheme was perfect, if she *did* say so herself.

'Say no more!' Lady Honoria beamed all over her dead, white face, and fair bobbed with anticipation. 'She shall do nothing in this house but what we'll know of it, and if she leaves we shall follow.'

'Do not let her see you, if you can manage it,' Gussie warned. 'I want her to imagine herself entirely above suspicion.'

'Shan't see hide nor hair of us,' said Ivo. 'Guarantee it.'

'You are both very good.' Gussie smiled upon them, very well pleased. 'I shall shortly be interviewing the lady myself, and you are quite welcome to attend if you wish. In your new, secret capacity, of course. You may tell me if you observe anything unusual in her.'

With which words, she soon had chance to observe the extent of their talents. They faded from view almost immediately, and Gussie retreated down the stairs without the smallest reason to imagine herself anything but alone. That she was, in fact, flanked by two disembodied beings might be indubitable, but no one short of Nell herself could have detected it, she was sure.

She paused on the upper landing, considering. Where should she expect to find their guest? It might be awkward to descend upon the actress in her own bedchamber, and interrogate her; they were not on such terms as that, and Gussie could think of no more effective way to advertise her suspicions.

'You would not chance to know where she is to be found?' she said, in a whisper.

No immediate reply came. Gussie waited, and after a few minutes there came a ripple of movement at her elbow. Lady Honoria's head shimmered into brief and hazy view. 'The drawing-room,' she hissed.

'Chance favours us. Thank you, Aunt.'

The head disappeared again, and Gussie proceeded to her aunt's withdrawing-room. She found not only Mrs. Everleigh there, but Lady Werth as well, the two enjoying a cosy tête-à-tête.

'Why, Gussie,' said Lady Werth in some surprise. 'What a pleasure.'

If there was a hint of inquiry, or even suspicion, hidden behind her aunt's pleasant words, Gussie flattered herself that Mrs. Everleigh was unlikely to perceive it. 'Yes, I felt desirous of company this morning,' she said airily, and took a seat opposite to the actress. She had a clear view of the lady from there, and could watch her reactions closely. She thought, belatedly, that she ought to have brought some needle-work with her; it would have made a convincing appearance. But it was too late now. 'I was hoping to have a little conversation with you, ma'am,' she said to Mrs. Everleigh. 'I am so powerfully fond of the theatre, as my dear aunt will tell you!'

Her dear aunt did not appear disposed to make any such declaration, knowing her niece to be only passingly interested in spectacle. She cast Gussie a look of mild reproof, which Gussie serenely ignored.

Mrs. Everleigh must be used to exciting such interest. She inclined her head, a gesture Gussie was quite ready to take for permission.

She had, at last, opportunity to examine the deceased actress up close, and without the distraction and confusion of so many other persons about. The actress's attire at the time of her death had been handsome enough, but the garments she had since adopted were so different, Gussie was disposed to think her first outfit may have been a costume. Had she been interrupted as she prepared herself for a rehearsal?

She was handsomer, too, now that she was less bloodied, and more animated. She was some dozen or so years older than Gussie herself, perhaps, with guinea-gold hair and arrestingly green eyes. Death had given an interesting pallor to her complexion, which suited rather than detracted from her beauty. The wounds upon her neck were hidden under the high neck of her gown: an attractive piece wrought from ivory silk, and with coquelicot trimmings.

'*Do* tell me all about your life at the theatre,' Gussie gushed. 'I'm quite enraptured.'

'Ah, as to that,' murmured Mrs. Everleigh in her rich voice. 'I have been some time away from the stage, as you must have heard, though I was a sensation for many years before. Perhaps you had occasion to see me perform, prior to my absence?'

'I'm afraid not. We are but recently arrived in London, you see, and were never here before. *Buried* in the depths of Norfolk, only think how tedious!'

'Such retirement,' agreed Mrs. Everleigh. 'You must have been fair smothered with boredom.'

Thinking of the events of the past few months, Gussie could not agree; boredom had been the last of her troubles, for once. She could see similar thoughts passing behind her aunt's eyes, though neither chose to enlighten Mrs. Everleigh. 'Yes!' she declared mendaciously. 'Only imagine my excitement at finally removing to London! And my cousin, too, is so fond of the theatre. Why, he was in the audience, you know, last evening, when you were to perform.'

'How sorry I am to have disappointed him,' said Mrs. Everleigh, with perfect calm; she might have missed her performance due to a sore-throat, or a headache.

'Do say you will be returning to the stage,' Gussie pressed. 'My uncle will be so pleased to have been of assistance.'

Mrs. Everleigh's attention seemed arrested. She sat up a little. 'Lord Werth has been a great benefactor,' she said. 'I could hardly have hoped for so advantageous an outcome to so distressing an event.'

Gussie's eyes narrowed a little. It entered her mind that, if Mrs. Everleigh had known of Lord Werth's particular talents, she might very well have hoped for exactly such an outcome. Had she had *herself* deposited in this of all houses because she had heard of his Wyrde, and anticipated that the mystery of her appearance there would prompt him to exercise them?

She had embarked upon a renewed career upon the stage, after all, but she was no longer a young woman. Her preservation now that she was undead — that could be more lasting than the youthful looks which had won her some of her popularity. Had that motivated her?

Besides which, the tale of her gruesome murder and subsequent revival would be in all the newspapers; what better publicity could she hope for? Strangewayes would be packed with eager theatre-goers, as soon as she chose to appear.

Gussie decided upon a frontal attack.

'When you think about it, everything has worked out charmingly for you,' she remarked. 'You were tragically slaughtered! A black mark upon any woman's career, to be sure! But, by some kind twist of fate, you were abandoned under the roof of the one person in London who could have reversed the general effect. What fortune, after all! And as the star of Strangewayes, of all theatres, your present condition can only increase your appeal.'

'It was lucky, was it not?' said Mrs. Everleigh, inclining her elegant head. 'Fortune sometimes shows her favour in unexpected ways.'

She showed no signs of wanting to dissemble, nor any discomfort at the line of questioning. No signs, in short, of a guilty conscience. With an inward sigh, Gussie abandoned this mode of attack. She was talking to an actress, after all; the infernal woman need not make a display of her discomfort, if she felt any.

'How curious I am as to how it came about!' said Gussie instead. 'Perhaps you may like to meet the instrument of your unusual good fortune.'

'My murderer, you mean?' Mrs. Everleigh smiled still, but her eyes had gone a little cold.

'Why, yes. Or whoever it was who conveyed you here, if they are not the same person.'

'Are you disposed to discover the identity of this person, or persons, Miss Werth?'

'Yes,' said Gussie firmly, and without further pretence. 'I do not know precisely how the law will view such a crime as this, when the victim declares herself well pleased with the result; but you were still murdered, Mrs. Everleigh, and whoever did it has cast suspicion upon my family by leaving you in our house. I need not tell you, I am sure, that this is a situation we find unacceptable.'

Mrs. Everleigh hesitated, and looked at Lady Werth.

'My niece has the right of it,' agreed that lady. 'The truth must be uncovered, Mrs. Everleigh, or I shall have to fear for my son.'

Lady Werth was far too gentle-mannered to make anything like a palpable threat. But she spoke with an iron will underlying her words, and with a steadiness of gaze and purpose which clarified her point perfectly: no threat to her son, or any other member of her family, would be permitted to exist.

'I understand you,' murmured Mrs. Everleigh. 'Pray believe I shall be ready to do all in my power to assist you.'

'Capital,' said Gussie. 'You have already spoken to Mr. Ballantine, I collect?'

'Another member of our family,' put in Lady Werth. 'He is most kindly representing our interests in this matter.' This was not strictly true, as Mr. Ballantine would be the first to assert. He represented the interests of Justice and the Crown, not those of any private citizen. But Mrs.

Everleigh need not know of it.

'I see,' said Mrs. Everleigh. 'Yes, I told Mr. Ballantine all that I know, but I am afraid it is very little. I do not remember much of that day.'

'You went to Strangewayes,' Gussie prompted. 'Preparing for your debut?'

'It could hardly be called a debut, more of a reappearance—' Mrs. Everleigh stopped herself. 'Yes, I — I suppose I must have done so. I had been going there every day, for we had daily rehearsals all week.'

'You are not perfectly certain?'

'I have no clear recollection of it.'

Curious, Gussie thought. 'Perhaps you did not, after all. Or if you did go there, you must have been interrupted,' she suggested. 'For you were not wearing any stage make-up when I discovered you in the parlour.'

'No,' said Mrs. Everleigh, rather hesitantly. 'I was not. I wonder what can have happened?'

Her curiosity did not appear to be any source of great discomfort to her. She sat placidly with her hands in her lap, and offered nothing more.

'The gown you were wearing, when we found you,' Gussie pressed. 'Was it your own gown, or part of your stage attire?'

Mrs. Everleigh frowned. 'Mr. Ballantine had no such question to ask of me.'

'That is because Mr. Ballantine is uninterested in matters of dress, and not like to think of such things. He will be grateful to me for thinking of it in his stead. The gown, ma'am?'

'The truth is—' Mrs. Everleigh hesitated, and paused in thought. 'The truth is that I do not know,' she finally answered. 'It was not the costume I was to wear for the performance, but I do not imagine I was wearing it when I arrived at the theatre.'

'What *were* you wearing upon arrival, if I may ask?'

'I fail to see the relevance, ma'am.'

47

'Oh, me too,' Gussie agreed affably. 'But one never knows, does one?'

Mrs. Everleigh paused in momentary thought. 'The last gown I clearly remember wearing to the theatre was a muslin. Blue.'

'Thank you. If we may return to the lustring gown: why might you have altered your attire?'

'I am afraid I don't recall. That gown was not my own at all, in fact. I had never seen it before the moment of my revival.'

'But how fascinating!' Gussie was enchanted. 'What a capital clue! I shall find out more about it. If you would be so good as to relinquish it into my possession? I suppose you won't be too concerned about its being returned to you, if it is not your own?'

'You may have it with my good will, Miss Werth.'

'Perfect.' Gussie beamed. She opened her mouth to say something else, but whatever it was flew out of her head, for the gown in question came floating into the room under (apparently) its own power. Mrs. Everleigh's pelisse followed it, and the bonnet she had been wearing.

'Oh,' Gussie faltered. 'There it is.'

The gown and pelisse proceeded to perform a gavette for the amusement of the company, before draping themselves at last over Gussie's lap.

'Great-Aunt Honoria,' Gussie sighed.

'Honoria,' Lady Werth said in disapproving tones. 'It is quite improper to enter our guest's bedchamber without her leave.'

'Oh, but they were not *in* her bedchamber!' Lady Honoria protested, her head materialising in a puff of indignation. 'One of the maids must have taken them for laundering. I have *rescued* them.'

'They certainly must not be laundered,' Gussie agreed, handling the liberally bloodied garments with a little distaste. 'Any clues that might be gleaned from them would be wiped away.'

'Precisely! Have not I done well?' Lady Honoria would not rest until she had been duly praised, it appeared, so Gussie relented.

'Extremely well, and I thank you. Mrs. Everleigh, have you made my great-aunt's acquaintance?'

'We have set eyes upon one another,' said Lady Honoria, nodding wisely. 'Last night. But how delightful to be introduced! Your servant, ma'am.' The odd bobbing of her head that followed probably betokened that a polite curtsey was being performed by her mostly incorporeal form, even if most of it went unperceived.

Mrs. Everleigh received this with unruffled calm. As a performer at Strangeways, she must be well used to the Wyrde in all its forms, from the shocking to the mundane; nothing Lady Honoria might do could discomfit her. 'A pleasure, Lady Honoria,' she said. 'And I thank you for retrieving my garments. I left them in my chamber when I dressed this morning, being uncertain what to do with them.'

'Mr. Ballantine will want them eventually,' Gussie said. 'But first I will do a little investigating of my own.'

'Gussie, do please try to remember,' put in Lady Werth. 'We are desirous of finding the culprit, and it does not matter who receives the credit for it.'

'You mean I ought not deliberately exclude Mr. Ballantine in order to investigate on my own account?' Gussie waved this off. 'Yes, yes, my dear aunt, you are perfectly right. I shall behave myself very well, I assure you.'

Lady Werth did not appear in the least bit reassured by this handsome statement.

SIX

At more or less the very moment that Gussie and Lady Werth were interviewing Mrs Everleigh, the very dressing-room of which the actress spoke was also under scrutiny.

'I wonder if they are all like this,' mused Theo, surveying Mrs Everleigh's abandoned dressing-chamber with a little distaste.

'I could not say,' answered Ballantine. 'I was never in an actress's private chambers before.'

Despite appearances, they had not arrived at the Strangewayes theatre together. Theo had gone there directly after breakfast, thinking to get a head start on the business before anybody could much disarrange Mrs Everleigh's possessions, and potentially spoil any clues. But Ballantine had got there before him.

'You surprise me, Lord Bedgberry,' the Runner had said, when Theo had walked in. 'I did not know you had a fancy to turn investigator, like your cousin.'

Nor had he, at first, but a few things had changed since the discovery of Mrs. Everleigh's remains upon the carpet. 'You forget,' Theo had replied, coolly. 'It appears to be my neck that's on the line.'

'I shall take it upon myself to prevent anything untoward happening to your neck.'

'And while I appreciate the sentiment, I don't choose to sit at home with a book and wait for Fate and the Runners to decide between you whether I shall live an exonerated man, or die a murderer.'

'Your cousin appeared to suggest that the latter might appeal to you.'

'That is only Gussie's funning,' sighed Theo. 'Can you imagine the reception I would meet with in London, and elsewhere, were I to become the revived and mysteriously undecayed Lord Bedgberry, hanged for the murder of a celebrated actress?'

'Besides, I don't suppose the process of *being* hanged is so very pleasant.'

'No, indeed.' Theo permitted himself an eloquent shudder.

Now they stood in Mrs Everleigh's dressing room, somewhat at a loss, for the chamber was in a state of disorder. A cramped space, for the theatre was not large, it possessed a surfeit of such articles as gowns, splendid hats, dominos, capes, and assorted accoutrements Theo supposed were intended for the painting of the face; and, unfortunately, a dearth of suitable furniture in which to properly store such things. Most of them were dumped upon the floor, or piled into the embrace of a sagging arm-chair that occupied one corner.

Another chair sat before a dressing-table, equipped with a large, if cloudy, mirror. The chair stood a little askew, as though it had been pushed back in a hurry, by whoever had been sitting in it. The table-top was littered with small bottles and jars, some of which smelled odd.

'I'm given to understand that Mrs Everleigh never arrived at the theatre that night,' offered Ballantine. 'She was last seen upon the previous day, when she attended the final rehearsal before the opening performance. Perhaps interestingly, nobody remembers seeing her leave again afterwards, and no one could tell me where she might have gone.'

Theo thought back to the night at the theatre. 'I was in the audience, for her debut performance,' he said. 'There was a long delay before it began. I suppose they had been hoping and expecting she would arrive after all, however late, and had to rush to replace her at the last moment.'

Ballantine nodded. 'Who replaced her?'

'I think her name is Mrs. Daughtry. I've seen her on the stage before. Capable enough.'

'I had better try to speak to her.'

Theo didn't reply. He was thinking over the events of the previous evening, with a gathering sense of unease. 'Whoever you spoke to,' he began. 'Did they say anything else?'

'How do you mean?'

'About that night? Anything else they thought... odd?'

'I don't believe they did.' Ballantine regarded Lord Bedgberry intently, and added, 'You've something in your mind, I perceive.'

Theo hesitated, unsure how to articulate his thoughts. 'It's only that, when the performance finally began, I thought it — off, somehow. The actors seemed — perturbed. They were not at all themselves, and performed atrociously.'

Ballantine nodded thoughtfully, his quick mind rapidly perceiving Theo's line of thought. 'All they could have known at that time was that their star actress had failed to appear, and was nowhere to be found. This must have been disappointing, perhaps aggravating, but at *that* time, they could not know what had become of her. We were slow to identify her remains, and the newspapers were not yet reporting her demise.'

'No. Any number of mundane occurrences could have prevented her from showing up. Surely their first thought would not have been that something so terrible had befallen her?' Theo thought, briefly, of Miss Manning, whose horrid little mind had flown straight to just such a conclusion; but she was an over-imaginative Miss with a fondness for romances. He did not at all suppose that the entire performing body at Strangewayes would have concluded the same.

'Unless they had some reason to fear for her,' said Ballantine slowly. 'Or something else had occurred to distress them.'

'Don't forget,' put in Theo. 'She was not killed in our house. Have not you said so?'

Ballantine's eyebrows rose; he paused, gaze distant, as he considered. 'I have said so,' he agreed. 'I believe it. While there was a quantity of blood left behind by her remains, considering the state of her throat I do not imagine it was enough. Had she been killed in that room, and in such a fashion, there ought to have been a lot more.'

'Well, then. Do you think it possible she was killed *here*, and somebody from this theatre removed her to our house?'

'It's possible. Yes, it is quite possible.'

That would explain the palpable discomfort of the actors, Theo thought. They *had* known what had befallen Mrs Everleigh. 'But why should they cover it up?' Theo thought aloud. 'You have spoken to some of them, and nobody mentioned anything of the sort. If they *did* know that she'd been killed, they are lying about it now.'

'An intriguing puzzle.' Ballantine took another, keener look around the disordered dressing-room. 'If she was killed at Strangewayes, it might have been in here. This mess might have been arranged to conceal the signs of it.'

'Better talk to the actors,' Theo recommended. 'I'd attempt it myself, but I hardly think they will talk to me.'

'Perhaps they won't speak honestly to me, either,' said Ballantine. 'But I'll attempt it. Your information has been useful, Lord Bedgberry.'

'Don't tell Gussie. She delights in thinking me useless, and might be disappointed.'

'We certainly can't have that,' Ballantine agreed.

It seemed to Theo that the Runner was regarding him in a speculative fashion. 'Well,' said he. 'What is it?'

'You say the actors are not likely to speak openly to you, but I wonder? Whatever made them uneasy that night, they have not chosen to share that information with me. Some folk do not like to imagine themselves investigated, whether or not they have anything pertinent to hide. But a wealthy and fashionable gentleman, now—'

'Fashionable?' gasped Theo, appalled. 'I am nothing of the kind!'

'No, that epithet might more reasonably be applied to that friend of yours,' Ballantine agreed. 'But you are certainly wealthy, and the heir to an earldom, besides.'

'I do not see what you are saying,' declared Theo. He saw it quite clearly, in fact, but did not choose to admit it.

'I understand it is the *fashion* among wealthy gentlemen to enjoy the, ah, attentions of actresses.'

'If you mean to suggest I should take some kind of mistress just so that I can question her—'

'No, no,' said Ballantine. 'But if you don't already have someone of that sort, then you might be seen as a prospect. And were you to host one or two actresses at some salubrious address, they might be more likely to talk freely with you than they appear to be doing with me.'

Theo's spirits sank rather low. The mere idea of carrying on in that manner, puffing off himself and his money, as though he might take advantage of his position to secure an actress or two — perfectly revolting.

But Ballantine had the right of it. If they wouldn't talk to the Runner, then something else must be attempted.

'Very well,' he said, rather curtly. 'I'll begin with Mrs. Daughtry.'

'Thank you,' said Ballantine, with a sincerity that immediately put Theo and his sour temper to shame.

'And what will you be doing?'

'I shall attempt an enquiry among the staff here anyway,' answered Ballantine, with a slight shrug of one shoulder. 'They might be induced to give me something of use, whether voluntarily or otherwise. Besides that… I don't suppose it will please you to hear it, but questions must be asked at your father's house.'

It did not please Theo at all, but he could hardly object. 'I see that there must,' he acknowledged. 'Though Gussie will already be up to her neck in all of that, depend upon it.'

'Perhaps it won't be so bad a thing if she is,' the Runner allowed. 'Who better to discover anything untoward going on at home than someone who perfectly understands the daily workings of the place? And who must have the confidence of at least some of your father's servants.'

'I don't suppose she has anything of the sort, but being an inquisitive sort of person (besides perfectly shameless) she'll soon find a way to prise information out of them.'

'That will be satisfactory.'

'Don't encourage her too much,' Theo warned. 'Or you'll ever hear the end of this Bow-Street-Runner business.'

'It could be said to be rather a pity that she cannot join us, in point of fact.' Ballantine's smile was rueful. 'Were she a man, she might be just the sort of person we would like to recruit.'

'What? Interfering, rampantly curious, reckless and entirely without dignity or shame?'

Ballantine's smile widened. 'Forthright, fearless, and practical, with an enquiring mind. And unencumbered by notions of propriety or appropriate behaviour, which are important among the gentry, I'll allow, but would be a grave obstacle in an investigator.'

Theo threw up his hands and turned away. 'If she grows unmanageable my mother will not be pleased. On your head be it, Ballantine.'

'Forgive me if I err, but I have not been under the impression that Miss Werth has ever been *manageable*.'

55

Despite himself, Theo had to agree. 'No, that's perfectly true.'

Though he would never have owned it, Theo was a little struck by Ballantine's view of Gussie's character. To him, she had always been the rather tiresome child who had never given him a moment's peace; as a boy, he had resented her interfering ways, her boundless energy, and her blunt honesty. She had shared none of his tastes, and having frequently found him dull, had never hesitated to inform him of it.

As a grown woman, she had traded that tactless honesty for a devastating irony, too often turned upon Theo. The mode might have altered, but the effect remained the same: Theo experienced Gussie as an invading army, against which he must defend himself.

But perhaps Mr. Ballantine had the right of it. Perhaps Gussie's nature was not at fault; she was merely formed for an active, vigorous career which her gender had denied her.

No wonder she stuck her nose into everything interesting that might be going forward.

'Does it strike you that my cousin is... bored?' Theo ventured.

Ballantine did not hesitate to agree. 'Oh, undoubtedly. I would say Miss Werth has been staggeringly bored, probably for the majority of her life. The sooner she secures employment enough to occupy her talents, the better for us all.'

SEVEN

Mrs Everleigh's Turkey-red gown did not prove so valuable a clue as Gussie had hoped, being a featureless sort of garment, with no maker's mark, nor any way to identify its provenance. It was handsome enough, but in no way remarkable; a passably fashionable thing, such as any female with a little money and some pretensions towards modishness might wear.

The sort of attire one might don if one wished to go about unremarked in decent company, Gussie thought. If she were to adopt such a purpose, she might choose such articles herself.

But she could conclude nothing else from the gown, the pelisse or the bonnet, and so she regretfully dispatched them to Bow Street, for Mr. Ballantine's inspection. She included a note:

Cousin Ballantine, enclosed are several articles of feminine attire lately removed from Mrs Everleigh's person (rescued from the laundry by Great-Aunt Honoria, though Mrs Everleigh denies having sent them for washing). Nothing to tell us where they came from — a question of some import, for I have shocking news for you. The lady claims never to have seen them before! What a mystery!

Perhaps your men can make something of them; the bloodstains, if nothing else.

A. H. W.

Having carefully wrapped the bloodied clothing in paper, and set her note upon the top, she went in search of Mrs. Gavell for assistance.

'They must go out at once,' she said, soon afterwards, having cornered the good lady in the housekeeper's room. Mrs. Gavell sat with a pair of spectacles upon her nose and a quantity of knitting in her lap; rather a vast quantity, Gussie noted in surprise, for Mrs. Gavell's own form was almost entirely obscured beneath gouts of sage-green yarn knitted up in neat cables.

'Oh— of course, Miss,' said the housekeeper, and began the process of extrication.

Gussie foresaw that the procedure might prove to be a long one. 'Ah— may I perhaps be of assistance?'

'God love you, Miss Werth, I can manage,' said Mrs. Gavell, and though it seemed to Gussie's fascinated eyes that the yarn actively resisted its makers attempts to subdue it — those cables positively *writhed* in protest, she was almost sure of it — the blanket was soon folded up, and tidied away upon the capacious shelves of a nearby cabinet. 'Now, then,' said Mrs. Gavell, accepting the parcel, and reading the direction.

Gussie had printed upon it, in her best and boldest handwriting: **Mr. H. Ballantine, Bow Street.**

'It is very important,' said Gussie.

'I'll see that it goes out at once, Miss.'

'And it had better be done secretly, I think,' Gussie added.

'Secretly, Miss...?'

'Very secretly. This household is crawling with intrigue, Mrs. Gavell, and who knows but what we have a spy somewhere in our midst?'

'A spy!' The good lady considered this prospect with palpable dismay. 'On account of somebody having got into the parlour, think you?'

'That is it, exactly. Which puts me in mind of a question I wanted to ask you: what do you make of my aunt's new servants?'

Mrs. Gavell darted a nervous look at the door to her room. The white-washed passage beyond led straight to the kitchens, and anybody might pass by it at any moment.

Gussie stole over, and quietly closed the door.

'I know of no reason to doubt any of them,' said Mrs. Gavell. 'But I shouldn't like to say that as certain, Miss. There's several of them as is strangers to me, and what they get up to on their days off, well, I couldn't say.'

'You will inform me if you see, or hear of anything untoward?'

'I don't know as I understand what you mean by *untoward*, Miss.'

'Oh, anything you wouldn't expect of a servant in this household! Creeping about in the drawing-room, say, with no cause to be there. Wandering into places they shouldn't. Meeting with suspicious characters at the stroke of midnight. That sort of thing.'

'I see.'

'Demon-summoning. Infant sacrifice,' Gussie went on. 'Any of these might be distinct possibilities if there is a shadowy villain about.'

'Yes, Miss.'

'And if anybody at all — including Theo — should be discovered to be holding dark rituals in the cellars at the witching hour of the night, I must be informed of it *immediately.*'

Mrs. Gavell appeared to give this possibility some serious consideration. 'I can't say as I've noticed any such carryings-on in the cellars, but I have not cause to go down there very often. If we had a butler, now—'

'Good Lord. Haven't we got one?'

'No, Miss. I do believe your lady aunt has been interviewing candidates, but has not yet filled the position.'

'That must certainly be resolved,' Gussie decided. 'No butler to manage the wine stock! I am no longer surprised that people have been leaving bodies in the parlour. I shouldn't wonder at it if there are several more below stairs.'

'I am sure there is nothing down there but bottles and dust,' said Mrs. Gavell reassuringly. 'Don't you worry yourself about that.'

'Oh, no. The cellars are bristling with corpses, I'm sure of it.' Gussie smiled hopefully. 'Does not it seem probable? I should like it of all things, if they were.'

'I shall send somebody to look, Miss.' The words held a note of weary resignation.

'No, no! Do not trouble the servants about it. I am sure they have enough to do already. I'll go and look myself.'

She was not to be dissuaded, despite Mrs. Gavell's best efforts (*It will be fearful dirty down there, Miss, and you with such a fine gown on today*). As it happened, Gussie was very fond of her rose-print sprig muslin, but what investigator worth her salt balked at a little dirt?

'Gowns may be laundered,' said she stoutly, and, duly armed with the cellar keys and a lanthorn, she descended directly.

The cellar door proved to be closed, but — unlocked.

Gussie's heart quickened. Someone had been down there recently! Someone might be down there still! She hastened her steps, regretting that the poor light below obliged her to carry the lanthorn. Its light must advertise her presence to whoever skulked there, and it would have been so much more entertaining to be stealthy, and come upon the intruder by surprise.

Since a secret advance was out of the question, she thought it best to call out, as she reached the bottom of the stairs: 'Whoever you are, you are fairly caught, and so I warn you! There isn't a particle of use in trying to escape, for I am in the way of the staircase.'

'Miss Werth?' came a soft, familiar voice.

'Frosty...?' Gussie turned towards the sound of her erstwhile governess's voice, and entered a small antechamber, a dank little room equipped with a dusty (and empty) wine-rack, and little else.

Therein she discovered Miss Frostell in a state of minor distress. The poor woman wore an expression of exaggerated dismay, and was actually wringing her hands in turmoil.

'Why, Frosty, whatever is the matter?'

Miss Frostell beheld the approach of her protégé with something like dread. 'Oh, dear! I am sorry, Miss. I was about to come and tell you, only she has been *so* persuasive, and seemed so very upset at the prospect, and as you know I don't *like* to disoblige anybody—'

'Calm yourself, do,' Gussie said, as soothingly as she could. 'Whatever has happened, I am not at all likely to be angered with you. Pray start from the beginning?'

Miss Frostell took a deep breath. 'Well, it was as I was talking to Gabriel Footman,' she began. 'A good lad, that. Happy with his position, he says, with no cause for complaint. And such nice manners! Even if I am not one of the family myself, he treats me quite as though I am, and—'

'Frosty,' Gussie interrupted. 'You *are* one of the family, and if you persist in claiming otherwise I fear I shall break my promise, and become quite wrath with you.'

'Be that as it may,' said Miss Frostell, passing the point by. 'There was one thing he said that I did think odd. Cook sometimes sends him down for a bottle of something, and did so this morning. Something about a sherry-pudding, for his lordship's dinner. Well, Gabriel came down — just for a minute, like, he had no cause to linger — but he thought he heard an odd noise, he says. He had no time to investigate, having a great deal to do, and the matter went out of his head entirely, until I asked.'

'See!' crowed Gussie. 'I *thought* there must be something! It is another dead body, is it not? Say that it is!'

'Well—'

'In fact, if I may be granted my wish I should prefer *two* bodies. But one mustn't be greedy, must one?'

'It is not a body,' Miss Frostell persevered. 'At least, I suppose it is, only this one is still — wandering about.'

'A living person.' Gussie thought this over. 'I am a little disappointed, I confess, but one must accustom oneself. Who was it?'

'Ah— well, I do not think you will be quite pleased…'

'Oh no! On the contrary. Only tell me this person had no right whatsoever to be poking about in our cellar, and I shall be perfectly happy.'

'I should say she doesn't, indeed,' said Miss Frostell, rather unhappily.

'She—?' echoed Gussie, rapidly adjusting her ideas. 'A villainess! That is much better than I had hoped, after the disappointment about the corpses.'

'A villainess?' said somebody behind Gussie. 'Famous! Where is she?'

Gussie knew this voice, too. Her head came up; several thoughts at once passed through her mind, none of them charitable. 'Miss Selwyn?'

She turned.

There was Miss Selwyn indeed, clad in breeches and top-boots and a handsome cutaway coat. She had an uncorked bottle in one hand, and a lanthorn in the other, and was liberally coated in dust.

'I have *asked* and *asked* you to call me Clarissa,' said she, shaking her head. 'Really, one would almost be tempted to think you didn't want to be bosom-sisters at all.'

'*Clarissa*,' Gussie growled. 'Just *what* are you doing in my uncle's cellar?'

'Oh! Investigating,' said Clarissa vaguely. 'I was almost

sure there had to be something nefarious going on down here, but there appears to be nothing at all. I have scarcely ever been so cast down.'

'Nefarious?'

The dangerous note in Gussie's tone appeared to pass Clarissa by. 'Why, has the possibility never occurred to you? I must say, I am surprised.'

'What interests *me*,' said Gussie, 'is why the possibility occurred to *you*.'

'Why, because there have been all manner of dark carryings-on in *our* cellars,' said Clarissa brightly. 'Why not yours?'

This promising revelation caused Gussie to forget some of her outrage. 'There have? Marvellous! What kinds of carryings-on? I hope something frightful.'

'A corpse!' Clarissa beamed her delight. 'An entire corpse, whole and intact. Stone-cold, as one would expect. Quite *emptied* of blood. I remember thinking, at the time: what a pity it is that my bosom-sister is not here. How she would have enjoyed it!'

Several thoughts chased themselves around Gussie's head, none of them quite making it to her lips. She had not known that the Selwyns were in town, and had no idea at all of their present place of abode. And if Clarissa pined for her "bosom-sister" so terribly, why had she not come to inform Gussie, either of their arrival or of the discovery of the corpse?

But all such practical questions and considerations melted away in the face of that one, dazzling fact: the Selwyn household had sprouted a corpse soon after the Werths' had.

It could not be a coincidence.

'Why, we have had a corpse, too!' Gussie gushed. 'Only, ours was not left in the cellar. Our mysterious benefactor deposited ours in my aunt's favourite parlour, and who do you think it is? No less a person than a celebrated actress!'

63

Clarissa's face brightened at the beginning of Gussie's speech, and then fell again. 'Yes, the newspapers have been very full of it! And I am so *envious*. Ours is not a famous person, I don't think, though we are not perfectly sure yet who it is. Not a woman, either. Youngish man, unremarkable. Nothing much to identify him by. It's quite the *best* thing that has happened to us since Christmas at least, even if ours does happen to be a nobody.'

A disquieting thought occurred to Gussie. 'Clarissa. You did not happen to mastermind this delectable scheme, I suppose?'

'You mean did *I* leave the corpse of a beautiful actress in your aunt's favourite parlour, and land my own family with a mere nobody? La! No.'

'Very well,' Gussie allowed, for this made rather more sense than it didn't.

'Though I rather wish that I was responsible for so scintillating a scheme. Would not you admire me excessively, if I had come up with it?'

'I daresay I should. Just *one* further question, before I let you return to your activities. Why are you investigating in this clandestine fashion? You could have come in by the front door, I feel bound to point out, and conducted your investigations by my aunt's invitation.'

'I could have,' Clarissa agreed, nodding. 'But where would be the fun in that?'

A sentiment with which Gussie could not, in all honesty, disagree.

The air rippled oddly near Clarissa's elbow, the lanthorn's yellow light illuminating some ethereal disturbance. A head materialised, ghastly-pale, and wreathed in cobwebs. The face scowled horridly at Gussie. 'And look, you have intercepted my intruder!' cried Great-Aunt Honoria. 'I but *just* turn away for a moment to fetch dear Ivo, and when I return, *what* should I find but that the game is up! I had every expectation of bringing you the most delightful surprise, my dear, once I had discovered

64

what Miss Selwyn was about.'

'I perceive you are taking your duties as scout very seriously, Aunt,' Gussie approved. 'I am quite contrite, I assure you.'

'I suppose there will be other intruders,' Honoria allowed, somewhat mollified.

Clarissa smiled. 'Oh, there cannot be a doubt of it. It's only a matter of time.'

'What was Ivo doing, if he was not with you?' Gussie enquired. She did not altogether like to think of her aunt's mysterious companion drifting about the house by himself, undetectable.

'He has been keeping an eye on Mrs. Everleigh, and bid me leave him be. Not that it appears she has been doing anything so *very* fascinating.' Great-Aunt Honoria huffed an indignant sigh.

'This is what comes of keeping beautiful actresses in the house,' Clarissa said wisely. 'Though I do not see why she was to be kept an eye on, if she's a corpse. What could she possibly be doing?'

'My uncle has rectified her unfortunate condition,' Gussie supplied. 'To a degree.'

Clarissa's frown cleared; her face lit with delight. 'But of course! I cannot think how it came about, but I had rather forgotten that talent of his. He must come instantly to Mamma's, and revive *our* corpse, too.'

'Doubtless he would enjoy it very much,' Gussie allowed. 'But I do not know that my aunt would approve. My uncle is no longer a young man, you know, and she does not like him to tire himself.'

'Cook is making a lemon syllabub for dinner,' Clarissa offered.

Unable to perceive the relevance of this line of argument, Gussie waited.

'Perhaps that might satisfy your aunt?' Clarissa persisted. 'I asked for it especially, you know, for it is wonderfully rejuvenating. Mamma has sustained quite a shock. I have not seen her so elevated since Henry became a dragon.'

Ah yes, Lord Maundevyle. Gussie wondered whether his lordship had also removed to London, and then asked herself, a little severely, why she should care. 'Elevated?' she echoed. 'The corpse's identity may be a mystery to you, Clarissa, but your mamma may know better.'

Clarissa beamed. 'You are envisaging some scheme of revenge. How scintillating. Mamma is even the killer, perhaps! Is that what you are thinking? How sorry I am to pour cold water over such charming ideas. But Mamma would never stoop to murder so featureless a person. She would have one of the servants do it.'

'She would still be culpable, if she did,' Gussie pointed out. All things considered, she rather fancied Lady Maundevyle as the villainess of the piece. The woman was equal to anything. And considering what Gussie had (however unwittingly) done to her at Christmas — all her airy dreams of a draconic destiny ended in a half-hour's crushing disappointment — perhaps her ladyship was harbouring dreams of revenge, after all.

But Clarissa was shaking her head. 'Perhaps she may have wanted our hapless young man dead — why not, after all? He may have done something perfectly *awful* to her. But to dispose of the lifeless remains in our own cellar, and suffer them to be discovered there? The clumsiness of such a scheme! No, no. It could never be Mamma.'

Upon reflection, Gussie had to agree. Whatever else may be true of Lady Maundevyle, she had a cunning mind, and an attention to detail that could not abide such a mess.

'I must admit, investigating murders is a lowering experience,' Gussie sighed. 'No sooner do I hit upon a possible suspect than all my ideas are dashed down at once. It is very disheartening.'

She found her hand pressed by Miss Frostell. 'Never mind, my dear. You are doing your best, and no one could ask more.'

'A poor best it is,' Gussie replied. 'All I have uncovered so far is more questions! But perhaps this corpse of yours will help, Clarissa. Do tell us about him. Was he very bloodied?'

'Oh, positively drowned in blood,' she said. '*Bathed* in it. I shouldn't think there was so much as a drop left in his veins.'

'Much the same as ours!' said Gussie triumphantly. 'Though Mr. Ballantine does not think she was killed in the parlour. Somebody put her there on purpose, and very likely did the same with yours. You do not yet know how such a person might have got in?'

'Oh, anybody might have got in,' said Clarissa carelessly. 'Mamma is planning a party, and all manner of persons are coming and going all day long.'

Gussie heard the word "party" with a sense of foreboding. The last time Lady Maundevyle had undertaken to arrange a large celebration, it had all gone very wrong for Gussie. And her unfortunate elder son, too, though he had since reconciled himself to the outcome.

Miss Frostell was shivering. Gussie noticed this because the poor lady's teeth began to chatter. 'Poor Frosty, we will freeze you to death with all this talk. Clarissa, I collect your investigations are over?'

'Yes,' came the answer, with some disgruntlement. 'There isn't a thing to be found. I should have thought of the parlour as a superior location, but I confess I did not.'

'Then I should like very much to meet your corpse,' said Gussie. 'For if I do not do so at once, I feel sure someone will seek to prevent me.'

'Y-you have consulted the Runners, I suppose?' put in Miss Frostell, in her gentle way.

'And a magistrate, and a coroner, and all those sorts of things?' added Gussie helpfully.

Clarissa waved all this off. 'What on earth for?'

'It is the custom,' Gussie said. 'I believe it may even be the law, in some one or two points.'

'Such fuss over a mere dead person,' sighed Clarissa. 'When in a city as large as London, there must be hundreds of new ones made every day.'

'It is not *law* to consult Mr. Ballantine, of course,' Gussie continued. 'But he will be positively savage with me if he isn't included.'

'Ballantine?' echoed Clarissa. 'The ogre? We will invite *him*, with my good will. I'm dying to get to know him.'

There came an odd gleam into Miss Selwyn's eye; it was the words *savage* and *ogre* so neatly juxtaposed, Gussie supposed. If the woman could develop a fancy for such a person as Theo, small wonder that she found Mr. Ballantine's combination of qualities attractive.

A flurry of activity saw all the ladies retreating back up the stairs to the kitchens, Great-Aunt Honoria deigning to lead the way. Once the cellar door was suitably bolted, and the key relinquished into Miss Frostell's keeping, a stray thought entered Gussie's head. Indeed, she felt passingly ashamed that it had not occurred to her before.

'Frosty,' she began. 'Did you go down into the cellar quite alone?'

'Yes, my dear?'

'To investigate a possible threat lurking among the wine-bottles?'

'Yes, I did.'

'You did not happen to think to take Gabriel Footman with you, by chance? Or someone else vigorous and doughty?'

'Gabriel Footman was so busy this morning, and I could not find anyone else that was at leisure.'

'What I am attempting to get at, *dear* Frosty, is that you might have been in considerable danger. What if the interloper had not been only Clarissa, and had proved to be a murderer?'

'*Only* Clarissa,' interrupted Miss Selwyn, scowling. 'You

make me out to be just nothing at all, Gussie. I can be *quite* terrifying at need, I assure you.'

'I do not doubt it for a moment, but *you* would never harm our dear Miss Frostell. Another might, Frosty, and very easily. I do not mean to impugn your capabilities, of course. Only I should be so very unhappy if anything untoward were to happen to you.'

'Well. Perhaps some one or two things *untoward* might be permitted to happen,' said Clarissa. 'How frightfully dull life would be, otherwise.'

'I see what you are saying, my dear,' said Miss Frostell. 'And I shall be more careful in future, I daresay.'

'I shall be glad of it.'

Miss Frostell hesitated. 'Ah— did *you* happen to have company, when you came down?'

Gussie had no immediate answer to make, not having known beforehand that her Great-Aunt Honoria was down in the cellar. 'Well— no, I did not, but— but— I am rather more *hale* a figure, I suppose? And Wyrded besides, even if in no particularly useful fashion. I was in no danger, I am sure.'

Clarissa was unkind enough to smile. 'A very palpable hit, Miss Frostell. I have never until this moment seen Miss Werth at a loss for a convincing answer.'

Gussie, to her indignation, was blushing with discomfort. Good lord! Was Frosty taking her cues from Gussie's own behaviour? Shameful, if so. Her example, if followed by an elderly and unWyrded lady such as Miss Frostell, could only deserve the name of recklessness.

'If I propose to preach good sense, I suppose I must endeavour to exercise some of it myself,' she allowed. 'Only it is most inconvenient! And I *refuse* to be so incommoded as to have to ask Theo for assistance. A more unreliable person I have never met in my life.'

'We will be each other's support, Gussie,' offered Clarissa. 'I shall be positively savage in your defence.' Her smile might have struck terror into the hearts of the most brutal of murderers.

'And me,' put in Great-Aunt Honoria. 'I am always on the watch, my dear niece. No harm shall come to you under this roof, while I live and breathe!'

No one thought it worth pointing out that Lady Honoria had neither lived nor breathed in many years.

'You are all very kind,' Gussie forced herself to say. She supposed Miss Frostell had a point: if she *were* to run face-first into whichever brutal killer had emptied Mrs. Everleigh of her life's blood, she might be in a spot of trouble.

She resigned herself to operating, henceforth, as part of a pack.

EIGHT

Theo's first thought was to invite Mrs. Daughtry to attend him at his father's house, being by far the most convenient scheme. But a little reflection persuaded him that it would not answer. Mrs. Daughtry would soon hear whose house Mrs. Everleigh had been discovered in, if she had not already, and she may not be comfortable walking into that same house of apparent danger herself. And she would be unlikely to speak openly about Mrs. Everleigh if she felt uncertain of her own safety.

There was also Gussie, of course. If Mrs. Daughtry appeared on their own doorstep, his interfering cousin could not help but stick her oar in.

Hmm. Well. Were Theo perfectly honest, the prospect was not wholly unattractive, precisely because of Gussie; Ballantine's confidence in his powers of persuasion were not echoed by any particular confidence Theo felt in himself. If wringing secrets out of cagey thespians was to be the order of business, it might be possible that Gussie would do a better job than he.

But he would never hear the end of it, if so.

So he consulted Hargreve, and secured a set of rooms for himself at an unexceptionable address. A bachelor's abode, handsome enough to hint at wealth and plenty, but unostentatious. He only wanted to attract Mrs. Daughtry's attentions for an hour or two, no more.

Having done this much, he soon ran into difficulties again. He had never made *advances* towards a lady before; how did one go about issuing such an invitation? He reflected, with some bitterness, that Hargreve would have no trouble at all. Perhaps he could learn to be a little bit more like his handsome, sociable friend.

'Visit her after the performance,' Hargreve recommended, upon enquiry. 'If you ask to wait on her in her dressing-room, she is unlikely to refuse.'

'She is?' Theo said, blankly. He'd brought Hargreve to inspect his new rooms before he ventured to invite any ladies there, and his friend lounged in the arms of a particularly good wing-back chair positioned near the fireplace. The rest of the décor achieved a similar balance between comfort and sumptuary: a divan, rather elegant, for a lady to recline upon; another good chair; a few console-tables devoid of ornament ('Nothing that might suggest a lady's touch,' Hargreve had recommended. 'You want your guests to feel uniquely sought-after.').

No problem there, Theo had sourly reflected. They *were* uniquely sought-after, and he had no intention whatsoever of taking up the pursuit of women as a habit. But despite this, he hadn't even been permitted to dispense with the inconvenience and expense of setting up a bedchamber. 'I won't need one,' he had protested. 'I won't use it.'

'But it will look strange if you don't have one.' Hargreve had said it gently enough, but he had been firm. Inexorable. 'Do you want to present a compelling appearance, or not?'

His friend derived some unholy amusement from the process, Theo concluded, quite unconnected with the business at hand. Damn him.

Thus had Theo arrived at the peculiar set of challenges which now faced him, upon which topics his long-suffering friend continued to advise.

'Oh, she won't refuse to see you,' Hargreve said confidently. 'Come off it, Bedge. You are the son and heir of an earl, and the scion of one of the most sensationally Wyrded families England has ever known. Why, if I had half your credentials, I would have the whole of London at my feet.'

With half Theo's "credentials" together with his angelically handsome looks, perhaps he would. Not to mention his facility with words and women.

Theo found the entire business wearying beyond words.

'Very well,' he said, capitulating to inevitability with a sigh. 'I will do as you suggest.'

'Buck up, do,' Hargreve said, catching sight of Theo's grave face. 'Much as it would entertain me to see you turn charming seducer, that is not what you are setting out to do. You are in the service of Bow Street.'

The reminder was a percipient one, for it removed much of Theo's uncertainty. When he attended the theatre that night, he sat through the performance of Daggett's *Revenge* with a feeling of grim purpose. He felt no qualms whatsoever at sending his card round to Mrs. Daughtry, and requesting admittance; he was not a supplicant, nor was he a wooer, but an instrument of justice. He would put Mrs. Daughtry to the question, and uncover the sordid truth. She would be quite unable to hide.

He arrived at her dressing-room door puffed up with purpose and perfectly free of trepidation; a state of being he rather enjoyed.

Unfortunately for Theo, it did not last.

Why?

Well. For a start, she was appallingly beautiful.

Somehow, he had never noticed this from his seat in the audience. She was so distant and so distorted under the lights, covered in her make-up and arrayed in her elaborate costumes; he had never seen her, or thought of her, as simply a woman underneath it all, and a beautiful one at that. Up close, her stage make-up removed, she was younger than he had imagined, and divinely fair. She had delicate features, prismatic blue eyes, and the sweetest smile he had ever encountered in womanhood.

Besides this disarming quality came others, equally devastating, and Theo's breath entirely deserted him. He hovered in the doorway, stupefied.

She looked up at his arrival, and rather than displaying the smooth, cool manners of a woman of the world (as he had expected), she cast him a look of some distress, half-rose from her seat, and said: 'Oh, Lord Bedgberry! It is so good of you to come to visit me, but I confess I have been sitting in some dread of your arrival. I feel certain you are going to ask me about poor Mrs. Everleigh, and I am sure I do not know *what* to tell you.'

This robbed Theo of all the speeches he had half prepared for this moment, and rendered him mute. To be sure, she was an actress; perhaps this show of discomfort and distress was merely an act, intended to disarm him.

Whether truth or dissembling, it was damned effective.

'Ma'am,' he said at last, recovering his powers of speech. Somewhat. 'Er. I don't— that is, I'm not—' He blinked at the vision before him, all wreathed in lavender gauze as she was, and took a breath. *Think of Gussie. That ought to work.* Yes, yes it did: there, he was feeling irritated already.

'Your servant, ma'am,' he said, more composedly. 'Er, I wonder what led you to imagine I was here about Mrs. Everleigh?'

There; a circumspect reply, giving nothing away.

'Oh! But have not you seen the papers?' She got up, conducted a distracted hunt about her rosewood dressing-table, abandoned the endeavour and sat down again. 'I had some of them here about, I *had* thought, but no matter. It is in all the papers, Lord Bedgberry. That you are suspected of— oh, dear. *Do* forgive me, but you are suspected of having— of having effected her demise, they say. She was found in your home, was not she?'

'But—' Theo floundered, disarmed by so odd a mix of direct attack and earnest apology. 'But— but why the *Devil* would I kill Mrs. Everleigh? I'd never even met the woman!'

Mrs. Daughtry hesitated, twisting some hapless, fabric article about in her hands. 'They say— that you, being a known enthusiast for the arts, were in love with her; that you perhaps killed her in a jealous rage— oh, *dear*. I *am* sorry. I am sure it is all a monstrous lie, and you do look so unhappy.'

Theo, having enjoyed a brief spasm of thunderous indignation, subsided into indifference. 'Vicious slander,' he murmured — and stopped, for if either of them looked unhappy it was Mrs. Daughtry herself. She regarded Theo with a look of such limpid sympathy in her crystalline eyes, such passionate sadness — and for *him* — that he was, for a moment, silenced by it.

Nobody had ever looked at him like *that* before.

'Well,' he said awkwardly, after a moment. 'It will all be proved untrue, and the papers will be forced to retract, for I certainly did *not* kill Mrs. Everleigh.' He thought again, for an uncomfortable moment, of his treatment of Mrs. Everleigh's remains, and decided not to mention it.

Mrs. Daughtry appeared reassured, for she settled, and stopped torturing the defenceless article of women's dress she had been pulling about in her hands. Her expression turned contemplative. 'Really, it has been a clever scheme,' she observed. 'To involve *your* family was a brilliant move, for exactly this reason. All this speculation has completely obscured whatever might have been the true story.'

'And if the truth is not uncovered then *I* will be fortunate enough to hang for it.' Theo, at last, stopped hovering in the doorway, and ventured to enter the room. Mrs. Daughtry jumped up again, and ushered him into a seat; pressed him tenderly into it, before returning to her own.

Theo, bemused, exerted a strong effort to wrench his mind back to the matter at hand.

Yes. Mrs. Daughtry, and questions. This lady might have information. She might even know who had performed the dreadful deed, if the facts could be got out of her.

She might even be *involved*.

Every instinct he had cried out at the idea. *This* beautiful, tender creature, remotely connected with a brutal murder! Impossible.

But she was an actress. And he could hear Gussie's sardonic tones unfurling in his mind, almost as though she stood at his shoulder, coolly observing the scene. *This is all very lovely, is it not? What a sweet creature she is! Would never harm so much as a fly, I feel quite, baselessly certain of it.*

Hmm.

Theo eyed the ravishing creature before him, and regretfully abandoned his carefully-laid plans. He was no seducer, and this woman showed no signs whatsoever of hoping to be seduced. The scheme had been absurd from the start.

And, he had sourly to conclude, he was already out-manoeuvred. He did not *want* this lovely, delightful Mrs. Daughtry, who believed so deeply in his spotless character, and cared so much for his feelings, to be anything less than she seemed. Which meant that, in the space of a mere ten minutes, his judgement had been hopelessly compromised.

He would have to recruit the assistance of his family, after all.

'I admit, ma'am, I did come here with a few questions to put to you,' he said. 'I had hoped to discover what your impressions might have been about the night of Mrs. Everleigh's disappearance, and whether you saw or heard anything of use — that sort of thing, you know. But perhaps you would prefer not to speak of such things here? May I extend an invitation to call upon us?'

'To— to call upon your family?' she gasped.

She appeared, Theo ruefully observed, petrified.

'We are not at all alarming, I assure you.' He spoke stiffly; feeling, oddly, disheartened.

'Oh, no! I am sure you are not.'

'You will find my mother and cousin very welcoming.'

'Oh, certainly! I am sure I should.'

Theo perceived that this invitation had not had the effect he'd been hoping for. He had not made either of them feel more comfortable; more the opposite.

Perhaps his first conclusions had been correct, after all. He should have invited her to his own rooms — or dispensed with the invitations and simply interrogated her where she sat. Ballantine would have done the latter. Hargreve would have done the former.

He, Theo, had merely made a mess of it.

'I only need *information*,' he sighed. 'Will you not simply tell me why you, and the rest of the cast, were so uncomfortable that night?'

'U-uncomfortable?' she stammered. 'No, no! All was well at Strangewayes, except that Mrs. Everleigh's failure to appear *did* rather surprise us. There was such a bustle about it, and of course I had to be readied to go on at the last minute, and everyone was *so* angered with her.'

'Perhaps that was it,' he said. 'But I could not help but wonder whether there was more to it than that. Tell me honestly, ma'am: did you all know that she was dead? Was she killed here?'

Mrs. Daughtry covered her face with her hands, and wailed: 'I cannot speak of it here! But I see that I must.' She took a deep, shuddering breath, lowered her hands, and looked Theo full in the face. Her own, enchanting visage was contorted with some private agony. 'I accept your invitation, Lord Bedgberry. Your family has been deeply implicated by this sad event, and you all have a right to any information I can provide.'

'Splendid. Tomorrow, then? My mother will expect

you.'

'Yes. Tomorrow.' She took another, shaky breath, and straightened her spine. 'I promise you, I will not fail.'

NINE

Upon the following morning, Gussie arrived early at the breakfast table, perfectly unaware of the treat that lay in store for her. She had not slept well, her mind having persisted in turning the facts of the case over and over until she felt half-mad with it. Nor had the exercise blessed her with any flashes of inspiration, or new understanding; she had only given herself confused dreams, when at last she fell asleep, wherein various members of her family and acquaintance lay dead — only to revive again, and give her differing accounts of who was responsible.

The dream had ended with Theo hanging by the neck from a gallows-rope, while giving her a rather irascible account of a book entitled *Reflections on French Cuisine,* which he had lately been reading.

She had woken too early, as though her mind had despaired of itself, and decided that wakefulness would prove the less trying experience of the two. So when Theo appeared at the table, bright and early, and quite unexpected, she was too sleepy and (if we are to be honest) out-of-temper to remark upon it.

Theo sat with an empty plate before him, eyeing his cousin in a fashion she might have termed *nervous,* if it were anybody but Theo. And when Lady Werth came in soon afterwards, his agitation increased. He got up, served himself a portion of shirred eggs from the silver chafing dishes, and sat down again, only to toy with the unoffending comestibles in a manner even Lady Werth could not tolerate. His fork clattered loudly against the porcelain of his plate.

'For heaven's sake, Theo, whatever is the matter?' said Lady Werth at last, paused over a cup of chocolate she had, as yet, barely touched.

'Oh— nothing at all,' said Theo, pausing rather lengthily in the middle of this transparently mendacious statement, and casting a sideways glance at Gussie.

Gussie returned the glance with a cool stare.

Lady Werth appeared to accept this, and returned to her breakfast. But Theo's chair was soon discovered to be squeaky, a fact he thoughtfully made plain to the company by rocking back and forth upon it.

'Theo,' said Gussie at last. 'How you intrigue me. I had not thought you capable of anything so human as *agitation*, or— shall we say *guilt*? Yes,' she went on, for the look Theo cast at her positively reeked of something guilt-related; 'there is something you ought to tell us, but for some reason you hesitate. Do not keep us in suspense any longer.'

Mercifully, Theo stopped fidgeting in his chair; the squeaking stopped. But he only stared at his plate, and said nothing.

'If it has aught to do with the Selwyns, then permit me to reassure you,' Gussie persevered. 'Clarissa has been evicted from the cellar, and I do not believe she will make any more such forays.'

'What?' said Theo.

'Furthermore, I have already decided to attend upon them later this morning,' Gussie continued. 'I will investigate, and uncover the truth about this fresh victim.' She had been a little disappointed in her pursuit of the scheme, for by the time she had learned of the existence of Clarissa's corpse — as she was obliged to think of him, until some sort of name were discovered for him — well, the man had already been removed from the house, and put where she could not get at him. Not even Mr. Ballantine had been willing to let her visit the morgue. Vague thoughts of a covert infiltration floated through her mind at intervals, and might be pursued; but for the present, she was forced to put up with only a description of the corpse, and a social call later, under the guise of which she could examine the scene.

But Theo was staring blankly at her. 'What?' he said again.

'The new corpse?' said Gussie, politely. 'Gracious, Theo, have you not heard? Where can you possibly have been since yesterday?'

A conscious look, tinged vaguely with guilt again (or something like it) passed over Theo's face. 'I'll— get to that in a minute,' said he evasively, and Gussie perceived that his state of agitation this morning had something to do with whatever he had got up to yesterday. 'Go on. What's this about another corpse? I hope it was not in your parlour again, mother. That would be the outside of enough.'

'It would,' Lady Werth agreed, setting down her largely emptied cup. 'I should have been most upset, but fortunately this new corpse is not ours.'

'It's Clarissa's,' said Gussie, and added, disgustedly, 'and she is impossibly smug about it, too.' She went on to describe to Theo the events of the previous day, culminating in Miss Frostell's astounding discovery in the cellar. 'Only think!' she said in conclusion. 'If Clarissa had come straight here and told us all about it, I might have got a look at him! Instead she had to go poking about in the cellars, and goodness knows what else, and now I am most inconvenienced.'

'Doesn't trust you,' said Theo. 'Or any of us, I

shouldn't wonder. Thought we might have done it.'

Gussie, about to disclaim in indignation, paused. Honesty compelled her to admit that, if these were Clarissa's feelings, they were not unjust. Had she not herself considered that the Selwyns might have done the deed, if with no direct intention to cause serious trouble, then at least as some manner of ghoulish prank?

If the Selwyns had entertained similar suspicions of the Werths, could she fairly object?

'Well, we didn't,' she said. 'And I don't believe they did it, either, so we are no further forward.'

'Two corpses,' mused Theo. 'Killed in similar ways, and both left at the houses of prominently Wyrded families in London. There must be some connection.'

'That is what I think,' agreed Gussie. 'And now, Theo, I believe it is time for you to explain to us what has you so jumpy this morning. Or to speak plainly: *what* have you done?'

'Er.' Theo's gaze darted to his mother's face, but no help was forthcoming from *there*. 'It was Ballantine's thought,' he said, a little desperately. 'He asked me to, er, assist with one or two enquiries—'

'He did what!' Gussie exclaimed, outraged. 'The cheek of the man! Trying to prevent *me* from having anything to do with it while giving *you* carte blanche to investigate as you like! I must think of something awful to do to him.'

'You, er, would not have been qualified for this particular endeavour,' Theo said, his desperation increasing. 'The thing is— well, what happened was— er—'

Gussie waited, and out came a halting tale of attempted subterfuge and failed seduction and angelic fairness and something about *dressing-tables*— by the time Theo stopped speaking she felt hopelessly confused.

One point, though, lingered in her mind.

'You set up rooms?'

Theo gave an awkward nod.

'And you were going to take a *lady* to them?'

'I was *going to* ,' Theo snarled. 'But I *didn't*.'

Gussie began to laugh. 'Mr. Hargreve can have no very accurate idea of you,' she managed, once the initial paroxysms of laughter had subsided. 'To imagine you capable of—'

'Gussie,' said Lady Werth, mildly, but with an implied reproof her niece had no trouble in perceiving.

'My apologies, Aunt. Theo, I applaud you. This was an instance of utter heroism in you.'

Theo merely cast her a suspicious look — and then glanced at the clock.

'Oh, dear,' said Gussie. 'That was not quite the whole story, I perceive?'

'Well, no,' Theo admitted. 'The thing is that— er, well—'

'Out with it, Theo,' said Gussie, beginning to feel rather wearied.

It was at that moment that the doorbell rang.

'The thing is that she's coming here,' said Theo all in a rush. 'Today.'

Mabel appeared at the door. 'There's a... lady to see you, ma'am,' she said, hesitating, almost imperceptibly, over the word *lady*. 'I'll put her in the— er, the library, shall I?'

Mabel, uncertain of the visitor's genteel credentials, hesitated to conduct her to the drawing-room.

Lady Werth cast her son a speaking look, and rose from her seat. 'No indeed, Mabel,' she told the maid. 'I will receive her in the drawing-room.' She glanced, briefly, at Gussie and Theo, and added, by way of explanation (if not defence): 'It is far more comfortable in there.'

The Werths processed to the drawing-room in some state, collecting Great-Aunt Honoria on their way up the stairs. Lord Werth was encountered, coming down them.

'What's all this?' he asked, brows rising at the unlooked-for sight, so early in the morning, of his wife, son and niece apparently forming a council of war.

'I will tell you all about it later, my dear,' said Lady Werth. 'Don't let your beef-steaks get cold. Cook has made a fresh batch especially.'

Thus dismissed, Lord Werth met Gussie's gaze for a short, helpless moment, then shrugged up his shoulders and retired to the breakfast-room, clearly deciding not to interfere.

Upon entering the drawing-room, Gussie beheld Theo's actress ingénue, reposed upon a small sofa near the bay window, and gazing pensively into the street. The steel-grey light cast a wan, pallid colour over her complexion, and turned her hair very pale, but nothing could dim the scintillating beauty she patently possessed.

And she knew how to use it, Gussie thought at once, for upon hearing the door creak slightly as it opened, and the footsteps of her hosts entering the room, Mrs. Daughtry turned — an artlessly graceful gesture — and rose from her seat, her face a study of conflicting emotions.

Nothing could have been prettier than the smooth and deferential curtsey she performed before Lady Werth, Lord Bedgberry, Lady Honoria, and the Honourable Gussie. It spoke of a charming humility, and a gratifying sense of their condescension in admitting her to their home.

And, indeed, their best drawing-room.

Gussie transferred her attention from the actress to her cousin, and did not miss the stupefied look that transformed Theo's face as he beheld this performance.

Good Lord. She had not thought any woman had the power to rearrange Theo's wits, and when at last he succumbed to the combined powers of beauty and fine tailoring, he must needs choose a conniving actress?

For conniving she undoubtedly was; every gesture, every change in her expression, was palpably chosen to create an ingratiating effect.

It seemed to be working on Great-Aunt Honoria, too.

'Oh, my love for the theatre is *inexhaustible*, I declare!' cried she, once pleasantries had been exchanged, and the ladies (and Theo) had all taken seats. 'I am sure you adorn it charmingly, my dear! How delighted I should be to witness a performance of yours.'

Mrs. Daughtry, a true daughter of Strangewayes, was not in the least perturbed by the absence of most of Lady Honoria's body. 'I would take the greatest of pleasure in numbering you among my audience,' she said prettily. 'What an honour it would be!'

Great-Aunt Honoria, to Gussie's disgust, simpered.

'How kind of you to visit us, Mrs. Daughtry,' said Lady Werth, taking control of the conversation with her usual grace. 'And so promptly,' she added.

'I *am* unfashionably early, I know,' answered the actress, colouring prettily. 'I pray you will forgive me. You see, I knew I had not dealt fairly with Lord Bedgberry, and I could hardly rest for thinking of it! My lord, I ought to have owned the whole truth last evening, when you were so good as to call upon me after the performance. I cannot think why I did not, only I was—' She broke off and gazed into space, her pose and expression hinting at some nameless torment. 'Oh, but the past few days have been so very perturbing!' she burst out. 'And I have had *no one* to talk to, no one I felt I could trust. Can you understand?'

Theo looked ready to fall at her feet, which irritated Gussie immensely.

Her aunt, however, retained the full use of her wits. She did not answer immediately, and when she did, her voice was cool. 'I can imagine it has been a very trying experience, ma'am — losing a cast member, and in such a fashion. You are not experiencing any great distress at finding yourself in this, of all possible houses, I trust?'

'Oh, no, no! How could I be so disobliging as to— and you have been *so* good to welcome me, even at a time of such affliction among your family.'

Lady Werth appeared somewhat at a loss.

'I believe she is referring to Theo's status as prime suspect, Aunt,' Gussie murmured. 'The newspapers having been so obliging as to broadcast the fact all over London.'

'Indeed. I feel for him so very, very much,' said Mrs. Daughtry, and the look she cast at Theo was brimming with unshed tears.

'Your belief in my son's innocence touches my heart,' said Lady Werth, expressionlessly.

'Oh, who could believe otherwise? One has only to look at him to understand — to *know*, that he could never be capable of such a terrible deed.'

There followed a brief silence, in which each individual member of the Werth family engaged in private reflections upon the deeds of which Theo had, in fact, proved heartily capable.

Gussie could not resist.

'He has never been *proven* guilty of anything very terrible,' she said, adding, after a moment's apparent thought, 'not yet, anyway.'

Mrs. Daughtry turned luminously-blue eyes upon Gussie. 'You jest, Miss Werth?' she said, her breath catching. 'At *such* a time!'

'I believe you will find I jest at any, and indeed, *all* times,' Gussie answered, smiling. 'If one is not to be out-faced by the innumerable trials of life, one must invariably find a way to laugh at them.'

'To laugh at Death!' declared Mrs. Daughtry, and achieved a shudder. 'I am not equal to it, I admit.'

'Then you have come to the wrong house,' Gussie said crisply. 'Permit me to direct you to any one of our neighbours' establishments. They are all perfectly unobjectionable dwellings, with not a single corpse between them, bloodied or otherwise.'

Mrs. Daughtry's angelic face darkened, but before she could speak, Lady Werth intervened.

'You had something of importance to tell us?' she

prompted, casting a quelling look at Gussie.

'I— yes. Yes, I must.' Mrs. Daughtry took a deep breath; her bosom swelled. Gussie did not trouble herself to observe the effect this manoeuvre might have had on Theo. 'It will not surprise you to learn, my lady, that your son is a man of far more than ordinary perspicacity.'

Since this fact came as a decided surprise to Lady Werth, she was not able to favour Mrs. Daughtry with any immediate response.

'He witnessed our performance, the night of Mrs. Everleigh's unfortunate— event,' the actress continued. 'And, talented thespians though we all are, we could not conceal from *him* that something— unusual had occurred. Something that disturbed us very greatly. He concluded, very cleverly, that the two things must be connected — that it was some knowledge of Mrs. Everleigh's— *event*—'

'Demise,' interrupted Gussie. 'One may as well use plain words. An *event* cannot be made one jot less terrible by applying some obfuscating term to it afterwards.'

'Mrs. Everleigh's— demise, then,' said Mrs. Daughtry, the syllables uttered reluctantly, as though the word itself pained her. 'You thought, my lord, that she must have died at Strangewayes; that we must have discovered her death when we discovered her body. Perhaps you even imagined we might have had something to do with her— demise. But the truth is—' She hesitated, again, and Gussie fought an urge to catch up the nearest heavy object and brain her with it. A porcelain vase was within easy reach, and looked weighty enough to do a charming degree of damage.

'The truth is,' said Mrs. Daughtry, after a steadying breath. 'We *were* aware of her— distress, but not in the way you imagined.' Her eyelashes fluttered; she looked down at her hands. 'Have you ever heard mention of the nature of my Wyrde, Lord Bedgberry?'

Theo, hearing his name, started, and blinked. His gaze never moved from its absorbed contemplation of her face. 'I haven't.'

'I am... some would say I am *blessed* with a degree of foresight,' she said, looking up again, and bravely meeting the stares of her audience. 'I might rather call it a curse, and no more so than I have had occasion to do this week!' Her words gathered in pace; she launched into an impassioned speech. 'I knew it was to happen! I saw it all! But too late, *too late...* oh, shall I ever forgive myself? It was not until I arrived at the theatre that I knew — I *knew* that something terrible was to happen, or had already happened; something *deadly*, and that it would befall our dear Arabella — Mrs. Everleigh. I expected her to arrive at any moment, for she was, as you know, to be on stage that night. But she did not appear, and as time passed I grew more and more agitated. I could not conceal it, I own, and I fear my very natural concern must have increased that of those about me, for as time passed and Arabella did not arrive, we became— half maddened with fear for her. *That* is what you witnessed, Lord Bedgberry, and your instincts did not deceive you.' She bit her lip, her celestial eyes shimmering with tears. 'How I *hoped* that I might be proved wrong, somehow! I did not sleep a wink all night. But the morning brought such terrible news...'

Theo looked ready to lunge in Mrs. Daughtry's general direction, with what aim in mind Gussie could not have said. She read more apparent emotion in his face than she had ever seen there before.

'How trying,' she murmured.

Lady Werth said, 'An affecting story, Mrs. Daughtry. Is that the extent of it?'

'No!' cried the actress. 'I very much fear there is more to come, my lady. For I have received similar feelings — forebodings — about another member of our precious theatre. He is young yet, Robert Pile, but great things are predicted for his future upon the stage, and he *must* live to fulfil that promise!'

'He *is* missing, I suppose?' Gussie put in, interested.

'Yes! Nothing has been seen or heard from him in near

two days, and I am afraid—'

'Oh yes, he is quite dead,' Gussie confirmed. 'At least, I feel strongly persuaded of it.'

'Clarissa's corpse!' gasped Great-Aunt Honoria.

'Quite so, Aunt,' Gussie agreed. 'What a relief to be able to put a name to him at last. "Clarissa's corpse" has been such an unwieldy moniker.'

Mrs. Daughtry's face crumpled. She accepted the handkerchief Theo thrust into her hands, and buried her face in it. 'I— f-feared it must be so,' she sobbed.

Lady Werth's crisp voice sliced through her paroxysms of grief. 'Have you had any other premonitions, Mrs. Daughtry?'

The afflicted lady raised her face from the handkerchief. She cried beautifully, Gussie noted with dispassionate interest; gracefully, serenely, her tears glittering on her pale cheeks like clear jewels. 'I have,' she confessed brokenly. 'And it pertains to—'

Another great, shuddering breath. Gussie thought again, wistfully, of the heavy vase.

'It pertains to— to *me*, my lady. I very much fear that there is more death to come, and the next victim of it will be my own self.'

Theo gave a strangled cry, and started up from his chair. 'No! That cannot be!'

'Sit down, Theo,' said Lady Werth icily.

Theo sat, only to sit gazing at Mrs. Daughtry with naked anguish. 'You must be protected,' he gabbled. 'Something must be done.'

Gussie did not understand quite what the actress had done to Theo, but it had been done masterfully well. Perhaps she might herself take notes, or request some form of tuition. Who might not she enslave, with such arts at her disposal as Mrs. Daughtry possessed?

Lord Maundevyle's face floated through her thoughts, and was promptly banished.

'But this is perfect!' Gussie said, beaming. 'How

practical your premonitions prove, Mrs. Daughtry. We need only set some kind of watch over you, and when you come to be murdered we will know at once who the culprit was. Our good Mr. Ballantine can swoop upon the fellow without the smallest delay, and do away with him.'

Mrs. Daughtry stared at Gussie with horrified reproach, apparently shocked speechless.

'Or perhaps Theo would enjoy that particular honour,' Gussie amended, handsomely making over the task of violent retribution to her cousin. 'Provided the miscreant is suitably punished, I do not suppose it matters greatly who administers it.'

'It *does* appear,' interrupted Lady Werth, 'that somebody has a quarrel of some kind with Strangewayes.'

'Quite true, and *quite* shocking,' said Great-Aunt Honoria. 'Two thespians despicably slain, and a third in line for a like fate! It is just like a play.' Her beaming smile aptly conveyed her delight in the prospect.

Gussie gave the matter some deeper thought. Her aunt was right. Gussie had been disposed to assume that the murderer, whoever it was, had a quarrel with the Werth family, a theory which she had since widened to include the Selwyns. But if all three victims came from the only theatre in the country dedicated to Wyrded performers and attendees alike, the truth must run deeper. 'Somebody has a quarrel with the *Wyrde*,' she said. 'All of the victims, or potential victims, came from Strangewayes, which means they were— or *are*— Wyrded. And two of the three were left at the houses of prominently Wyrded families. If one wanted to make some kind of statement of opposition to the Wyrde itself, and did not especially mind bloodying one's hands a little, I could hardly think of a more impactful way to make it.'

'To what end, however?' asked Lady Werth. 'Is it intended as some form of protest? Against what?'

'Perhaps we are to be all tidied away, like last year's gowns,' said Gussie lightly. 'Half of us murdered, and the other half hanged for it.'

This piece of wit was not much to Lady Werth's taste, for she stared at her niece, stone-faced and silent.

'You may be right, Gussie,' said Great-Aunt Honoria, slowly. 'Are there so very many Wyrded souls in England, after all?'

'No, but the numbers are on the rise.' She stared down at her own hands, folded in her lap, as a number of unpleasant ideas unfurled in her mind. The numbers were indeed on the rise — thanks to her own efforts. If somebody wanted to cull the Wyrded of England, Ireland and Scotland, what did that mean for Gussie?

The same idea had occurred to her two aunts, for both were now staring at her in some horror.

'Surely someone would already have tried,' Gussie said, answering their unspoken question. 'Surely I would have been the very *first* victim.'

'Your unique Wyrde may not yet be widely known,' suggested Lady Werth. 'Your efforts among the military notwithstanding.'

'You ought to take care, Gussie,' said Great-Aunt Honoria. 'Oh, dear! I shall have to keep a close watch on you, shan't I? I'll tell Ivo at once.'

She was as good as her word, disappearing in an instant.

Lady Werth said nothing more, but sat in palpable disquiet, her mind apparently busy.

Everyone had forgotten Mrs. Daughtry. Except, perhaps, for Theo.

'I see I have brought unhappy news,' uttered the actress into the silence. 'If it is of any comfort at all, I have suffered no dire forebodings regarding *your* fate, Miss Werth. Only my own…'

'Your forebodings came rather too late to be of any use to Mrs. Everleigh,' Gussie pointed out.

Lady Werth rose abruptly. 'I must consult with my lord,' she said. She cast an abstracted look at Mrs.

Daughtry, who rose, belatedly, from her chair. 'Forgive me for cutting short this meeting, ma'am. We are grateful for your information.'

'But, Mother,' interposed Theo. 'What are we to do for her?

'For Gussie? That is what I wish to consult with your father about.'

'No. For Mrs. Daughtry.'

Lady Werth looked at the actress in some surprise. 'Do?' she echoed.

'It appears to be *her* life that is in imminent danger, not Gussie's.'

Lady Werth did not appear to be overpowered with concern.

'Why, we will keep her as well,' Gussie suggested brightly. 'She may like to room with Mrs. Everleigh.'

Mrs. Daughtry looked up. 'Arabella is here?'

'Of course. Having so rudely returned her to life, we could hardly turn her straight out into the street again. It can take a little time to adjust to so altered a state of being.'

'You have? *How* I should like to see her!' declared Mrs. Daughtry.

'Then you shall,' said Lady Werth. 'Theo, please escort our guest to… wherever our other guest is to be found.'

Theo, obviously displeased, did not reply. He offered his arm to Mrs. Daughtry, and the two left the room together, leaving Gussie alone with her aunt.

'A fine imbroglio this is turning out to be,' Gussie said cheerfully.

'I do believe there is greater danger than I had at first perceived,' answered Lady Werth. 'Gussie, I know you are wont to be careless of risk, but in this instance—'

'I promise, Aunt, I shall keep a wary eye out when I am abroad. And Great-Aunt Honoria has already pledged herself to my protection while I am at home.'

Perceiving her niece unmoved, Lady Werth gave a short sigh. 'I must speak to your uncle,' she said again.

'And, somebody must inform Mr. Ballantine of this new information.'

'I daresay he would like to know his latest corpse's name, at least,' Gussie agreed. 'So might Clarissa. Shall I go?'

'I am not sure that—'

'I'll go,' Gussie decided. 'It is not far to Bow Street, and if anybody tries to murder me on my way there, I shall have a most invigorating walk.'

She was gone before her aunt could make any further remark. Curse the dramatic Mrs. Daughtry! If her warnings and her premonitions were to worry Lady Werth, Gussie might find her movements severely curtailed, and she had had enough of *that* to last a lifetime.

Ten

'So much emotion!' Gussie said, later that same morning, for Clarissa Selwyn's entertainment. 'How *exhausting* I should find it.'

Clarissa nodded wisely. 'The thing is that they're paid to have emotions.'

'Actresses? Why, yes, I suppose they are. But she might save them for the stage, and spare *my* patience.'

'Oh, but she was on stage.' Clarissa's smile turned sly. 'By your account, she turned in a rousing performance.'

One might be forgiven for assuming that the two young ladies reposed themselves somewhere comfortable for this conversation— respectable, even. Civilised. Like Lady Maundevyle's drawing-room, or a charming parlour.

In fact, upon arrival at the Selwyns' townhouse, Gussie had asked for Clarissa and then been obliged to wait for some time. When the maid had reappeared at last, she had conducted Gussie up a flight of stairs, and then another, and a third, and finally delivered her to a cobweb-ridden garret at the top of the house. Clarissa sat upon an array of threadbare cushions strewn in front of the window, clad as always in her breeches and top-boots. The window was small and the chamber cramped, but the view it afforded of the streets below was considerable.

'She has set her cap at Theo, I fear,' Gussie said.

'Who could blame her,' Clarissa replied, with a wistful sigh.

'And it appears to be working.'

Clarissa's eyes narrowed at that. 'No, is it? Who could have predicted that Lord Bedgberry would fall victim to a watering-pot?'

'Not I.' Gussie shook her head. 'It doesn't hurt that she is transcendently beautiful, of course, but Theo has come across beautiful females before without seeming much affected by it. It is quite unaccountable.'

'I begin to dislike your Mrs. Daughtry rather excessively.'

'She is not "our" Mrs. Daughtry, and I am determined that she never shall be.' She spoke truly. If she had to choose between Clarissa and the actress for a sister-in-law, she would choose the former in a heartbeat. Top-boots and all.

Clarissa sniffed. 'She sounds a suspicious character.'

'That is what I think,' Gussie agreed. 'Far too insinuating! And her effect upon Theo is positively shocking. Who *could* have predicted that he would fall for such a display, indeed? It is unthinkable. He is acting quite unlike himself, and I refuse to believe that he has fallen in love.'

She had wanted to say the same things to Mr. Ballantine, only an hour ago, but he had not been at Bow Street, and nobody would tell her where he had gone. Gussie was officially out of all patience with him.

'We must join our forces,' Clarissa decided. 'I have given up hope that *you* might prove to be behind it all, and as such—'

'Me?' Gussie interrupted. 'Theo I could understand, but you suspected *me*?'

'No,' Clarissa sighed. 'I *tried*, of course, but I could not persuade myself that it was your style of thing.'

95

'I *am* sorry to disappoint you.'

'It is all right. One must bear one's disappointments with fortitude.'

'Would it have been so very diverting, if it had been me?'

'To be sure! Were you to turn miscreant, you would think up the most shocking schemes. Now, would not you?'

'So I would,' Gussie said, much struck by the idea. 'Really, I cannot think why it has not occurred to me to turn criminal before.'

Clarissa smiled. 'We will think up some shocking schemes together, one of these days. But first we must confirm the author of this week's pretty little mess, and rescue your absurd cousin into the bargain.'

'My *absurd* cousin? I thought you were dying of love for him.'

'I was, but I confess your divine Mr. Ballantine has quite turned my head.'

Gussie could only shake hers, bewildered. Clarissa had the strangest taste in gentlemen. 'He is an ogre,' she informed her friend.

'I know,' sighed Clarissa, fervently.

All this talk of men brought Gussie's thoughts back around to Lord Maundevyle. It would have been the easiest thing in the world to enquire after him. She could say something like: *speaking of gentlemen, has your charming brother accompanied you to London?* And Clarissa would say something like, *Why, yes, and he is sick with longing for you,* and then Gussie could say—

'You've had an idea, have not you?' Clarissa interrupted. 'Your eyes went faraway. Tell me all about it.'

'No,' said Gussie hastily. 'I wish I had. What are we to make of all these clues? I shall never wish for anything for the whole rest of my life, for look what comes of it. I wanted a single, good clue, and now we are drowning in far too many of them.'

'The mysterious gown,' Clarissa nodded. 'The actress's forebodings. The connection with Strangewayes. The Wyrde. The attempt to implicate your family, and also mine.'

'The lack of a trace left by the perpetrator in either of our houses,' Gussie added. 'And have you discovered how, or when, they got in?'

Clarissa shook her head. 'They came in disguised as some person relevant to Mamma's party-business, I suppose.'

'Or they also must have had a key, or had somebody open the door for them! Perhaps we both have traitors under our roofs.'

'How exciting! I hope it is Frederick. A repulsive fellow. I cannot think why Mother keeps him on as footman.'

Gussie did not answer. She had wasted little time on the servants at her own house; she relied upon Frosty to uncover the truth, aided, perhaps, by Great-Aunt Honoria and Ivo. But what about the Selwyns' house?

Before she could raise the thought, however, Clarissa sat up. 'I want to go to Strangewayes,' she announced.

'What? Now?'

'Yes. Look at it any way you like, Strangewayes has to be at the heart of it.'

'You may be right, but Mr. Ballantine has already combed the place quite through. In fact, he is probably there even now, enquiring about Robert Pile—'

'Excellent.' Clarissa was up in an instant, and dashing for the door. 'Do hurry up!' she called back over her shoulder. 'I shall have the carriage at the door in five minutes.'

* * *

Mrs. Daughtry leant on Theo's arm like the delicate creature she was, still in some distress as he conducted her

97

out of the drawing-room. 'It is all so unpleasant,' she sighed, as the door shut lawfully behind them, leaving them alone in the passage. 'I feel quite disordered. And I cannot help but feel that I have been the means of bringing further misfortune upon your family! Lady Werth was not pleased, I am certain of it, and who could blame her?'

Assigned the duty of reassuring the poor lady, Theo did his best. 'Come now, it isn't as bad as all that,' he offered.

'Two people have been killed, and you are likely to hang for one of them,' she reminded him.

That *was* an unpleasant prospect, to be sure. But what, then, was one supposed to say to a lady in affliction, if things were every bit as bad as she feared? 'Quite so,' he produced.

'And *I* shall be next!'

Ah. Yes. Recalled to a sense of impending tragedy, Theo recollected that he, too, was disturbed by this prospect. The sensations of distress and alarm washed over him again, powerfully affecting. 'That will not happen,' he said firmly. 'I won't permit it.'

Mrs. Daughtry smiled tremulously up at him. 'How *kind* you are.'

No one had ever called Theo "kind" before, nor gazed at him with such tender gratitude. He found that he liked it. 'Not at all,' he said, gazing back. 'You are in the safest house in London.'

Her fingers tightened upon his sleeve. 'But what shall I do when I am no longer—'

Footsteps approached, brisk and loud, and Mrs. Gavell came around the corner. *No longer what?* thought Theo, dimly bemused, but had not time to pursue the thought, for Mrs. Gavell was making her curtsey.

'Forgive me, my lord. I hadn't meant to disturb you,' she was saying, looking rather hard at Mrs. Daughtry. 'I was on my way to her ladyship's room, and—'

'It's quite all right,' Theo interrupted. 'Carry on.'

She curtseyed again and went on her way, casting a last, keen look at Mrs. Daughtry as she passed.

'Who was that?' said the lady, softly.

'The housekeeper.'

'She looked at me as though I were— but one can hardly wonder at it, can one? Oh! Why did I ever come to this house!'

Theo began to feel rather at sea. 'You, er, wanted to talk to Mrs. Everleigh?' he said after a moment.

'Dear Arabella! Yes, it would greatly ease my poor heart to see how she has borne with this calamity.'

Theo was perfectly ready to assist her with this — and, indeed, anything else she might desire — but found himself at a loss. 'I do not know where she is to be found— oh, hullo Gussie.'

Gussie emerged from the drawing-room behind him. She, too, directed a flinty look at Mrs. Daughtry as she swept past. 'You'll likely find her in the garden,' she said, rapidly disappearing down the passage. 'Chilly weather for it, but the dead do not feel the cold as you or I.'

'The garden, oh, dear,' said Mrs. Daughtry. 'And it is such a cold morning! Never mind. I am sure I will not catch a chill.'

'Perhaps Mrs. Everleigh might be so good as to come in for a— oh, hullo Mother.'

Lady Werth erupted into the passage and marched past Theo, chin high. 'When Mrs. Daughtry's business is concluded, Theo, come and find me. I shall be with your father.'

Theo had not time to reply before she, too, was gone. The ladies of the house appeared to have important matters on hand.

'Well,' said he, avoiding Mrs. Daughtry's eye. 'Shall we go to the garden?'

The weather was freezing, of course, and a penetrating rain hurtled out of a slate-grey sky on purpose to render the interlude more miserable. How Mrs. Everleigh could endure it, let alone *enjoy* it, Theo had not a notion. But there she was, strolling about among the drenched shrubbery, only a wide-brimmed bonnet and a heavy pelisse protecting her from the elements. The face she turned towards them as they approached was white with cold, or perhaps only with death.

'Lord Bedgberry,' she said serenely. Her composure flickered when she discovered the identity of his companion, and her brows rose. 'Marianne?'

'My dear Arabella!' Mrs. Daughtry clasped her hand in both of her own and wrung it feelingly. 'I heard the news, of *course*, and I have thought of nothing else since. How I have felt for you! And how very, very sorry I am that I could not reach you in time.'

'In time?' echoed Mrs. Everleigh, frowning. Gently, she retrieved her hand from Mrs. Daughtry's grip.

'If I had only known sooner! But fate, it would seem, was not in our favour. Never mind. I see that you have come about, with Lord Werth's very able assistance. Shall you be returning to the stage?'

Mrs. Everleigh did not immediately reply; she appeared to be thinking. 'Perhaps, yes,' she said, withdrawing her hand from Mrs. Daughtry's. 'I have not yet finally decided.'

'Oh, but you must! What a disappointment if you do not! I do not know how the play could go on without you.'

'I am sure you performed excellently,' answered Mrs. Everleigh, coolly. 'The night after I was killed.'

'She did, indeed,' put in Theo.

He was rewarded with a dazzling smile, and his heart performed an odd gallop. 'How *kind* you are, Lord Bedgberry!' she declared, and that was the second time she'd said that in only ten minutes. Theo experienced a warm, glowing feeling.

Mrs. Everleigh missed nothing of this exchange. 'I did not expect to encounter anybody else out in the garden this morning,' she said, easily enough, but her eyes were watchful. 'The weather being inclement.'

'Oh, but we came in search of you,' said Mrs. Daughtry earnestly. 'I could not go away without seeing you. I had to know—'

'Yes?' prompted Mrs. Everleigh, when she paused.

'How you are,' finished Mrs. Daughtry, laying a hand on Mrs. Everleigh's arm.

Mrs. Everleigh took a slight step back, a subtle movement, but the effect was immediate: Mrs. Daughtry's hand slid off her sleeve. 'I am touched by your concern,' she announced, 'but I am as you see me. Quite well.'

Mrs. Daughtry's smile was radiant; indeed, her whole face shone with pure, disinterested happiness in her dear friend's recovery. Theo wondered that Mrs. Everleigh should be so unmoved.

But she was. She could even be so unfeeling as to say, 'The morning has turned cold, and I am chilled to the bone. I had better go inside.' Having said as much, in her usual cool tones, she made the barest of curtsies in Theo's general direction, and retreated.

Mrs. Daughtry watched her go, her shoulders drooping.

Theo shook his head. 'I thought you said you were friends?'

Mrs. Daughtry hesitated. 'I fear that she— has come to dislike me.'

'Dislike *you*?' Theo said. How could that be? Mrs. Daughtry was sweetness itself!

'Oh, do not blame her!' she cried. 'She was so long away from the stage, you see. Others' stars have risen in her absence, and she is no longer *quite* young, and— and the performance that was to reintroduce her to London was so tragically delayed. It is, unhappily, *I* who took her place, and *I* who—' She stopped, with a little sigh, and shook her head. 'She cannot forgive me, but I can hardly wonder at it. I dare say I should feel the same, in her shoes.'

'You are generous,' Theo said, staring after Mrs.

101

Everleigh in disgust. 'More generous than I should be, in your place.'

'It… is an attitude I often encounter,' Mrs. Daughtry admitted, colouring prettily.

'Jealousy, you mean.' Theo remembered the stony look Gussie had directed at the actress as she'd stalked off down the passage. Even Gussie resented the poor woman her beauty and sweetness! Really, he would never understand women at all.

'Come inside,' he told her, offering her his arm again. 'You had better stay until you are quite dry, and I shall send you home in the carriage.'

He received another glittering smile for his solicitude, and his heart squeezed painfully. Really, if she were to go on smiling at him like that, there would be nothing of him left. 'How kind you are,' she said, and that was three times in a single day, and the next time Gussie called him selfish or oblivious he would remind her of it.

But all thought of a cosy interlude with the enchanting actress were soon dashed, for upon their return into the house, Theo heard the distinctive, faintly Scotch burr of Mr. Ballantine coming from the parlour. 'The news caught me just as I was leaving Bow Street,' he was saying. 'I cannot remain long; I'm bound for Strangewayes in a moment. It is a matter of some urgency.'

The door was only half-closed, but Theo had hopes of being able to sneak Mrs. Daughtry past it without being observed. He attempted this, but had not gone more than three steps towards the staircase when Miss Frostell came out of the library, and all but collided with him. 'Oh!' she gasped. 'Lord Bedgberry, I *am* sorry. I was looking for Miss Werth.'

'It's my belief she is not here,' he said. 'But she may be, for all I know.'

Unhappily, Miss Frostell was blocking his retreat. He hoped she might take herself off in search of Gussie, but instead she took in Mrs. Daughtry's presence with a long

102

look, and said: 'If I'd known you had company I would have been more careful, I'm sure. Forgive me, ma'am.'

Theo rather thought that an immediate withdrawal would be more fitting than an apology, and more in-keeping with Miss Frostell's rather self-effacing character. But she stood her ground, curse her, while Mrs. Daughtry (with her usual generosity) hastened to reassure her.

'We were just on our way to—' he began, but his mother's voice cut him off, emanating from the parlour with the ringing tones of authority.

'Theo!'

Sighing, Theo glowered at Miss Frostell, and turned himself about. 'Yes, Mother?'

'Do come in, if you please. Mr. Ballantine has some questions to put to our guest.'

Mrs. Daughtry's countenance registered dismay.

'It won't be much,' he told her, resigned. 'Ballantine's a good enough fellow.' He conducted the reluctant actress into the parlour, and found himself skewered at once with the kind of unforgiving stare he had never before encountered from the Runner.

'Lord Bedgberry,' said Mr. Ballantine, with a perfunctory bow. 'And Mrs. Daughtry. How interesting to find you here, ma'am.'

'Is it?' faltered the lady, looking to Theo for support. 'I came here to share my story with those who— who found my dearest Arabella, and have been *so* kind as to assist her—'

'Yes, well,' interrupted Ballantine. 'That's as may be. What *was* the story, pray?'

Nobody even invited Mrs. Daughtry to sit; she was to be interrogated on the spot, it seemed, like a— why, like a common criminal! Theo swelled with indignation.

'Look here, Ballantine—' he began.

'Not now, my lord,' answered the Runner curtly. 'Your turn will come.'

My turn ? Theo entertained brief, wild notions of fleeing

the house, though he could not have said why. He was guilty of nothing, after all! Only Mr. Ballantine was so grim, and his mother and father so quiet...

He suppressed the urge, and remained quiet himself as Mrs. Daughtry repeated her account of the night of Mrs. Everleigh's disappearance, together with her subsequent forebodings regarding her own fate. Theo's breath caught again at the prospect: this poor, sweet woman slain and bloodied, her lifeless remains dumped carelessly in some rich house. His father would instantly revive her, of course, should such a fate befall her, but still! It was the *principle* of the thing.

'An interesting story,' Ballantine said once Mrs. Daughtry had finished. 'It did not occur to you, ma'am, to contact a constable, or even Bow Street, when Mrs. Everleigh failed to appear? Considering your certainty as to her macabre fate, surely your concern would have led you to some course of action.'

'It... I thought about it, of course, but— oh, could I have expected anyone to come to our aid? We are but poor players, of no consequence to society, and my premonitions, you know, are not often taken seriously.'

'Your fellow players appear, by your account, to have done so.'

'They are accustomed to my ways.'

'Well then, did none of them attempt to assist?'

Mrs. Daughtry hesitated. 'A boy was sent to Arabella's rooms, I understood, but she was not there, and no one had any notion as to where else she might be found.'

'A boy?' Mr. Ballantine's interest sharpened. 'Who was it?'

'I am sure I do not know.'

'No matter. Thank you, Mrs. Daughtry. You may go.'

The actress looked helplessly up at Theo. 'Oh, must I indeed?'

Lady Werth rang the bell. 'The carriage will take you home, Mrs. Daughtry.'

'Mother—' Theo began. He was silenced by a cool stare.

One of the maids came, and took charge of Mrs. Daughtry. Once the door had closed behind her, Theo found Mr. Ballantine's penetrating stare turned upon him.

'Yes, what is it?' he said impatiently. The sooner the interview was completed, the sooner he could reassure himself as to Mrs. Daughtry's safety.

'I find myself obliged to ask you some questions, my lord. You may not find them pleasant, for which I apologise.'

Theo, surprised, looked to his parents for elucidation, but found nothing. His father appeared grim, his mother coolly composed. 'All right, but do get on with it,' he answered.

'Your association with the lady who has just left this room,' Ballantine began. 'Is it of long standing?'

'No, I— I had never met her before last night.'

'You're certain of that?'

'Am I certain? Of course I'm certain. How could I forget such a woman?'

'How, indeed,' murmured Ballantine. 'And had you previously encountered Mrs. Everleigh, before her scheduled appearance at Strangewayes?'

'No,' Theo said shortly, his impatience growing.

'Or a young actor known as Robert Pile?'

'No! Look here, what is all this about?'

'You *did* assure me that you had nothing to do with Mrs. Everleigh's death,' Ballantine said.

'Nor did I.'

'Even though you admit to attempting to dispose of her remains?'

Theo looked wildly at Lord Werth. 'Father! This is preposterous.'

Lord Werth merely said, 'Please answer the questions, Theo.'

'But—' Theo sighed. 'I did not kill her,' he said through

gritted teeth. 'I cannot imagine why I *would*.'

'An amorous engagement got out of hand?' Ballantine suggested. He smiled in such a fashion as to expose his teeth, prompting Theo to think of his own.

'You mean you think that I had some *involvement* with the woman, and that this *liaison* involved my— no! Good heavens, no! I am not at all given to such *escapades,* as my mother and father must surely have told you. And if I was, why would I— why would I do something like *that* when I might simply go to Stebbington's, and have as many glasses of refreshment as I wish, and without having to lift a finger for them?'

Theo expected another, relentless question from Mr. Ballantine, but the Runner merely looked at him. Narrowly, consideringly.

'I say, Ballantine, this is all a bit too much,' Theo protested. 'What is this all about?'

It was his father who spoke. 'I have just returned from an interview with Mr. Robert Pile, not that he was much disposed to answer my questions.'

'Wonderful,' Theo answered. 'Who is that.'

'The young man whose body was recently discovered in the cellar at the residence of Lady Maundevyle,' said Ballantine. 'As I gather you have recently deduced.'

Theo tried to remember if he had heard mention of such a development. Possibly Gussie told him; he might not have been listening. 'And?' he prompted.

'Like Mrs. Everleigh,' Ballantine went on, 'Mr. Pile does not remember the events that led to the ending of his life. However, the last person he remembers encountering was, in fact, *you*.'

'Me?' For a moment, Theo was too astonished to speak. 'But how could that be?'

'How indeed,' said Ballantine.

Theo looked helplessly from face to face. 'Come, Father,' he said, beginning to feel desperate. 'Mother? You cannot imagine me capable of all this.'

'Of calculated destruction, no,' said Lady Werth. 'Never, Theo. But of carelessness, perhaps? Of getting a little— carried away? London is new to you, and has been such a revelation—'

'Do you think me so altered as to be carrying-on with actresses and— and using them for— no! A thousand times no! Devil take it, who do you think I am?'

His mother visibly relented. The tension went out of her face, and she exchanged a considering look with Lord Werth. 'I think it most unlikely, Theo,' she said, more gently. 'But the fact remains that you *did* try to dispose of Mrs. Everleigh, and this Mr. Pile appears to remember you. You are certain you did not— make a mistake, and get into a panic— or engage in a little carelessness, knowing that your father could be relied upon to rectify any unfortunate outcome?'

Theo's indignation had faded; he simply felt weary. 'No,' he said again. 'No, and no.'

'Very well.' Mr. Ballantine's hard expression faded. 'I am sorry, my lord. It is my duty to ask unpleasant questions sometimes, as I hope you will understand.'

Theo waved this off, and collapsed onto the nearest divan. 'I suppose I would do the same, were I you. But I cannot make sense of it, Ballantine. I've never heard of this Mr. Pile before. What can he possibly have remembered me doing?'

'He claims to have seen you leaving Strangewayes in Mrs. Everleigh's company,' Ballantine answered.

'When? Yesterday? That is not what happened—'

'Not yesterday, my lord. The same evening that Mrs. Everleigh was killed.'

'But that's impossible. I had never met her before yesterday.'

Lady Werth intervened. 'Mr. Ballantine, if Theo does not recall ever encountering Mr. Pile, then answer me this: how is this pestersome young man so certain of my son's identity?'

'A fair question, my lady, and one that ought to be asked.'

ELEVEN

Having failed to materialise at Bow Street, Mr. Ballantine was not to be found at Strangewayes either. It was most disobliging of him.

'I believe I have lost interest in investigating,' Clarissa declared, once the unhappy truth could no longer be denied. 'It makes me lose all heart.'

'But if we do not find the killer, there will in all likelihood be several more corpses dumped all over London,' Gussie protested.

Clarissa merely yawned. 'What of that? Most of the people of London are boringly alive. The city can very well find space for a few more dead ones.'

'Go if you choose, then,' Gussie said. 'I want to look around.' She marched off, without waiting for a reply.

The two ladies had tumbled out of the Maundevyles' coach at the door of the theatre and bustled inside, Clarissa asking for "that handsome Bow Street Runner" before they had even got across the entrance hall. The query had produced a general negative from everyone, though Clarissa had marched down a quantity of corridors, opened every door she had come across, and invaded more than one dressing-room.

A few, hapless theatre-folk had attempted,

unsuccessfully, to throw them out, but Clarissa had borne down every objection with a mixture of obliviousness and an inflexible will. 'Nonsense. We are here to help,' she'd kept saying. 'You *are* in terrible trouble, are not you?'

She had operated upon Strangewayes as an unstoppable whirlwind, and scarcely needed assistance. Nonetheless, Gussie had contributed her mite, here and there. 'We are assisting Bow Street,' she had said, airily but firmly, to one indignant fellow (a scene-painter, by the bedaubed look of him). And when an imperious actress had, in resonant tones, attempted to expel them, Gussie had said: 'We are on the trail of a killer, ma'am. You do not wish to go the way of Mrs. Everleigh and Mr. Pile, I suppose?'

But all of this was to no avail, for Clarissa's mind had fixed upon Mr. Ballantine, to the exclusion of all else. *Good riddance to her*, Gussie thought, and went off in the direction of the playhouse's theatre.

'Oh, but wait!' Clarissa called, and came running after her. 'Mr. Ballantine may be here later, after all.'

'Clarissa,' Gussie said firmly, without stopping. 'One mustn't chase men. It encourages them, and they are incorrigible enough as it is.'

'Is that why you have not even enquired after poor Henry?' came the answer. 'He is most cast down, you know. He believes you have forgotten him entirely.'

'I had the same idea, probably on account of having heard nothing from him in many weeks. But I make it a point never to be cast down; it is lowering, and I really have far too much to do. Ah. This begins to look promising, do you not think?'

They had not arrived at the theatre. Clarissa's complaints had distracted Gussie, for instead of venturing into the heart of the building, and discovering the red-curtained stage, they had instead disappeared into the depths of a warren-like maze of cramped, white-washed corridors lined with doorways. One of them stood open, and emanating from within came a babble of voices. A rehearsal in progress? Efficient, if so: Gussie might ask her questions of most of the troupe at once, and carry her information back to Bow Street (and her aunt) all the sooner.

But as she formed the thought, a panelled door at the end of the corridor opened and a man emerged. He wore a neat black coat and snowy cravat, and walked with a hurried air. He had recently come in from outside, perhaps, for he was pale with cold, his skin stark-white against the black of his too-long hair.

...or was he pale for some other reason? Gussie realised, almost too late, where she had seen that pallor before — and recently.

'Er. Good morning!' she called, hurrying after the man (for he had passed her already, striding off at some speed). 'I was wondering if—'

She stopped, for the man had ignored her entirely, and disappeared around a turning in the corridor.

'What's the matter?' Clarissa hissed.

'Do you recognise that fellow?' Gussie said, hastening to follow her quarry.

'I do not know, I hardly looked at him. Should I?'

Gussie turned the corner. There he was, still in view, though rapidly disappearing. Was he running from something — or *to* something?

'Mr. Pile!' Gussie shouted. 'Mr. Robert Pile?' Her voice echoed off the empty white walls, and at last, the man stopped, and turned.

'Yes?' he answered, frowning.

'Ohhhh,' Clarissa gasped. 'My corpse!'

'I see you have become acquainted with my uncle,' said Gussie to the actor, advancing with a smile. 'Rather recently, I fancy?'

'Your uncle, ma'am?' His gaze flicked to Clarissa, but without recognition.

She, however, was rushing forward. 'Mr. Pile!' she cried. 'Capital! You won't remember me, but we *have* met.

You were dead at the time, stone dead, and who do you think it was that got you out of our cellar, and into the good coroner's care? Yes! It was me. How fortunate it is, our running into you like this. We have been trying and trying to discover who it was that left you there — and in *such* a state! I have rarely been more shocked! Perhaps you can help us?'

Mr. Pile bore this barrage without flinching, though he appeared more bemused than gratified. 'You're Lady Maundevyle, then?' he said, when Clarissa paused to draw breath.

'No, alas. The title would suit me, would not it? I am Miss Selwyn, though since we have already met, and on such peculiarly intimate terms, I feel you must call me Clarissa.'

In the wake of this effusion, Gussie discovered two things: one, that Mr. Pile possessed a certain handsomeness of feature unmarred by his recent demise and resurrection; two, that Clarissa's wild nature in no way balked at devoting herself to three men at once, two of whom were not even gentlemen. *Why* she might do so in this instance must remain a mystery, for Gussie had no inclination to enquire into it.

'I am Miss Werth,' she interrupted. 'And you owe your restoration to life to my uncle's ministrations.'

'Werth.' Mr. Pile's eyes glittered; he did not seem as grateful as Gussie had expected. He bowed, a belated (and, judging from the minimal degree of the obeisance, grudging) acknowledgement of their eminence, and seemed on the point of departing again.

Gussie hastened to intervene. 'We do need your help, if you do not mind? Members of your estimable playhouse do *keep* turning up dead, and somebody ought to do something about it.'

'As I have already told your uncle,' answered Mr. Pile, with a trace of impatience, 'I remember very little.'

'Oh no,' cried Clarissa. 'You are not also struck with an

obliterated memory? How unlucky!'

It was, Gussie thought, most unlucky. Watching Robert Pile's preternaturally composed face, she began to wonder whether it was not also rather convenient. 'Anything at all that you remember could be of use,' she said. 'However insignificant.'

'You had better interrogate your cousin, ma'am, rather than me,' said Mr. Pile.

'My cousin?' Gussie said sharply. 'Why?'

'Because I saw him with Arabella Everleigh, on the day she were killed.'

'Where?'

'Here. They were getting into his lordship's carriage, bold as you please. On their way to some tryst, I imagine.'

Gussie's mind raced. 'It was Theo? You are certain?'

'No mistaking that carriage, ma'am. If you want to know who killed Mrs. Everleigh, look you to your cousin. And his father rushes to revive the both of us, don't he? Before there can be any inquest.' He took a step nearer to Gussie, his eyes dark and cold. 'If you're here looking for someone else to pin it on, you are wasting your time. Lord Bedgberry's responsible, and I reckon your family knows that right enough.'

He turned his back on them and stalked away, his boot-heels ringing on the tiled floor.

There was silence between the two ladies for a moment; Gussie was too thoughtful for speech.

'Well!' Clarissa said at last. 'Your cousin always did have that dangerous look to him. I own, I like him the better for it.'

'Theo didn't do this,' Gussie said.

'Your loyalty does you great credit, but—'

'No. I should be the last person to defend Theo out of blind partiality; he is capable of creating disaster out of sheer abstraction and carelessness, never mind deliberate intent. But there are flaws in Mr. Pile's story.'

'What are they?' Clarissa breathed, avid.

'Theo has never engaged in a tryst in the whole course of his life, and certainly would never engage in a scandalously public affair with a renowned actress. The whole notion is preposterous.'

'You greatly relieve my mind.'

'And then? *No mistaking that carriage, ma'am,*' Gussie said, mimicking Mr. Pile's rough tones. 'What does he mean by that, pray? Theo has no carriage of his own, so he must either have used my uncle's for this alleged outing, or hired a vehicle, either of which I should think most improbable.'

'He may have used your uncle's, in which case Mr. Pile must have recognised your coat of arms,' Clarissa replied.

'A reasonable explanation, one would think. But firstly, I might ask *how* an ignominious actor at the bottom of the Strangewayes' troupe should be so familiar with the Werth arms as to recognise them at a glance.'

'Excellent question.'

'Secondly, our carriage is unmarked.'

'Your uncle does not choose to have his arms displayed upon it?'

'It is not easy, being the most Wyrded family in England,' Gussie said. 'My uncle does not choose to be gawked at, pursued, or stoned to death whenever he stirs from home, and as such chooses to keep a plain carriage.'

'So there *is* no recognisable Werth equipage.'

'Precisely. So our plausible Mr. Pile cannot have seen Theo and Mrs. Everleigh getting into it, can he? In which case, what is he about?'

'He may have been mistaken,' Clarissa said. 'But it is a curiously specific mistake to make.'

'Yes, and how should he recognise Theo, either? And he called him my cousin; his familiarity with the Werth family tree seems out of place, does not it?'

'Highly.'

'It is my belief the whole story is a lie.'

'Mine as well,' Clarissa agreed. 'But why on earth should he lie? He was himself murdered. He is a victim.'

'I wonder?' said Gussie.

'Besides, we may easily clear up this little matter. We may go and ask Lord Bedgberry, *and* Mrs. Everleigh. He must know that we have it in our power to do so.'

'Theo, certainly, and he will of course deny it. But Mrs. Everleigh? He may deduce that she has been restored to some semblance of life, just as he has himself, but can he know that we have her with us? This fact has not, I believe, appeared in the newspapers. Which means, he may be unaware how easily his tale can be contradicted.'

'We must speak to her,' declared Clarissa. 'At once!'

'Yes, but I would also like very much to speak to Mr. Ballantine.'

'Oh, me too,' said Clarissa fervently.

'This web becomes tangled, and I would be glad of his insights. And, of course, to share ours. Shall we to Bow Street, and see if he is yet returned?'

Clarissa, of course, was all enthusiasm for the plan, but it soon proved unnecessary. No sooner had Gussie retraced her rambling steps and emerged from the maze of dressing-rooms and costume cupboards, and got out into the street again, than she ran into Mr. Ballantine himself. He had the dark look of a man in a temper, and was striding towards the playhouse with such single-minded speed, he almost knocked Gussie down.

'Miss Werth,' he said, halting abruptly. 'And Miss Selwyn. I ought to have known.' His expression blackened further.

'Ought to have known that we would be tireless in our pursuit of truth and justice?' Gussie said.

'I ought to have known that you would prove to be exactly where you should not. Are you never concerned for your own safety?'

'You appear to be preaching good sense, Mr. Ballantine, which is impolitic, for nothing makes a man more tiresome.'

'Are you never concerned for *your* safety, sir?' breathed

Clarissa. 'Heroes never are, are they?'

This piece of flattery won her a penetrating stare, and his mouth twisted in annoyance. 'Let us take it as read that I told both of you to go home, and you ignored me, which doubtless you would do.'

'We would,' Gussie agreed. 'And we have discovered some one or two things of interest—'

'Might it wait, Miss Werth? I must find Robert Pile, before he has a chance to vanish on us.'

'Oh, we've just seen him!' said Clarissa.

'Yes, and he told us the most vicious lies about Theo,' put in Gussie.

'You are certain they were lies?'

'Perfectly.' Gussie quickly related the actor's allegations, and her own conclusions as to their veracity. 'So you see, he is at best mistaken. And at worst—'

'Lying, with the direct intention of incriminating Lord Bedgberry,' Mr. Ballantine finished grimly. 'I've heard this story already, and Lord Bedgberry has roundly contradicted it. Do you know where Mr. Pile went?'

'No, he did not say anything about that.'

The Runner looked around, rather helplessly. They stood out in the grey-befogged street some little way from the entrance to Strangewayes; nobody apart from themselves was in evidence. 'He could be anywhere by now.'

'You think him likely to abscond?' Gussie asked.

'The thought entered my mind. The more so, from what I've just heard.'

Gussie felt a momentary chagrin. If she had known this, she might have been able to delay Mr. Pile long enough for Mr. Ballantine to find him. This was what came of excluding her, and refusing to tell her things!

'If it is some manner of scheme,' the Runner mused, 'what might he be likely to do next?'

'He has chosen to invoke Mrs. Everleigh's name in his iniquitous tales,' Gussie said. 'But is she a willing partner of his, or unconnected? I cannot know until I have had a chance to question her. If she verifies this false story, then I shall know what to think.'

'He might have come here to meet her,' Clarissa put in eagerly. 'Perhaps they are plotting some fresh scheme of infamy, between themselves.'

'Her dressing-room,' said Mr. Ballantine, apropos of, apparently, nothing. He paused in momentary thought, then strode towards the theatre's entrance. 'Pray go about your business, ladies. I will inform you later as to my success.'

He vanished inside.

Gussie exchanged a look with Clarissa.

'Are we feeling obedient?' said she.

'Are we *ever* feeling obedient?' Clarissa replied.

The question answered itself.

Gussie and Clarissa hurried after Mr. Ballantine, and re-entered Strangewayes.

* * *

Following his uncomfortable encounter with his esteemed parents and Mr. Ballantine, Theo felt unaccountably disordered.

'It was a deal of nonsense,' he reminded himself. 'There is no need to be in a pelter about it now.'

He thought of going into the book-room, and consoling himself with a little reading. There was a decent volume on the process of decomposition which he had not yet perused; a favourite of his father's, by report. That ought to disperse the morning's various confusions, and restore him to himself.

But if he were to *remain* in the book-room, someone was bound to discover him there, and plague him with more questions. Or, still worse, find him all sorts of unpleasant things to do. He would just creep in for a moment, retrieve the volume, and—

117

'My dear Theo!' The voice hailed him the moment he opened the door, and Honoria's head materialised, greeting him with a ghastly grin. 'Just the man we want! Come in.'

'No, I was only—' Theo tried.

'You *must*,' Honoria hissed. 'It is a matter of the gravest *urgency*.'

'It is to do with those infernal actresses, I suppose,' Theo sighed, resigned, for the moment, to his fate.

A cold wind swept through the shadowed room, raising a cloud of dust, and the door slammed behind him.

Theo sneezed, surprised. Where had the wind come from? The windows were closed. He saw only Ivo Farthing hovering over the hearth, and smiling.

'Infernal?' Unusually, Lady Honoria manifested the rest of her corporeal form, bit by bit, a slightly stout figure in an outmoded, half-decayed gown. Her full skirts raised whorls of dust as she swept across the book-room, and stood frowning at Theo, her arms folded. 'You have been cosy enough with *one* of them, hm?'

'Hardly,' Theo protested.

'Don't trouble to deny it! I saw the whole thing, and so did Ivo.'

'That's right,' said Farthing.

Theo cast his mind back. He supposed they were speaking of Mrs. Daughtry, for he had spent a quantity of time in her company that morning, had he not? He recollected crystal-blue eyes, and a sweet smile. Her gown, too: a pale grey, he thought, and embroidered with—something. But these ideas swam hazily through his befuddled mind, and brought few other memories with them.

'Er,' he said. 'What did you see, exactly?'

'Why, you and that young lady, thick as thieves!' said Honoria, with strong disapproval. 'Hanging on her every word, you were, and ready to jump down the throats of anybody as merely asked her a question!'

Theo said nothing, racking his brains for some

corroborating recollection. 'Er. You are certain it was me, I suppose?'

'As certain as that I stand here! What can you mean by such a question? Really, Theo, this dissembling is beneath you.'

But Ivo Farthing drifted nearer, and looked keenly into Theo's eyes. 'I am not certain he is dissembling, my dear,' he said, his ordinarily amiable face grave.

'Of course he is, how perfectly absurd—'

'What was it you wanted?' Theo interrupted. 'You said it was a matter of urgency, and I want to read.'

'It is that actress,' intoned Honoria.

'I have told you, I was *not* making love to her—'

'Not that one. She is gone, thank the spirits of West and North. The other one!'

'Mrs. Everleigh?'

'Yes! We have been watching her all this morning, and yesterday, and there is something of the most suspicious about her.'

'Cannot you take this to my father, or to Gussie, or—anybody? I want to read.'

'Yes, and so we *shall*, Theo, but it is you that fortuitously happened to come in! What do you think, but—'

'I came in because I wanted a book,' Theo interrupted, his impatience growing. 'A not uncommon reason to enter a book-room, I should think, and I hardly expected to find the two of you haunting the place. What *are* you doing?'

'Watching,' said Farthing.

'Watching what? There's no one here—'

The words cut off in a startled cry, for he found himself summarily seized by Lady Honoria, and shoved towards the far window. The garden lay beyond, a dreary vision of faded verdure, and standing in it was— Mrs. Everleigh.

'Yes,' said Theo testily. 'She likes to take the air; what of it?'

119

'In *winter*?' said Lady Honoria.

'The dead don't feel the cold.'

'Then they can have no need to take the air either, can they? Pay attention, Theo. What do you think she is doing out there?'

Foreseeing that he would have no peace until he satisfied his importunate ancestress, Theo suppressed a sigh, and fixed his attention on the figure of Mrs. Everleigh. She stood still, preternaturally still. Not even breathing. She wore a pelisse and bonnet, but more as a matter of form than because she appeared to need it; the hard frost of the morning coated the sleeping shrubberies in a thick, white coat and the air was bitter, but she gave no sign of feeling it at all.

Her face was turned to the side, away from the book-room, and as far as Theo could tell, she did not even blink.

Something about her pose, and her stillness, and her rapt attention, suggested that Honoria was right: she was not merely disporting herself among the shrubs.

'What can she see from there?' he asked.

'The front door,' said Farthing. 'And a little of the street.'

'She's watching our front door?'

'She has been doing so for some time,' said Lady Honoria. 'She saw Mrs. Daughtry come in, and came in herself, after which she found a variety of reasons to linger in the passage outside the drawing-room. Once Mrs. Daughtry left, she returned to her station in the garden, and has not moved since.'

'She was eavesdropping?' Theo said, startled. He had escorted Mrs. Daughtry outside to see Mrs. Everleigh, without having the smallest suspicion that the woman already knew of their visitor's presence in the house; indeed, had taken steps to find out her business in coming. Nor had she given any sign of it during the subsequent encounter between the two ladies. Why not?

'I believe she heard every word of your Mamma's

conversation with the actress. And what's more, I have run into her in some odd places in the house. I could make little sense of it before, but I now think that she has been—'

'Spying on us,' Theo finished.

'Yes. That is it, exactly.'

'But what possible cause can she have to do so? And when father was so good as to snatch her from the grave! How ungrateful.'

'I do not know. I have asked, of course, but she is quick to dissemble, and I fear I have made her suspicious of me.'

Theo foresaw what was coming next. 'Oh, no,' he said. '*I* can't talk to her. I tried that, this morning, and she would hardly speak two words to me.'

'You had Mrs. Daughtry with you at the time,' pointed out Lady Honoria. 'If you were to speak to her alone—'

'Why me? Cannot Gussie do it? She could wheedle secrets out of a stone.'

'Gussie is not here. And I am persuaded you, as a personable young man—'

'No!'

'But we are in *crisis*, Theo!' wailed Lady Honoria. 'And it is *your* neck that shall be stretched if we do not find something to *do* about it!'

Theo appreciated this reminder about as much as might be expected. He swallowed, thought with brief, fervent regret of the book on the stages of natural decay, and sighed. 'I suppose you expect me to be *subtle* about it.'

'Of course. She must not discover that we are wise to her ploys—'

Theo did not wait to hear the rest. He strode out of the book-room, went around to the side-door, hurled it open, and marched over to the still, silent figure of Mrs. Everleigh. The cold bit at his ears, and the wind swept straight through his swallow-tailed coat. If his neck were to be stretched in the near future, he thought bitterly, at least he would be spared any more unfortunate encounters with inclement weather.

'Madam,' he said, stopping before Mrs. Everleigh. 'I have been sent by my interfering relatives to enquire into your business, and I shall have no peace until I produce an answer. What can you mean by watching our front door?'

She turned her head, slowly, to look at him. There was no consciousness of wrong-doing in those cool eyes, no chagrin at being caught out. She merely blinked, once, and said: 'I am seeing who goes in and out, of course.'

'Watching for anyone in particular?'

'Yes.'

'Well? And who is that?'

'I don't believe I will tell you.' Her head turned again, slowly, smoothly; she resumed her vigil over the front door. 'I do not yet know if you are to be trusted.'

'If *I'm* to be trusted? Forgive me, madam, if I point out that it is *you* abusing my father's hospitality by spying upon us.'

'It is necessary.'

'And if I should have you thrown out of the house in consequence?'

'You are free to do so, if you wish.'

The woman was maddeningly unflappable; Theo's impatience rose. 'If you told me what you are looking for, I may be able to help.'

'Surely you must be able to guess the answer to that question, Lord Bedgberry.'

'It appears not.'

'I am looking for the man who killed me.'

'And you expect to find him waltzing into our house?'

'He has done so once before, has not he?'

'Yes, but he had a corpse to dispose of. Why on earth should he do so again?'

Her reply did not appear to be in answer to his question. 'Prominent families build alliances,' she mused. 'They stick together, guard each other's interests. Cover for one another.'

'I do not understand you.'

'It was not by your hand that I was murdered,' she said. 'But I may still have been so with your knowledge, perhaps even with your complicity.'

Theo threw up his hands. 'This is the outside of enough. I have been interrogated by my parents, had my motives questioned by a Bow Street Runner, and my character impugned by every newspaper in London. Am I now to be accused by the finest actress in the west end?'

She turned her head at last, slightly. A twinkle of amusement lurked somewhere in the depths of her eyes. 'And what do you propose to do about it?' she murmured. 'Kill me?'

'The prospect grows more appealing by the moment,' he growled.

She nodded sagely. 'A man of temper makes a poor murderer. He may commit the deed, in a moment of anger, but he has not the cool nature necessary to cover his actions afterwards.'

Theo's frustration dissipated; he was thinking. What had she said, a minute ago? 'Permit me one question, ma'am. How are you so certain it was *not* by my hand that you were murdered? I had thought you were unable to remember.'

She looked steadily at him, perhaps turning over her response in her mind. She opened her mouth, preparing to speak— and stopped, her attention arrested. 'Someone seeks entrance.'

'The footman will answer the door,' said Theo, impatiently. 'My question, ma'am, if you please.'

But she shook her head, and her voice dropped to a whisper. 'It will be of no use to answer the door, sir, for your guest appears to be entering through the window.'

TWELVE

'What an appalling mess,' declared Gussie, who had taken one look at the disordered state of Mrs. Everleigh's dressing-room and recoiled.

'No. Is it?' said Clarissa vaguely, stepping over a discarded straw bonnet, only to tread heavily upon the sleeve of a dark blue velvet gown.

'I suppose your chamber would look much the same, had you no maid to tidy it for you.' Gussie spoke with a little scorn; such chaos was only too fitting for the abominable Clarissa. 'Do watch where you step, or something is bound to be—'

A *crunch* of shattering glass interrupted her. Clarissa lifted her foot, shedding shards of some destroyed costume-jewellery.

'—broken,' Gussie finished, with a sigh.

'Ladies, did I not ask you to wait outside—' Mr. Ballantine began, and cut himself off with a shake of his head. 'Never mind. I do not know why I bothered to try.'

'No, neither do I,' Gussie agreed. 'You did not happen upon one Mr. Pile when you came in, I collect.'

'And find him furtively engaged in planting, or concealing, evidence for or against Mrs. Everleigh? Alas, no. And I cannot see that anything in here has changed, since the last time I came in—'

'You mean you were here before, and left it in this state?'

'It is not for me to tamper with possible evidence, Miss Werth. Nothing ought to be moved, for who knows what damage I might do if I tried?'

'But if nothing is moved, how can you *see* anything? Have you, in fact, uncovered any evidence in here?'

'No, but that may be because there is nothing to be found—'

'Nonsense,' Gussie said stoutly. 'How can you know that, if you haven't looked? Clarissa, our mission is clear. We will tidy up.'

'Oh, must we?' sighed Clarissa, surveying the sea of discarded garments with palpable dismay.

'It will take no time at all, if you assist me suitably,' said Gussie, stooping to collect an armful of evening gowns. 'If you do not, then it will take me all morning, and I shall be in the devil of a temper by the end of it.'

Mr. Ballantine looked as though he would like to intervene, but he reckoned without Gussie's capacity to perform as a human whirlwind, when it suited her. By the time he had taken two breaths, she was halfway across the floor, clearing swaths of carpet as she went. She and Clarissa worked methodically, folding gowns and cloaks, heaping bonnets and gloves upon arm-chairs and returning felled jewels and cosmetics-pots to the dressing-table.

'It seems to me that this is too much disorder,' Gussie said, as she worked. 'A degree of untidiness one could certainly allow for in a spoiled actress, but this is something more. I believe someone may have done this deliberately.'

'Precisely,' said Mr. Ballantine, rather wearily. 'That is why I wanted to search *carefully*.'

'If you find anything in a blue muslin,' Gussie said to Clarissa, ignoring this. 'Pray hand it to Mr. Ballantine. Oh!

No, there will be no need, for here it is.' She selected a pile of cornflower-coloured gauze from beneath a rose-coloured mantle, and held it up. The vivid, floral colour bore a streak of spilled face-powder upon the bodice, but the gown must surely be the same as Mrs. Everleigh had described.

'May I ask the relevance of this particular gown?' said Mr. Ballantine.

'I believe it is the one Mrs. Everleigh was wearing, the last time she arrived at the theatre.' Gussie shook the creases out of the dress, and handed it to the Runner. 'Which could mean a number of things.'

'It might well mean that she changed her dress herself, on purpose, before she left the theatre,' said Mr. Ballantine, accepting the gown with care.

'Yes, and perhaps she cannot remember the Turkey-red gown she was slaughtered in for the same reason she does not remember who killed her. It falls into that part of her memory that appears, unhelpfully, to be faulty.'

'Yes,' Mr. Ballantine agreed. 'Or—'

'Or!' interjected Clarissa. 'It means that somebody has put this gown here on purpose, in order to give the impression that she altered her own dress.'

'Mr. Pile, perhaps,' offered Gussie. 'Though he had not a gown about him, when we saw him.'

'And I saw this dressing-room before, remember,' said Mr. Ballantine. 'Days ago, shortly after the lady was killed. And it was already in this state.'

'So if the gown was concealed here intentionally, it was done shortly after the dreadful deed was committed.' Gussie beamed. 'This is capital! What progress we make.'

'It seems to me,' said Clarissa, 'that we have only produced more questions.'

'Yes,' Gussie allowed. 'More questions — and a fresh piece of evidence, by way of the gown.'

'Two gowns, now, both worn by Mrs. Everleigh shortly before— or during— her death,' said Clarissa. 'Neither of them offering answers.'

'Yet! Neither of them offering answers *yet.*'

Clarissa adjusted her three-cornered hat. 'I am tired of tidying,' she announced.

'I must find Mr. Pile,' answered Ballantine. 'I've to go all over the theatre, and enquire of everybody if he is here, or if anybody might know where he has gone. And if not, I must go again to his lodgings, and anywhere else he might be found. It will, I expect, be dull.'

Gussie recognised a hint when she heard one, even if she did not often choose to act upon them. 'We will go home,' she announced.

Mr. Ballantine appeared surprised, as well he might be, by this unlooked-for success.

'Go home?' he echoed. 'Just like that?'

'Yes, because Mrs. Everleigh is there, and I want to talk to her again.'

'Ah. Naturally.'

'In particular, I want to ask her about Theo. I am perfectly certain that she was *not* getting into a carriage with him shortly before her unfortunate demise, but if she is not minded to confirm the ridiculous story, then she may have some idea as to why Mr. Pile might say such a thing.'

'I have already enquired with her about Mr. Pile,' said Ballantine. 'She claims they were unacquainted, for that young man was not part of the production she was due to begin starring in.'

'How mysterious,' Gussie said, delighted.

'In that case, we shall remain,' decided Clarissa. 'And assist Mr. Ballantine.' She bestowed upon him a dazzling smile.

Mr. Ballantine appeared bemused. 'I imagine Lord Bedgberry would be glad of your company,' he suggested.

'By which you mean that you would not! You break my heart.' Unusually for Clarissa, she did not speak with her usual flippancy, but with an element of real feeling. Or at least, what seemed like it.

Mr. Ballantine appeared affected. The Runner may have faced down any number of desperate criminals over the course of his career, but the Honourable Miss Selwyn appeared to be too much for him. He looked uncertainly at Gussie, and she realised — to her vast amusement — that he was pleading for help.

'Intriguing,' she said, with high enjoyment. 'The great Hugh Ballantine, Ogre and Bow Street Runner, proves to be highly susceptible to guilt.' Or perhaps it was Clarissa herself he was susceptible to. She may be perfectly maddening, but she was pretty enough, and perhaps he had a taste for wilful females.

No, surely not. He had only ever threatened to throttle Gussie, and she was as wild as they came.

Her remark annoyed him enough to stiffen his spine. 'I cannot and will not take a delicately-nurtured young lady along with me on Bow Street business,' he said firmly, and scowled when both Gussie and Clarissa went off into peals of laughter. 'What is the matter now?'

'Well-bred young women do not wander about in gentlemen's dress,' Gussie pointed out. 'Will you not take her along? She may be of great use to you.'

Mr. Ballantine's look expressed his deep sense of betrayal. 'No.'

'Then we must stick together, Clarissa,' said Gussie. 'Never mind. I believe Theo may be at home.'

Clarissa's head came up. 'He is?'

'Why yes, where else should he be?'

'Oh! He is!' she said, and a smile appeared. 'Delightful. We will go at once.' To Gussie's bemusement, she suited action to words, and abandoned Mr. Ballantine on the spot.

Gussie traded a puzzled glance with the Runner. Volatile behaviour, even for Clarissa Selwyn, but what could be taking place inside that chaotic mind, Gussie would not attempt to guess.

With a shrug of her shoulders, she followed in Clarissa's wake, and turned her steps for home.

* * *

'The window—?' Theo uttered a muffled curse, and took off in the direction the interloper. By the time he reached the side wall of the house, however, the man had vanished inside.

He had chosen a lower window, and as Theo stood peering in through the foggy glass he discovered that it was the same window he had been looking out of himself only a short time before. The window Lady Honoria had dragged him over to, in other words: the book-room window.

Presumably, Honoria and Ivo Farthing remained on the other side of it.

Mrs. Everleigh came up behind him. 'Are you not going in after him?'

'No immediate need,' he replied. 'I don't suppose there is much left of him by now.'

'Oh?'

'Some of my ghastlier relatives are in that room.'

She smiled. 'What a delightful family you do have.'

'I am quite sure no one has ever expressed such a sentiment before.' He offered her his arm. 'Shall we?'

She took the proffered arm, and promenaded with him back into the house.

And into chaos, for the moment Theo stepped over the threshold he became aware of a ruckus in progress. A clattering and banging and shouting emanated from the book-room, Lady Honoria's voice rising over the noise — 'Oh no, my good man, you shan't run away from *me* — ah! Now I've got you!' — all this followed by a fresh round of clattering, suggesting that Honoria's confidence might have been misplaced.

'Perhaps they do need a little help,' Theo murmured,

dropping Mrs. Everleigh's arm. 'If you will excuse me for a moment, ma'am.'

'Of course,' she said, politely, though she did not hang back as Theo sallied forth into the book-room, as her words implied. Instead, she was right behind him, and he had not a moment to discourage her, for the mess that met his eyes proved occupying.

The window, of course, hung open, and a cold wind blew into the room. There had been a mighty scuffle, for a great many books had plummeted off their shelves and lay scattered about the floor. A small, formerly elegant reading-table lay askew, one of its legs broken, and some terrible fate had befallen Lord Werth's preferred reading-chair. It seemed to have encountered a wall, and had doubtless been moving at some speed when it did so.

Ivo Farthing had developed limbs at last; indeed, an entire body. He proved to be a rotund man, clad in a fine, if worn, coat of crimson velvet, and pale breeches. Neither his age, nor his size, nor indeed his state of undeath appeared to have slowed him down, for he had hefted another of the hapless reading-chairs over his head and stood ready to hurl it at—

Charles Selwyn. The identity of the interloper broke upon Theo all at once, somewhat delayed; the fellow had his head down, fighting to extricate himself from the merciless grip of Lady Honoria. What's more, he had grown a quantity of extra hair since last Theo had encountered him. He wore a full beard now, rather unkempt, but it was undoubtedly Selwyn.

'What the—' Theo gasped, and barrelled into the fray.

The next few minutes proved both noisy and confusing. Theo received a clout to the chin (from Honoria, mistakenly); narrowly avoided a braining as Farthing's chair hurtled past his head; suffered a ringing blow to his shoulder and another to his midsection, leaving him rather winded; and finally ended face-down in the dust, from which ignominious position he endured the

130

final humiliation of Lady Honoria's foot planted squarely in the middle of his back as she ran after the fleeing intruder.

Theo was not ordinarily so easily bested, but Selwyn fought like a cornered tiger, and with prodigious strength. What he was doing breaking into Lord Werth's book-room in the middle of the morning was a question that would have to wait; at present, the chances of catching him were diminishing by the moment—

'Ah. We are already acquainted, are not we?' came Mrs. Everleigh's voice, and there followed a dull thud, as of a heavy object (or body) hitting the floor, together with a sharp cry. Selwyn.

Theo looked up.

Mrs. Everleigh blocked the door, cool as ever, her chin high as she beheld the felled and prone form of Charles Selwyn before her. She had delivered a sharp blow, expertly judged, and blood flowed freely from Selwyn's nose as he lay there, cursing. The fight seemed to have gone out of him, which puzzled Theo, until he sat up a bit. Then he beheld the positioning of Mrs. Everleigh's delicate foot: she had planted it somewhere *very* delicate indeed, as far as the male anatomy was concerned. As Theo watched, she mercilessly exploited her advantage.

Selwyn howled.

'I have been expecting you,' Mrs. Everleigh informed the writhing man at her feet.

'You have?' said Theo, hauling himself to his feet. 'Why didn't you say so?'

'What would you have done, if I had?'

Theo thought about this, but not very deeply. His head swam, and he had not yet caught his breath after Selwyn's pummelling. He permitted the question to pass.

'Capital!' cried Lady Honoria. 'A slippery fellow, but no match for the ladies, hm?' The battle seemed to have invigorated her, for she was in high fettle, and joined Mrs. Everleigh with alacrity. 'Ivo, you may put the chair down.

Yes, that's it. Lord Werth would prefer to retain the use of it, I daresay.'

Ivo Farthing set the chair down with great care, looking a little sheepish. 'Yes, my dear.'

'Well.' Lady Honoria and Mrs. Everleigh made a formidable pair, Theo thought, gazing down upon Charles Selwyn with matching expressions of bleak condemnation. 'It is time you accounted for yourself,' commanded Honoria. 'Who are you, and what are you doing breaking into Lord Werth's book-room?'

'It is Charles Selwyn,' Theo said, moving (carefully) to join them. 'Though he looks somewhat altered since Christmas, I grant you.'

'Why, so it is.' Lady Honoria stooped down to inspect her captive's face. 'There seems something frightfully odd about him.'

Theo saw what she meant at once. It was not just the beard, or the long and unkempt hair. There was a feral look about him, all long, bared teeth and wild eyes. Indeed, he looked only half man, and half a wild animal; a wolf, perhaps. He returned the stares of his captors with no sign of recognition, snarling deep in his throat.

'What's the matter with him?' Theo frowned.

'He cannot hold his Wyrde,' Mrs. Everleigh said, her voice very cold. 'A gentleman-lycanthrope ought to have better manners than to scurry about slaughtering women.'

'Slaughtering?' Theo echoed. 'What?'

'And men,' added the lady. 'Though how young Robert Pile came to be drawn into this, I could not say.'

'You mean *this* is the chap who murdered you? *Charles Selwyn?*'

'Certainly. I remember it very clearly.'

'Forgive me, ma'am, but I thought you remembered nothing. The fact has been quite obstructive.' Theo felt unaccountably annoyed, at Mrs. Everleigh and Selwyn both. Honestly, *murder?* Was there no end to the man's poor taste?

'Nor did I, at first,' answered she, unruffled. 'Not until later.'

'You could not have mentioned it *then*?'

'I didn't know his name, and could not have clearly described him,' she said. 'Besides, I wanted no interference. This *gentleman* is mine to destroy.' She remained as cold as ever, but there remained nothing of serenity about it. It was now the killing cold of a freezing winter, and Theo hoped no one would ever look at *him* with such blistering anger.

'Stop a moment,' he said. 'If this miserable specimen killed you, then *he* is the person who deposited your body in my mother's parlour.'

'I imagine so,' agreed Mrs. Everleigh.

Which was a fine thought to anger a man, and Theo developed one or two airy dreams of revenge on the spot. 'But *why*?' he said. 'Why would he kill you? Why would he frame me? What on earth has it all been *for*?'

If Charles Selwyn heard or cared for these questions at all, he gave no sign of it. He didn't answer. He continued to snarl, like an enraged beast, and looked ready to spring at Mrs. Everleigh again— until her foot twisted, reducing him once more to miserable howling.

'He had better be restrained,' Theo decided. 'Who knows what mischief he'll commit if he gets loose.'

Farthing had thought of this already, for no sooner had Theo uttered the words than he appeared behind Mrs. Everleigh with a length of fabric in his hands. A pretty pink colour, it looked torn from somebody's gown or pelisse. Theo hoped that it might be Gussie's. 'That's it,' he said, as Farthing trussed up the youngest son of House Maundevyle. 'That should hold him. Good. Now. We had better get hold of a constable.' Or better yet, Ballantine.

Farthing and Theo hauled the man out of the book-room between them. Selwyn still had not a word to say in his own defence, or upon any subject at all; Theo wondered whether he would ever trouble to account for

133

his actions. 'We will take him into the cellar,' he directed. 'This way— oh! Miss Frostell, this is really not the time—'

'Apologies, Lord Bedgberry,' said the good Miss Frostell, encountered on her way from the parlour to the drawing-room, perhaps, with an unwonted air of haste about her. 'But I did rather hope to speak to— oh dear, is that Mr. Selwyn? What has happened to him?'

'A great deal, I should think,' said Theo grimly. 'Can it wait, ma'am? We are urgently occupied, as you see.'

'Well, but it is about the matter of— oh, dear.' She took a hurried step back, for the prisoner, roused to some fresh frenzy by the sound of Miss Frostell's gentle voice, had made a lunge for her. 'Perhaps it had better wait.'

Theo wrestled Selwyn past Miss Frostell, coolly beating the man's head against the wall in the process. Selwyn subsided, at least enough to get him along the passage and down the cellar stairs (the door obligingly opened by an eager Lady Honoria). Motivated, perhaps, by vengeance, Theo chose the dankest, coldest chamber beneath the house for Selwyn's repose, and took great pleasure in dropping him onto its chilly, clammy floor, and turning the key upon him.

'Capital,' he decided, breathing hard. 'Now that we've got hold of the murderer, we'll have all this nonsense sorted out in no time.'

THIRTEEN

The moment Gussie stepped into her uncle's house, she knew that something untoward had occurred.

Something might be concluded from the air of bustle and alarm she'd walked into — there went a housemaid trotting across the hall, cap askew and her face registering some kind of dismay; and she could hear raised voices echoing from some indeterminable part of the house.

But the thing that really gave it away was simple.

Great-Uncle Silvester had, at last, woken up.

Ever since the disaster at Werth Towers, the haunted grotesque had remained in so deep a slumber Gussie had not truly expected him to rouse again. The carved and crumbling stone creature he had, for so long, inhabited, seemed reduced to a mere lump of granite again, not a flicker of life left in it. Lady Werth had placed him in a quiet corner somewhere up in the rafters, where his repose could continue undisturbed. Perhaps forever.

But here came the grotesque at last, swooping towards Gussie on stone-carved wings, and there could be no doubt that he was in something of a pelter.

'The door!' he cried, his rumbling voice like ancient rocks grinding together.

'Yes, yes, Uncle,' said Gussie soothingly. 'We shall close it directly. What a cold day it is, to be sure.'

Clarissa came in behind her, and obediently slammed the door shut against the freezing wind. 'There!' she called gaily up to the grotesque. 'Is that better?'

Great-Uncle Silvester never did, or could, answer a question directly, and this one proved no different. He fluttered around Clarissa's head in a frenzy, barking out assorted observations of no conceivable relevance — 'Excellent book! Not my area of expertise, but Theo's the man for it.' He added something Gussie did not catch, but which included peculiar words like *hirsute* and *scoundrel* oddly juxtaposed.

Gussie did not waste much time attempting to understand him.

'What is the matter, Uncle?' she called. 'If you cannot tell us what the matter is, then pray show us. I shall follow directly.'

'Oh! There you are, my dear,' came Miss Frostell's voice, and here came the lady herself, hurrying out of the parlour. 'I thought it was your voice I heard. I have been wanting to speak to you this age—'

'Just a moment, Frosty,' said Gussie, keeping her eyes on the flapping form of Great-Uncle Silvester. 'My uncle appears to be in some distress, and I cannot at all determine why—'

'But that's just it,' interposed Miss Frostell. 'We are all in uproar! There has been an intruder, and it proved to be *Charles Selwyn*— begging your pardon, Miss Selwyn—' (This last directed at Clarissa) '—and what with Mrs. Everleigh saying as she remembers him after all, and poor Lord Bedgberry all in a temper—'

'Charles Selwyn?' Gussie stopped short, arrested. 'What, is *he* in London? How curious of you never to mention it, Clarissa!' The rest of Miss Frostell's rambling speech penetrated her consciousness, and she stared. 'Mrs. Everleigh remembers him? Surely you cannot mean—'

'But yes, precisely,' persevered Miss Frostell, 'And I really must tell you—'

'And, what, he is *here*?'

'Yes, and—'

Great-Uncle Silvester abruptly wheeled about and flapped away, and Gussie took off after him. 'A moment, Frosty!' she called over her shoulder. 'Pray, Uncle, not so fast! I cannot keep up with you.'

She spoke truly, for the dark little shape of the grotesque melded into the shadows in some cobwebby corner, and vanished. Gussie stopped halfway up the great staircase, frustrated. 'Uncle!' she called.

He did not re-emerge.

Gussie returned into the hall, muttering one or two of Theo's favourite curses under her breath. Something had roused Great-Uncle Silvester, and perhaps it was only the wretched Selwyns, after all.

'Now, where has Clarissa gone?' said she, perceiving that the hall had emptied of everyone but Miss Frostell. 'Impossible girl! But yes, Frosty, what is it?'

'I have been *trying* to tell someone,' said Miss Frostell, betraying a most uncharacteristic sense of grievance. 'I've found the person as opened the door to whoever killed poor Mrs. Everleigh, but I do not know what ought to be done about it. She is very young, and the villain threatened her family—'

'Who, Frosty?' said Gussie.

Miss Frostell moved nearer, and lowered her voice. 'One of the maids, my dear. Mabel. She cried ever-so, and I admit I was moved to pity, for all that she acted badly. I have not liked to take the story to Lord and Lady Werth as yet, for I fear they're like to be angry.'

'Like as not,' Gussie agreed, 'for she has caused a deal of trouble. But if she acted under duress, then I am sure they will be merciful.'

Miss Frostell hesitated, twisting her hands together. 'It is only that I had to promise, or she would not have talked to me at all.'

'Promise what? That you would not tell my uncle?'

'Yes, and it does not sit well with me to go back on my word.'

Gussie began to feel driven to some distraction. Too many competing demands upon her attention, and what to do about any of them?' 'Um,' she said. 'But can it matter all that much, now? For if Charles Selwyn is revealed as the culprit — and I cannot say as it surprises me — then Mabel's tormentor will soon be suitably dealt with.'

'Perhaps you are right, my dear. We have got him in the cellar, and there he shall remain until good Mr. Ballantine comes for him.'

'The cellar? What in the world—? Come, you had better tell me what has happened while I was gone.'

Out came a confused tale, the salient points being: Mr. Charles Selwyn had made an ill-advised and unsuccessful attempt at breaking into Lord Werth's house, and now reposed in the cellar, thanks to the combined efforts of Theo, Mrs. Everleigh, Great-Aunt Honoria and Ivo Farthing.

Gussie heard it with mounting incredulity. 'He did what?' she said, mouth agape. 'Broke into the book-room? In broad daylight? Why?'

Miss Frostell had no answer to give. 'He has not been himself, it appears, and has not made a great deal of sense.'

'You intrigue me greatly. Where in the cellar, Frosty? I will go and see for myself.'

But no sooner did she arrive at the head of the cellar stairs than she encountered Theo barrelling up them, clearly still in that temper Miss Frostell had spoken of. 'Gussie!' he said upon perceiving her, and quite without enthusiasm.

'You need not utter my name with such revulsion,' said she. 'I am here to help.'

'You've *helped* by bringing Clarissa Selwyn into the house,' answered he, with a snarl. 'With predictable consequences. I but turn my back for *five* minutes and what happens? Our prisoner is gone.'

Gussie thought rapidly. Clarissa had indeed disappeared. Had done so, in all likelihood, the moment Great-Uncle Silvester had distracted Gussie's attention. She had broken her brother out, had she? Hm. She had not wasted any time.

'Why, they have been in it together,' Gussie concluded darkly.

'I do not see how you can be surprised,' said Theo, disgustedly. 'You did find her poking about in the cellar, didn't you?'

'I did. But I remain uncertain as to why. What was she doing here, then? And why did her revolting brother break in today? It must be something desperately important for him to take such a risk, but even so it seems deranged.'

'He *is* deranged,' answered Theo. 'Your Wyrding of him has addled his wits, I'd say. He is all snap and snarl, not a syllable of sense left in him.'

'Then he must have killed Mrs. Everleigh in a fit of animal madness,' Gussie said, her confidence returning. 'How unfortunate.'

'Yes, but then to dump her in my mother's parlour?' Theo ushered Gussie back from the stairs, and slammed the cellar door with some force. 'That argues for greater sense and calculation than he appears capable of.'

'Perhaps he is shamming it.'

'That could be so, yes. Or perhaps he had help, just as he has had help today in freeing himself from just imprisonment in our cellar.' Theo glowered at her, quite as though it had been *her* doing.

'You mean to say Clarissa might have left us that charming little present?'

'Quite. Though a corpse is no light burden for a woman to bear, so it might just as likely have been Lord Maundevyle.'

'Henry! No, that cannot be the case.'

'Just because you have a *tendre* for him, doesn't mean he must be innocent of all wrong-doing.'

'I do not have a tendre for Lord Maundevyle.' Gussie spoke coolly, and with conviction, if not with the strictest honesty.

Theo pushed past her. 'We had better have everything set into order before my mother and father come home. There's been some little damage to the book-room.'

He disappeared in the direction of Lord Werth's library, where, Gussie hoped, Great-Aunt Honoria and Ivo Farthing might be already engaged in straightening up the room (but she doubted it). She might have followed, having some one or two questions to put to her great-aunt, given the chance - -and where was Mrs. Everleigh, by the by? The heroine of this morning's little drama was, as yet, nowhere in evidence — but there was Mabel, the disgraced maid, loitering beside the great stairs, her gaze fixed upon Gussie with a rather terrible mixture of hope and despair.

'Miss Werth,' whispered she as Gussie approached.

'Yes?' said Gussie, a little torn. To be sure, the girl made a wretched appearance, and could not more plainly have *repentance* written all over her whey-pale countenance. Then again, she had betrayed the household, and contributed to Theo's troubles in particular, and one could not simply let a thing like that go.

Mabel dipped her head. 'I heard what you was saying, about why that man might have wanted to get into the house.'

'And have you some information?'

'I may.' Mabel risked a look up into Gussie's face. 'I-I only kept it a little while,' she began, puzzlingly. 'I was going to turn it in sooner, I swear, only it were so pretty, and my mam being so sick, and I thought as I might— but I *didn't*,' she went on, passionately. 'It would ha' been so easy, just to walk it down to the pawn-shop on the corner. Mr. Babbage is said to be— accommodating, ain't he?'

'I know of no Mr. Babbage,' said Gussie. 'But do,

please, enlighten me. What was it that you did not choose to pawn?'

Mabel had something in her fingers, Gussie now saw. The work-worn hands opened, and revealed: a stick-pin, rather an elegant thing. Gold, and with a handsome diamond set into the crown.

'Ah,' said Gussie, enlightened. Just the sort of thing a Charles Selwyn might wear — and lose, during his inelegant tussle with Mrs. Everleigh's corpse. Doubtless this was what he had come in search of, and Clarissa too. Highly incriminating evidence.

Wonderful.

Mabel relinquished it into Gussie's keeping. 'Miss Frostell said as I should give it you,' she whispered. 'I am sorry, miss. I thought as it weren't belonging to the family, it might be all right, but I ought not to have kept hold of it.'

'No, that is certainly true,' Gussie agreed. 'But it is Miss Frostell's wish that I should be lenient, and so I shall be. What manner of threat did the miscreant make?'

'He said as it wouldn't take much to finish off me mam,' came the answer. 'Not that there were much blood in her, but enough for a snack. He were not kind, miss.'

'No, and it was not conduct befitting of a gentleman.' Gussie's feelings of disgust towards his lordship's younger brother grew. Really, to threaten a slip of a girl like that! Revolting.

'Oh, but he weren't a gentleman,' said Mabel.

Gussie blinked. 'No? How can you be sure?'

'Didn't talk like one, Miss. Nor did he have them pretty ways, like their lordships.'

Gussie's head began to swim. The pin *must* belong to Charles Selwyn, or what other reason could he or his sister have had for constantly trespassing all over the house? They must have been searching for it.

But if the pin was Selwyn's, that meant he must have lost it when he— or, perhaps, the pair of them— had dumped Mrs. Everleigh's corpse in the parlour. When else could it have gone missing?

In which case, it must have been he who had threatened Mabel into leaving the door open. Either he had been shamming it when he gave the appearance of being no gentleman, or he had some kind of assistant-in-malfeasance, besides his sister, and it was this underling who had approached the maid.

Either way, the vision of Charles Selwyn Miss Frostell had described — out of control, not making sense — did not much coincide with such machinations as that, which must require a clear head.

The situation grew hopelessly tangled, and Gussie began to feel out of her depth. Not that she would ever have admitted as much to Mr. Ballantine.

'I will see that this goes to Bow Street,' Gussie told the maid. 'And I shan't trouble my aunt about this matter, provided you do not plan to continue with this questionable career in petty thievery.'

'Oh, no, Miss,' gasped Mabel. 'I'm that sorry. Only don't turn me out, *please.*'

The flare of panic in the poor girl's eyes put Gussie to shame. 'Nobody will turn you out,' she said, more soothingly. 'And I shall ask Mrs. Gavell to ensure your mother is given proper care. Don't worry, nobody will be causing her the smallest harm.'

She was rewarded by the abject relief in Mabel's face. The girl crept away, profuse with gratitude, and Gussie was left to the contemplation of the diamond stick-pin.

If Charles Selwyn had killed Mrs. Everleigh: why? How had he come to be in sufficient proximity to the actress to cause her any harm at all? Why had he flown into such a rage, or a frenzy, as to tear her throat to pieces?

Moreover, what could possibly have prompted him to kill Robert Pile? Were it the same uncontrollable instincts that Theo attributed to his animalistic state, she had the same question as in Mrs. Everleigh's case: how had Charles

Selwyn known Robert Pile in the first place? Selwyn may well be an enthusiast for Strangewayes, as Theo was, but that did not answer all the questions. Mrs. Everleigh, for example, may not have been killed at Strangewayes, but somewhere else — wearing a gown that wasn't her own. And Pile had not, apparently, been killed at the playhouse either.

There was also the question of who had threatened Mabel, if not Charles; what Clarissa's interest in the situation might be, except perhaps tidying up after her brother; why Mr. Pile had tried to implicate Theo, with his lie about Mrs. Everleigh and the carriage; oh, and the maddening Mrs. Daughtry and her dark premonitions of disaster…

Really, there were too many questions floating about for Gussie's comfort, and she was becoming impatient.

She turned the stick-pin over in her fingers, thinking. Yes, it ought to go to Bow-Street, and without delay. But Mr. Ballantine was not present, and his search for Robert Pile may prove lengthy, in which case he would not likely return to Bow-Street for some hours yet.

In the meantime, Gussie might put it to use herself.

'Right,' she said. 'It is time to take action, I should say.'

She found Frosty engaged with Mabel, the hapless housemaid, and collected her up. Great-Aunt Honoria and Ivo Farthing had withdrawn to their attic hideaway; Gussie swept them into her train as well. Mrs. Everleigh was not to be found, but Theo lingered in the book-room, attempting (without success) to make something of the shattered remains of Lord Werth's favourite reading-chair.

'Theo,' Gussie said, bursting into the room. 'Come on. We are going out.'

He looked up, his face twisted with irritation. 'I can't. I have to mend this chair, or father will have my head.'

'I imagine he can live without a single chair, Theo, however well-favoured. Refocus your attention, if you please. We have this.' She held up the stick-pin. 'Likely the property of one Charles Selwyn, though perhaps not, and if you will give me the benefit of your assistance, I propose to stage an invasion of Lady Maundevyle's house. It's my belief a number of answers are to be discovered there, and I am rather tired of waiting for people to prove forthcoming about them.'

'Frontal attack?' Theo straightened, the chair forgotten.

'Why not? We might have the whole unsavoury business cleared up by tea-time.'

Theo smiled, showing his sharper teeth. 'For once, I do believe you have come up with an excellent idea.'

This was too patently absurd a reflection to warrant a reply; of *course* the idea was excellent. Gussie swept towards the door, pausing only to collect her bonnet, pelisse and gloves as she passed — and to let loose a vast, full-throated cry over her shoulder: 'Great-Uncle Silvester! Attend!'

FOURTEEN

Lady Maundevyle's townhouse was handsomer than that occupied by the Werths, this did not admit of a doubt. Considerably larger, and in excellent repair, it reeked of wealth and plenty almost as much as Starminster did.

None of which Theo noticed, or cared for, as he marched up to the front door, side-by-side with Gussie, and hammered loudly upon it.

When nobody leapt at once to answer — in fact, some two or three minutes passed without any discernible response — Theo grasped the door-knob, turned it, and shouldered his way into the house.

'Yes, we are not to be deterred by poor service,' Gussie agreed. The Werths spilled into the townhouse all in a gaggle: Gussie and Great-Aunt Honoria right behind Theo, Ivo Farthing close by, and Miss Frostell bringing up the rear.

'Oh, Lord Silvester,' Theo heard her say, in her soft way. 'Here, you might perch upon my shoulder, if you wish to. You're likely to be crushed to pieces, otherwise.'

A sound precaution; the Werths were in high gig and high temper, and anyone small and insufficiently wary might indeed find themselves at a grave, and permanent, disadvantage.

The house was as grand inside as it was handsome outside, smothered with such accoutrements as costly wallpaper, an ornate longcase clock, a glittering chandelier, and marble tiles all across the floor. Theo's footsteps echoed hollowly amidst all this splendour, and the clamour the family sent up as they spread out across the hall would soon attract notice. They had better get on with it.

'Right,' said Gussie, already striding off. A footman appeared at the far end of the hall, horrified in aspect; he soon vanished again, choosing not to remonstrate with six angry people, two of which bore every sign of a peculiar, and disconcerting, incorporeality, and one of which was an animated grotesque.

Sensible chap, thought Theo, but he had probably gone to warn the mistress of the house.

'Follow him,' Theo called to Gussie, who nodded, and directed her steps through the same door that had recently swallowed up the footman.

A passage was hastened down, the hapless footman glancing over his shoulder in perfect horror at finding himself pursued. Gussie's stride did not falter, and Theo was hard-pressed to keep up with her, despite his superior height.

The footman fled through a half-open door, and Theo heard some fragments of his words echo down the passage: '—couldn't hope to hold them— sorry, my lady— what to *do*—

'Never mind, my good man,' Gussie said cheerfully as she swept into the room. 'We are here now. You had better go about your work.'

Theo was barely a step behind her. He beheld: Lady Maundevyle, seated in a throne-like chair before a blazing hearth, and white with anger. Her swept-up hair was but plainly dressed today, and she wore a simple gown: no splendour about her, which, Theo dimly recalled, seemed uncharacteristic. 'Augusta Werth,' she said in quelling tones. 'And Lord Bedgberry! What can you mean by this intrusion?'

'We are looking for your horrible son and daughter,' Gussie answered her. 'By which you will understand me to mean Charles, and Clarissa. They will have returned to the house in the past half-hour, I imagine. Where are they?'

'They are not here— madam, I must *beg* you to stay where you are, and not commit so grave a solecism as to wander about my house unescorted!' Her voice rose to a shout by the end of this sentence, but to no avail: Lady Honoria had swept out again, Ivo Farthing in her wake, doubtless to search the rest of the house.

The footman, wisely, made no attempt to interfere.

Theo realised that Miss Frostell, also, was gone, Great-Uncle Silvester with her. He approved. The erstwhile governess had a way of going unnoticed, and consequently, of finding her way into all manner of quiet corners and secret doings. With the aid of the grotesque, there was no telling what she might uncover.

Gussie thrust a hand under Lady Maundevyle's nose. 'Do you recognise this?' she demanded. In her hand was something that glittered.

Lady Maundevyle plucked the thing out of Gussie's palm. It was the cravat-pin she had mentioned, a thing some gentlemen were fond of adorning themselves with. This one had a big, clear jewel in it — a diamond, doubtless. It was just the sort of showy piece a Selwyn would wear.

But her ladyship handled it as though it were an article of rubbish, and quickly dropped it back into Gussie's palm. 'No, indeed. Why should I?'

'Perhaps because it belongs to your younger son?' Gussie told her. 'And it was found somewhere highly compromising.'

Lady Maundevyle's lip curled. 'Charles has no need of paste jewels, and I wonder that you could be so foolish as to imagine it likely.'

'Paste?' Gussie, palpably startled, brought the pin closer

to her face, and fell into a silent study of it.

Theo, too, was surprised. The pin was a fake? 'Does it belong to Charles?' Theo demanded. If it did, then perhaps Charles had run through all his money, and fallen back on pawning his jewels, and substituting paste alternatives. But that would suggest that he had found his mother — or his elder brother — unsympathetic to his financial plight, and that did not ring true. Towards her children, at least, Lady Maundevyle was indulgent to a fault, and the family was rolling in cash.

'I have never seen him wear such an article,' said Lady Maundevyle coldly.

Theo met Gussie's eye, and saw in her an echo of his own chagrin. 'But if it isn't Charles's,' said Gussie, 'whose is it?'

If it did not belong to Charles, then the pin was not what the younger Selwyn had been looking for when he had infiltrated the book-room. Nor had Clarissa been in search of it when she had been discovered skulking about in the cellar.

'Devil take it,' Theo muttered. 'If you are concealing Charles and Clarissa somewhere in this house, madam, be sure that they will be found. My relatives are even now—'

The door burst open again behind him, thrown with such violence as to bounce off the adjacent wall. '*Mamma*,' somebody said, 'Charles is— oh, *no*. What are *you* doing here?'

It was Clarissa. She beheld Gussie and Theo with undisguised resentment, then threw up her hands. 'I give up,' she declared. 'If you are not to be deterred like *sensible people*, then I shall have nothing further to do with the nonsense of protecting you.'

'Protecting us?' Gussie's words dripped incredulity. 'From what, pray?'

'Why, have you fathomed nothing at all?' Clarissa flounced into the room, shaking her head. She did not seem disposed to explain further, for her next words were addressed to her mother. 'Charles is upstairs. I've ordered for him to be given his tonic. He is sorely in need of it.'

Briefly, Lady Maundevyle closed her eyes. 'What have these *Werths* done to him?'

'In justice to Miss Werth and Lord Bedgberry, Mamma, I do not think they have done anything to him that he did not deserve. He was discovered clambering through their book-room window, you know, and one can hardly blame a household for taking exception to such conduct.'

Lady Maundevyle's brows rose. 'Indeed? And what was his object?'

'He was looking for *that woman*, I imagine; he spoke of such an idea, last time he made any sense, and would not be dissuaded from it. But perhaps he had some other scheme in mind. He has deteriorated rather rapidly, since this morning.'

'What woman?' Gussie asked. 'Mrs. Everleigh?'

'No,' said Clarissa, rolling her eyes heavenwards. 'Mrs. Daughtry.'

Theo did not think he had ever seen Gussie's eyes open so wide in his life. His own, he imagined, were little different. '*Mrs. Daughtry*?' Gussie repeated, flabbergasted. 'You were looking for *her*? In *our* house?'

Clarissa looked at Theo, full of scorn. 'She has been dangling after Lord Bedgberry of late, has not she?'

'Dangling?' Theo protested. 'After *me*? No!'

'Yes,' said Gussie, disloyally. 'But she spent only some one or two hours in our house, and we sent her away again.' But a look of uncertainty crossed her face, and she added, more doubtfully: 'I do recall her angling for an invitation to remain with us, however. Something about her being in grave danger.'

Everyone was looking at Theo, now, and he recoiled. 'What?' he protested. 'I don't remember anything about it.' And he didn't. He recollected that he had visited Mrs. Daughtry's dressing-room, and he certainly recalled a quantity of smiles, and something about *kindness* — yes, she had repeated that word rather a lot. And she had come to the house, yes, and had tea with his Mamma, but what was there in that to justify all these reproachful looks at *him*?

'Grave danger!' Clarissa shook her head. 'She is not so much *in* grave danger as she *is* grave danger. Had not you realised?'

Gussie's uncertainty grew. 'I had not, I confess,' she said, and Theo knew well how much it would cost her to admit it. 'I suspected something, of course, for she was all too plausible, but I had not laid anything in particular at her door.'

'Nor I,' Theo put in. 'And if somebody does not enlighten me immediately, I shall grow savage.'

'He will,' Gussie corroborated. 'His teeth are sharpening already.'

'Mrs. Marianne Daughtry,' said Lady Maundevyle, with immense dignity, 'is a designing hussy who has already attempted to get her hooks into *both* my sons — unsuccessfully, I might add! But that she has some scheme afoot with regards to Strangewayes cannot admit of a doubt.'

'She certainly tried for Theo,' Gussie put in. 'successfully, I might previously have said, but he does not seem to be much affected by it now.'

'He wouldn't be, if she has not seen him in some little time,' Clarissa said. 'The effects wear off after a day or so, if not rather less.'

'What effects?' Theo asked, blankly. He was beginning to experience feelings of alarm, and that never did improve his temper.

'The effects of her mesmerism, or whatever it is that she does.' Clarissa looked keenly at Theo, as though she were trying to read something complex in his face. 'She must have dragooned Lord Bedgberry, to some extent, but I think it remarkable that the effect does not seem to have taken with the rest of you.'

'I recall that she was very focused on Theo,' Gussie offered. 'And he was acting most out of character, indeed! We were very struck by it. He came over all *chivalrous*, if you please. Theo! Protector to a poor, delicate flower of an actress! Now that you put me in mind of it, I ought to have enquired further into the matter. I suppose I was distracted.'

'Too ready to think the worst of your cousin, more like,' Clarissa said.

To her credit, Gussie did not dispute this.

'But what did she want?' Theo put in.

'Mrs. Everleigh. She had likely heard, by then, that the lady was not only brought back from the dead but sheltered under the Werth roof, and this did not at all agree with her plans.'

'She wanted Mrs. Everleigh gone?' Gussie said. 'A rival for her dominance of the stage, I suppose.'

'Oh, to be sure. The great, glittering Arabella Everleigh returns to the stage, and it is all that Wyrded London can talk of! Mrs. Daughtry is all but forgotten. *That* did not suit her notions of her own due, at all.'

'But I don't understand,' said Theo. 'If it was Mrs. Daughtry who had it in for Arabella, how came it about that your brother committed the deed?'

'Mesmerism,' said Clarissa shortly. 'Charles is a fool. Mamma persists in believing him too canny to fall for her wiles, but he wasn't.' Lady Maundevyle appeared ready to dispute this, but was, unusually, quelled by a glare from her daughter.

'Mesmerism.' Gussie frowned. 'And she told us her Wyrde was foresight! Came up with a deal of nonsense about having foreseen the danger to Mrs. Everleigh, and Robert Pile, and how she was like to be next— oh! I see it all, now.'

'Oh, she foresaw the dangers, all right,' Clarissa said grimly. 'Planned them, you mean. Mamma spoke truly, when she said the woman tried for Henry. He would have none of her, and we *all* interfered when she got her claws into Charles. She is not a woman to take a slighting lightly, and what better scheme of vengeance than to suborn the Selwyns into dirtying our hands for the sake of her horrible little plot?'

'But why drop Mrs. Everleigh's corpse in our house?' Gussie asked. 'It was only *after* that that she met Theo. He'd had no opportunity to slight her before.'

'Probably Charles's idea,' Theo put in. Nasty little man, Charles Selwyn. Would be just like him to try to implicate Theo in murder. Just the sort of thing he got up to in school.

But Gussie was shaking her head. 'Mabel — our maid — said it wasn't a gentleman that persuaded her to leave the door open. Either he had an accomplice, or it wasn't him. I can hardly suppose him capable of deceiving her about it.'

'It was not him,' said Clarissa. 'Poor idiot panicked when he realised what he had done, and fled. Once I'd got the sorry story out of him, Henry and I went looking for the corpse, but it was already gone. I hoped he had merely been mistaken as to the degree of damage he had inflicted, and Mrs. Everleigh had simply got up and gone home. Of course, we were soon disabused of that comfortable notion.'

'Henry?' Gussie said, startled. 'What, is he involved?'

'Of course he is. It is unwise to threaten the family of a dragon, Miss Werth; it tends to anger them rather, and once roused Henry can be quite implacable.'

'What of Pile?' Theo said, his mind turning over this flurry of revelations without much making sense of them.

'Another little gift from Marianne Daughtry,' said Clarissa. 'I fear Charles did away with him, too, though I am not sure why. Unhappily, our butler found him first, and the alarm had gone up before I was aware. It could not be suppressed.'

Theo frowned. 'What had this Pile done, to deserve

death?'

'I don't know, for the woman has disappeared. Henry has been trying to track her down. Your carriage restored her to her own lodgings — so says your coachman — but where she went after that is a mystery.'

'So,' said Gussie. 'We do not know for certain who killed Robert Pile (though it was probably your brother), or why Mrs. Everleigh's body was dumped in our house. Or by whom, for that matter, since it may or may not have been Charles's doing.'

'I have a further question,' Theo put in. 'What was her objection to *me* supposed to be? Why should she want to see me implicated for a murder she'd arranged for?'

Gussie frowned in thought, and shook her head. 'To be fair, Theo, she might not have predicted that it would be you who was implicated. The wounds Mrs. Everleigh and Pile had did not really match your Wyrde — Mr. Ballantine immediately drew a probable link with lycanthropy instead, which he was perfectly right about. Perhaps she was not trying to target you, specifically. Perhaps she simply wanted our family in trouble, like the Selwyns.'

'Maybe so,' Theo agreed. 'But I'd still say: why? She could have left the corpse where it was, and Charles Selwyn would likely have been condemned for it. Was that not the point of using him to commit the deed? If she wanted one of us to hang, why not mesmerise one of us into killing the woman?'

Gussie bit her lip. 'You're right, Theo. I cannot imagine what she has been about.'

'We'll find out,' Theo promised darkly.

'You are certain about all this, I suppose?' asked Gussie of Clarissa, dismissing the matter. "How did you find out the half of it?'

Clarissa turned upon her a look of withering scorn. 'Please, Gussie. You are not the only person capable of *investigating*.'

'It was Henry's doing,' said Lady Maundevyle, stiffly.

153

'For the most part.'

'*Mamma.* I had something to do with it, please recall.'

'You could not have included me, I suppose?' said Gussie tartly. 'We might have joined forces! You might at least have told me about your discoveries. Why, we spoke of Mrs. Daughtry this very day.'

'And once you discovered Charles to be guilty of at least Mrs. Everleigh's death, and possibly Robert Pile's, what would you have done? Would you have believed me about Mrs. Daughtry's culpability, before you had uncovered evidence of it yourself? I know you do not like Charles.'

'I don't,' Gussie agreed. 'But that does not mean I should like to see him hanged for a crime he had no choice in committing. Besides that, I did not like Mrs. Daughtry, either. Having had an opportunity to witness her peculiar influence over Theo, I do not find it difficult to entertain your theory.'

'Henry said you would feel that way,' Clarissa answered. 'And he said I ought not to have gone looking for more bodies without your leave, and perhaps he was right.'

'Oh, so you *were* in our cellar on a corpse-hunt? I had concluded you were after the pin, but if it was not Charles's then of course that couldn't have been it.'

'No. Having found another of Charles's possible leavings in our cellar, I had to make sure he had not left any more in yours. The newspapers made such a ruckus about the one in your parlour. I thought it would be nicer if they did not have cause to kick up a fuss about another one.'

Theo, oblivious, found himself staring at the cravat-pin in Gussie's hand. It glittered under the light, constantly calling his attention to it. Whose was it, if not Charles's? 'Who might wear so gaudy a jewel, when it's a fake?' he said aloud.

'Where *is* Henry?' Gussie said, almost at the same time.

'Henry left the house early, and would not tell me

where he was going.' Clarissa spoke with palpable disgust. 'I believe he went after *that woman*, as Charles did, but since he seemingly did not appear at your house then I have no notion where he expected to find her.'

'Should he be chasing Mrs. Daughtry about on his own?' Gussie's brow creased with concern. 'She does seem rather... potent a foe.'

'The pin,' Theo interrupted. 'I have an idea about it—'

'He ought to be found,' Gussie went on. 'What if he has got into danger?'

'Henry is a dragon,' Clarissa pointed out. '*She* had better be the one to look out.'

'But she did so enthral Charles as to—'

Theo gave up on trying to be heard, and simply snatched the cravat-pin out of Gussie's hands. 'Costumes,' he said, loudly and distinctly.

Gussie blinked. 'Why Theo, that is remarkably perspicacious. Yes. Perhaps this does not belong to any gentleman, but someone who dresses like one—'

'For a stage performance,' Theo finished.

'Like— Robert Pile?' Gussie's eyes opened wide. 'Now that I think of it, Clarissa and I ran into him at Strangewayes—'

'And he was coming from the costume cupboards!' Clarissa put in. 'At least, he could have been. There were certainly some in that part of the theatre.'

'He was wearing something passably gentry-like,' Gussie continued. 'Nothing excessively fine, but beyond what one would think a mere stage-actor of no renown might wear. A good coat, and a cravat, well-tied—'

'No pin, of course, but he would have lost this one by then,' Clarissa added. 'He might have been going to a rehearsal. A lot of the cast were in that day, judging from the noise.'

'If this belongs to the Pile fellow,' Theo said, 'then perhaps he is not merely a victim, as it appears, but an accomplice—'

'Mabel said it was not a gentleman that coerced her into unlocking the door,' Gussie went on. 'But she never said anything about him not looking like one, only that he didn't *sound* or act like one—'

'—So it could have been *Pile* who got into our house, and left us a fresh corpse,' concluded Theo. 'Losing his gaudy little bauble in the process.'

'So he must be under Mrs. Daughtry's thrall as well?' Clarissa speculated. 'If that is so, then Charles did right to savage him to death! No doubt he was skulking about in our house with some other scheme of infamy in mind—'

'*And,*' Gussie said, 'Mabel said something about our mysterious non-gentleman's having threatened her mother, even though there were "only enough blood in her for a snack", or some such. I wonder if Pile's Wyrde is the same as yours, Theo? If so, it is another count against him.'

Clarissa was bouncing on her toes. 'Yes! And Pile lied about Theo, Gussie, do not forget that. He tried to implicate him in Mrs. Everleigh's death, with that absurd carriage story—'

'So he has repeatedly tried to cast blame on poor Theo!' Gussie was beginning to look peeved, which was never a good sign. 'But why would he do so, I wonder, when Mrs. Daughtry had gone to such trouble to use Charles as a cat's paw?'

'We had better have words with Mr. Pile,' Theo decided.

'Yes, though Mr. Ballantine was having the devil of a time finding him,' Clarissa said. 'Perhaps he has already absconded.'

'As has Mrs. Daughtry, by your account,' said Gussie. 'Perhaps they have absconded together, which would be *too* inconvenient.'

'I doubt that,' Theo said. 'If all this was done to preserve the woman's stage career, she would hardly abandon it now.'

Gussie nodded. 'The papers still fancy Theo for the

culprit, after all, and we did not treat her with any suspicion, when she paid her little visit. She cannot know that we have come to suspect her.'

'Provided Henry has not been fool enough to inform her of the fact,' Clarissa said darkly.

'Henry,' said Lady Maundevyle majestically, 'could never be so foolish. You ought to know better, Clarissa.'

'You are probably right, Mamma. But then, where is she? Or Mr. Pile? Where is Henry, for that matter?'

'Or Mr. Ballantine,' Gussie added. 'They are lost somewhere in London, all four, and we have not much hope of finding any of them.'

She was right, Theo knew. Mrs. Daughtry's lodgings must already have been searched, by Clarissa's account, and likely Ballantine had gone after Pile's. They would not be at Strangewayes, or they would have been discovered long since.

He thought. Where might Marianne Daughtry go?

What might she be planning to do?

'Her scheme is not yet complete,' Theo said. 'The Daughtry woman, I mean. She hasn't done away with her rival.'

'Thanks to my uncle's interference,' Gussie agreed. 'If anything, Mrs. Everleigh's star will blaze all the brighter for it. What, then? You think she will make some further attempt?'

'She may indeed. Besides, Mrs. Everleigh's memory was coming back, wasn't it? And the fact she recalled so little before suggests that—'

'Mrs. Daughtry mesmerised her, as well as Charles!' Gussie concluded. 'Shortly before she was killed. Is that why she did not remember the gown? Why might she have done so?'

'But Mrs. Everleigh recognised Charles, after a time,' said Theo. 'Was that why Mrs. Daughtry asked to be taken to see her? She wanted to find out whether she remembered anything. Perhaps she thought she might mesmerise her again, if she needed to. Or do worse to her, if I had not been there.'

'No,' Gussie disagreed. 'If she were prepared to dirty her own hands in the matter, she wouldn't have gone to so much trouble to get Charles to do it. She went off to hatch some fresh plot to remove Mrs. Everleigh, I imagine, and more permanently.'

'But how do you kill a woman who's already dead?' Clarissa put in.

A short silence followed this remark, neither Theo nor Gussie having tested any particular method before. 'Fire, I suppose?' Gussie suggested.

'It worked on Lord Felix,' Theo agreed. 'Poor fool.'

Gussie met his eyes. Her own registered a rising alarm. 'But— Mrs. Daughtry knows that Mrs. Everleigh is a guest at *our* house—'

For an instant, Theo forgot to breathe. 'Oh, no,' he sighed. 'We cannot get *another* family property burned down. Father will never forgive us.'

'My aunt will never forgive us,' Gussie corrected. 'She has but just finished new-furnishing the drawing-room.'

'But we were there an hour ago, and Mrs. Everleigh wasn't, was she?' Clarissa said.

'No, but Mrs. Daughtry may not know that.' Gussie ran for the door.

'But where is she, then?' Clarissa said, her voice rising. 'Really, there are too many people adrift somewhere in London when we want to talk to them, it is most disobliging—'

Gussie was already out the door, Theo hard behind her. The whereabouts of Mrs. Everleigh did not interest him so much as the whereabouts of Mrs. Daughtry — and they had left the house unguarded.

* * *

It is time now to pay a visit to that worthy and long-suffering Bow Street Runner, Ballantine. We last encountered him shaking off the *helpful* interference of Gussie and Clarissa, and disappearing into the streets of London in pursuit of Robert Pile. What became of him after that?

He was as good as his word, and went all over the theatre, interrupting the company as they rehearsed and ruffling a good many tempers. He had at least his badge of office to assist him; a certain authority brought him answers and a grudging respect, even if he was very much in the way.

He had questioned the good folk of Strangewayes before, of course, without uncovering much of note or use. But today, something was different.

He had with him the gown Mrs. Everleigh had been wearing when she was killed, its Turkey-red silks still stained with blood. When he showed this around the theatre, it was recognised by more than one person — but the truth of its provenance came as a shock.

'Seen her in it a time or two,' he was soon told. 'Though how it came to get all that blood on it, I couldn't say.'

'How?' Ballantine said, surprised. 'This is the gown she was wearing when she died.'

'Mrs. Daughtry?' came the reply. 'What, has she gone and got herself killed, too?'

And Ballantine stood frozen for a moment, arrested, as all his ideas neatly rearranged themselves in an instant.

The gown was not Mrs. Everleigh's at all.

It belonged to the woman who'd served as her understudy on the night of the murder: Mrs. Daughtry.

Well, now.

The nature of his questions altered, and he learned some one or two other, salient facts in short order. His enquiries about Mr. Pile, for instance, elicited one or two of the self-same things Gussie and Theo have just been concluding: that there was, or had been, some association

159

between the celebrated Mrs. Daughtry, and Robert Pile.

'Aye, they were lovers, right enough,' said a costume-mistress around a mouthful of pins, busily engaged in pinning a ball-gown to a blonde actress. 'No secret about that. The way they carried on!'

'You would think she could do better,' put in the actress, with a sniff. 'Said to have one or two *gentlemen* in her train, but p'raps she lost them.'

'Perhaps she and Robert were *sincerely* attached,' said the costume-mistress, reprovingly. 'Hold still, ma'am, if you please.'

'Were they known to meet anywhere in particular?' Ballantine tried, but upon this point he received no certain information. Pile had often been seen going into, or out of, Mrs. Daughtry's dressing-room, and they had once or twice been seen leaving the theatre together. But as to where they were wont to go, nobody could say.

Still, the knowledge of prior — and close — acquaintance between the erstwhile star of Strangewayes and the murdered man set Ballantine's mind running along different lines. He began to enquire further about Mrs. Daughtry, a woman whose doings had not previously registered as relevant with him. He soon heard gossip enough to fan the flames of his theory.

'Oh, she were spitting *chips*,' said one young actress, with unseemly glee. 'Said as how an old fossil like Mrs. Everleigh had no business coming back to the stage. Not that she woulda said as much in public, like. She were all smiles about it to the papers, but I heard her raging about it in her dressing-room one night.'

And,

'It were positively sickening, the way she made up to Mrs. Everleigh,' opined another. 'All smiles to her face, and flowers sent into her dressing-room, and the like. And everyone knew she hated the poor lady.'

'Including Mrs. Everleigh?' Ballantine was quick to enquire.

'Reckon so. Not that you'd have known it, for she was a cool one, that Mrs. Everleigh. Didn't let on what she were thinking, so much. But you could see she weren't impressed.'

'Sometimes,' someone else contradicted. 'But I saw them going about together, a time or two. On the best of terms, they were.'

Ballantine had begun the morning with his suspicions fixed upon Mrs. Everleigh. Something about her story bothered him; there wasn't sufficient sense to be found in it. And her manner, too, was guarded, reserved, as though she were hiding a great deal from him. Had she truly forgotten everything that had led up to her death, or was she merely concealing the truth? She had not, after all, remained dead for long, and her fame had increased on account of it.

But an hour or two at Strangewayes entirely rearranged his ideas. He had only to enquire as to the nature of Mrs. Daughtry's Wyrde, and he grew increasingly certain.

For there seemed to be a curious lack of consistency as to the reports he heard. Mrs. Daughtry seemed devoted to her rival, but also seemed to despise her. Mrs. Everleigh seemed aware of this bitterness, but at other times appeared to befriend the younger woman. Curious.

'I don't rightly know,' came the common answer.

'She said what she had fore-seeing, or some such,' came another. 'Had us all going, the night Mrs. Everleigh disappeared.'

'Did you see much sign of that yourself?' Ballantine pressed. 'Had she often predicted things that then came to pass?'

Everywhere came the same answer: not often, no. Nor had she done much else to demonstrate any particular Wyrde, and at Strangewayes, it was not considered polite to ask.

Whatever the actress's Wyrde might be, he was not convinced that it had anything to do with foresight. What he did hear of was her strange persuasiveness; people spoke of having done favours for her, without understanding, afterwards, what could have possessed them to do so. People spoke well of her in one breath, and in the next expressed bemusement or condemnation for some action of hers that seemed out-of-keeping with her pleasant demeanour. The woman was a mercurial puzzle of a creature, right enough.

When he recalled that Lord Bedgberry had visited her after the performance only a day or two past, he began to grow alarmed. He had thought nothing of it at the time, but now—

He thought fast. If she proved to be the scheming, resentful woman she now appeared, could she be behind the death of Mrs. Everleigh?

She had not the equipment to commit the crime herself; he maintained the opinion that a wolfish set of teeth had inflicted the damage, and she had none. Had she persuaded or suborned someone else into making away with her rival?

Had she directed the corpse to be deposited in Lady Werth's parlour? Why?

Had her dead lover, Robert Pile, transgressed in some fashion, and fallen victim to the same merciless fate? Or was there something else afoot?

He could not answer these questions. But if she *was* responsible for this horrible scheme, one thing was clear: she possessed some kind of powerful resentment against not only Arabella Everleigh but also Charles Selwyn and Theodore Werth, and might be disposed to strike at them again.

But she was missing, and so was Robert Pile.

Where might she go?

Was she hiding? He thought not. As far as public opinion was concerned, Lord Bedgberry was still held responsible for the crimes; there had been an outcry at his continued liberty, and many had called for his incarceration. Mrs. Daughtry couldn't know that suspicion had finally fallen upon her. So if she had not chosen to return to her own lodgings after she had left the Werth house, then she had gone somewhere else by choice. Somewhere better.

He retraced his steps, back through the winding corridors of the Strangewayes theatre, looking for one in particular of the thespians he had interviewed that morning. The actress who had stood for the fitting of a handsome ball-gown. The one who had spoken of Mrs. Daughtry's *gentlemen*.

He found her at last, onstage. A rehearsal was in progress: she stood, tall and regal, playing the part of some wealthy society lady while a "gentleman" berated her for nameless but iniquitous crimes. The noise was tremendous, for in the midst of the staged confrontation someone was shouting directions; Ballantine had to stride right onto the stage to gain their attention. He stood firm against their reproaches, and said:

'I have only *one* further question to ask, and then I shall be out of your hair. It concerns Mrs. Daughtry. You, ma'am,' he said to the begowned actress, 'spoke of her having one or two "gentlemen" at her beck and call. Do you know who they were?'

The woman spoke with the sourness of some nameless resentment. 'Lord Bedgberry went back to visit her, this very week. Lord Bedgberry! He never goes backstage.'

'I am aware of Lord Bedgberry's fleeting interest, ma'am. Were there others?'

'There were always others.' She sniffed.

'Lord Havely,' said somebody else. The actor playing the irate gentleman. 'He was always in and out of her dressing-room, for weeks on end. Wouldn't leave her alone.'

'Did she encourage these attentions?' asked Ballantine.

'For certain,' said the actor.

The lady smiled, still sour. 'Any of us would've, at that.

He is rich, and well-looking.'

So he was. Ballantine was not personally acquainted with Lord Havely, but he was well aware of his reported wealth, and the man was still young. What actress in her right mind would turn him down?

'Does anybody know where his lordship is to be found?' Ballantine said, urgently.

This won him a look of incredulity from the actress in her ball-gown. 'Why, he has one of the finest houses in London. *Everyone* knows where Lord Havely resides.'

Ballantine, persisting in ignorance, was soon enlightened. Wimpole Street.

'I am obliged to you,' he said, sincerely, and took himself off at once. If he was in any luck at all, Mrs. Daughtry had gone to her wealthy admirer, and had spent the past day or so enjoying every conceivable luxury. If he hurried, he might catch her there.

FIFTEEN

The House of Werth was not on fire.

Standing on the street before his handsome abode, staring up at its solid grey walls shrouded in a late-afternoon fog, Theo experienced an odd feeling of anti-climax. Even something like disappointment. There had been a great rush to return home, a charging-through-the-streets in a state of high alarm, and while he was not *sorry* to find a perfectly intact house at the end of it, there had been a sense of certainty and purpose which was now all dissipated.

If the villainess of this horrid little tale had not chosen to smoke her rival out of her place of refuge, well then, what was she doing? Where was she? And what in the Devil's name was Theo supposed to do about it?

'Well,' said Gussie, climbing the two or three steps to the front door. 'I suppose it was an outlandish notion. After all, if she had decided to burn Mrs. Everleigh alive, and our family with it, she has had ample opportunity to do so before now.'

'Perhaps she had not sufficient reason,' said Great-Aunt Honoria. 'Her visit here confirmed that Mrs. Everleigh was present, but she seemed to be devoid of any unhelpful recollections — as was, doubtless, the aim. And

165

we did not behave towards her as though we suspected her. She had no cause to take up any dramatic course of action, at least not right away.' Her tone might be described as despondent — but then she brightened. 'Unless she is still inside, setting fires! I had better investigate.'

'Or perhaps it wasn't Mrs. Daughtry at all,' Theo said. 'Perhaps the whole story has been a fabrication of Clarissa's, to divert suspicion from her brother, and we need look no further than Charles Selwyn to find the culprit.'

'I know *you* would prefer it that way,' said Gussie, casting Theo a look of mild disgust as she rapped upon the door. 'That woman and her paralysing sense of your infinite *kindness*— ah yes, Gabriel, thank you. Absurd of us to require you to open the door to us in our own house, is not it? Letting oneself into one's place of residence is such a *low* thing to do, not when one has servants to remind us of our own elevated consequence. I believe I shall ask Uncle for a key.'

Gussie went inside, still rattling on in her odd way. Gabriel Footman bore it without comment, leaving his possible feelings a mystery. Wise fellow, thought Theo. Tended to be useless to engage Gussie on such questions; she would run on until a person grew quite exhausted.

Lady Honoria and Ivo Farthing had not waited for the door to be opened, the incorporeal having no need of ordinary portals. They had disappeared already, and since Miss Frostell and Silvester had elected to remain behind at the Maundevyle residence — for some reason — that left Theo standing on the street alone.

He felt a curious reluctance to vanish tamely inside, and return to the maddening business of *asking questions* and attempting, without information, to answer them. There would be more talking and *talking*, and Theo was exhausted with that, too.

He lingered in the thickening fog, feeling aimless.

Really, it was too much to be expected to go on caring about this miserable situation merely because someone had put his neck on the line for it. Mrs. Everleigh seemed contented enough with her new state, even if there had been some little lingering damage. Father had patched up the mess of her neck as best he could, and the stitches were really quite neat; the flimsiest little wisp of lace covered it up nicely, and Theo had a dim sense that such things were not necessarily considered unfashionable. Besides that there was hardly any alteration for her, and for an actress to exist in a state of ageless stasis might be considered an advantage.

She was chilly, Mrs. Everleigh. Unforthcoming, dead to all apparent feeling, and he wouldn't be surprised if she had done it all on purpose, just to get Lord Werth to make even more of an icicle of her. Perhaps it was not Mrs. Daughtry who possessed mesmeric powers, but Mrs. Everleigh. Nobody had offered any *proof*, after all.

It was in this frame of mind that he drifted along the street, feeling a curious sense of muffled isolation in the enveloping fog.

And it was in this frame of mind that he ran into another person; a fragile, female person, judging from the quantity of floating fabrics he encountered, and the way that the obstacle squeaked when his larger and clumsier form collided with it.

The creature fluttered in distress, and tried to dart away.

'Wait,' Theo said, catching at the trailing gown.

The lady, being fairly caught, stopped, and covered her face with her hands.

'Mrs. Daughtry?' he said, blankly. 'But what are you doing on the street without a coat?'

'I-I came to see Arabella,' she said, weakly. 'I only wanted to condole with her— to offer her my aid, if she wanted it— but... oh dear, I believe the experience she has gone through has changed her unalterably, for she would not hear me at all! She— she *attacked* me, drove me out of the house, and here I have been wandering all in a daze, I fear.'

Theo felt a momentary surprise, and a momentary suspicion. Mrs. Everleigh had not been at home when he and Gussie had marched off to the Maundevyle house, so how could she have attacked anybody? But she must have come back, of course, just in time to receive Mrs. Daughtry, and that the poor lady had been injured did not admit of a doubt, for she was bloodied and obviously shaken.

'Oh— thank you,' she whispered, as Theo took off his own great-coat and wrapped it around her. He found himself staring into a pair of grateful, tear-washed eyes, the lingering traces of shock and fear ebbing from them now. 'How fortunate that you came along, Lord Bedgberry,' she said.

It was, wasn't it? Some stray thought wandered through Theo's mind, too fleeting to be caught at. He let it go. Whatever had happened, Mrs. Daughtry was a wounded creature, and in need.

'You had better come in,' he suggested.

But this invitation produced a dismaying effect, for Mrs. Daughtry visibly shrank from the prospect. 'Oh, no! I couldn't! I could not face Arabella again, *pray* do not ask it of me.'

Theo ground his teeth, his impatience rising. All right, he couldn't take her into the house. Apart from the spectre of Mrs. Everleigh, the hunt was still up for her, and Gussie had accepted Clarissa's story entirely. She would never believe that Mrs. Daughtry could be the victim of Mrs. Everleigh's assault, rather than the other way around. She would frighten the woman still more.

He had those rooms, though, the ones Hargreve had got for him. He could take her there, get her out of the wet and the cold, and tend to her injury. Then, maybe, he could talk to her — more *talking*, and that would be a bore, but one good, proper conversation might get the whole truth out of her, and then the matter could be settled. Gussie would be doing the same with Arabella Everleigh, to be sure. Why, they could have everything sorted out by dinner time, after all.

'Come with me, ma'am,' he said solicitously. 'I will take you somewhere safe.'

'Safe from Arabella?' she said, shivering with fright and cold.

'Yes, yes, your precious Arabella hasn't set foot in the place.'

He was rewarded with a look of melting gratitude, and instantly set about finding a cab.

* * *

Lord Havely's Wimpole-Street residence really set the tone for the experience of entering it, Ballantine thought with disgust. The house's exterior was grand and forbidding, and those he encountered inside were scarcely less so.

The butler alone necessitated a thick skin and a strong stomach, for he looked at Ballantine in his Bow-street waistcoat as though he were little better than a ragged and importunate street urchin.

'Lord Havely has nothing to say to *you*,' he pronounced, icily over-enunciating every syllable with paralysing effect.

Or it might have been paralysing, to a man lesser — or at least, of lesser *impatience* — than Mr. Ballantine. 'I have not the slightest interest in Lord Havely,' he said curtly. 'I want to know if he has any house-guests at the moment, particularly of the female persuasion.'

'His lordship's personal arrangements can be of no interest or relevance to Bow Street,' came the lofty response.

'Except that they are, when we have reason to believe that he may be harbouring a woman suspected of two murders. Come, man, I shall have it out of you one way or another. I should infinitely prefer to remain civilised, but I am in no way bound to.'

He did not usually like to throw his weight around, for his weight was considerable, and he did not *like* to make a brute of himself. But the matter was urgent, and this top-lofty butler was rapidly aggravating his temper. He did not undergo the full shift from his human to his ogreish state, but he did permit himself to swell a bit about the shoulders; to grow a little taller, and a lot fiercer.

The butler seemed impressed, primarily, with Ballantine's teeth, for he stared at them with widening eyes even as he blustered, 'This is highly improper treatment! I shall be informing Lord Havely of this disgraceful visit, and I have no doubt that he will have a word with your superiors—'

'You may do as you choose, and so may he, provided that I receive an answer,' Ballantine ground out. 'His lordship's house guests. Does he have a lady staying here?'

There was no end to the butler's snobbery, but it might perhaps find a different outlet. He tore his eyes at last from the spectacle of Ballantine's mouthful of teeth, and his face puckered with disapproval. 'There is no *lady* staying here.'

'A woman, then. An actress. Marianne Daughtry?'

Stiffly, the butler nodded.

Ballantine's heart leapt. 'Is she here now?' he said urgently.

'She expressed herself wishful of going out, and his lordship ordered that the carriage should be made available for her use. But I do not know whether she has yet finished with her… callers.'

The butler's evident distaste at the prospect of Mrs. Daughtry's *callers* alerted Ballantine. 'Who has been calling on her? A gentleman?'

The butler's hauteur deepened into a full frost. 'Lord Maundevyle was admitted this morning.'

For a moment, Ballantine was surprised out of all

speech. 'Lord Maundevyle?' he said after a moment, recollecting his wits. 'Not Mr. Selwyn, his brother? You are certain?'

'*Quite* certain.' The butler's manner indicated the perfect impossibility of his mistaking a titled visitor's name or rank.

Lord Maundevyle had been here, expressly to call upon Mrs. Daughtry. Ballantine's head swam. Devil take the man, what could he be doing? Were there not interfering Selwyns enough in London already?

That Lord Maundevyle might have sought an interview with the woman on his brother's account made some sense, at least. That he might have been here on more nefarious business ought, at least, to be considered, if unwillingly, for Ballantine liked the odd, draconic lord almost as much as Miss Werth did.

'His lordship might still be in the house?' he prompted the butler. 'I had better be conducted to Mrs. Daughtry's rooms. It is *urgent*,' he added, over the top of the butler's renewed objections. 'Have I not said the woman is suspected of murder? His lordship may be in grave danger.'

This idea galvanised the butler, at least; let it never be said that a prominent member of the Quality had come to harm on *his* watch. Somewhat chastened, he personally conducted Mr. Ballantine up the grand stairs, quelling an astonished housemaid's stares with a frown, and led him to a nice suite of rooms not far from a handsome drawing-room. It was unusual for a lord to entertain a mistress openly, in his own house; ordinarily, the preference was for setting up alternative accommodation for them elsewhere, visits to be paid at his lordship's own leisure. Marianne Daughtry's mesmeric hold on Lord Havely was already considerable, then.

When the butler knocked upon the ornate doors, nobody answered.

The butler coughed, knocked again, waited, and finally

opened the doors. The room beyond — sumptuously decorated in jade and gold, beautiful, feminine — was empty of either Mrs. Daughtry or Lord Maundevyle.

'She must have already gone out,' said the butler. 'I will enquire of the stables whether the horses were taken out, and put-to.'

'I would be obliged to you,' said Ballantine. Perhaps some groom or stable-boy might have overheard where the lady expected to be driven *to*. He did not permit himself to be ushered out again, bearing down the butler's fussing with a calmly-uttered, 'I should like to look around, thank you.'

Once the impossible man had gone, Ballantine ventured into Mrs. Daughtry's borrowed bedchamber, and quietly shut the door behind him. The room might be empty of the two people he sought, but it was not empty altogether. There had been a slight sound as the door had opened, the faintest of footfalls; likely the butler, with his ordinary, unWyrded senses, had not perceived it.

'Hello?' he called. 'Whoever you are, you had better come out.'

He waited, all ogre now, braced for some attack. The likeliest explanation was that Mrs. Daughtry had not gone out, but had hidden herself, expecting an interrogation she would rather avoid.

But it was not Mrs. Daughtry. There came a small sigh, and a rustling of fabric. The person who emerged, fearless and unabashed, from behind a lustrous golden drape was, in fact, Arabella Everleigh.

'And what are you doing here?' he said.

She straightened, looking him coolly in the eye. She wore an elegant day-dress and pelisse, and an attractive silk bonnet; she looked every inch a lady, nothing of the unearthed grave about her, save, perhaps, her extreme pallor. 'The same thing you are, I imagine,' she answered. 'I am looking for Marianne Daughtry. She has gloated of Lord Havely's passion for her.'

'And what might you want with her?'

She thought for a moment before replying. 'You see, I have been remembering.'

'Ah.'

'Yesterday I remembered Charles Selwyn.'

'Your killer.'

'Yes. But today… today I have been remembering Marianne Daughtry.'

'Perhaps you had better tell me the tale, ma'am.'

And she did. It was a short tale, told without embellishment or emotion, of her return to Strangewayes, and the preparations made for her first performance, in *Revenge*. Of Marianne Daughtry's overtures of friendship, and shows of support. At first, the folk of Strangewayes had celebrated her for her generosity to her rival, the woman for whom she must give up the limelight. But rumours had begun to spread, of secret resentments and bitter plots, though Arabella had not paid them much heed. Theatre people, she said, did tend to gossip.

But then came the day of the final rehearsal. Marianne had come into her dressing-room, carrying some of her own garments over her arm: a fine silk gown, tinted Turkey-red, and a bonnet and pelisse. And somehow or other it had come about that Arabella had donned these, walked out wearing them; she had travelled, on foot, to an address she did not now recall, but she had found Charles Selwyn on the other side of that door.

And she had not lived long after she had gone through it.

Ballantine heard it in silence. It fitted, he thought, with everything he already knew. Mrs. Daughtry may wish her rival gone, but she was not a woman to sully her own hands in the doing of it — nor to risk detection in the crime, for nothing would more surely put paid to her career upon the stage. Hence, her use of another. And if she was a woman to nurse so bitter a resentment against a rival, she may well feel much the same towards a family

173

who'd scorned her. So far, so plausible.

But not everything fitted. 'Why the gown and such, however?' he enquired, once the tale was done. 'It was to encourage *someone* to mistake you for Mrs. Daughtry herself, I suppose, but it cannot have been intended to fool Selwyn, surely? If she had him in her power, it can hardly have mattered who he thought you were.'

'No, I do not believe it was a deception aimed at Mr. Selwyn,' Arabella agreed. 'He would have been enlightened the moment he saw my face, which he could hardly be prevented from doing. I believe the change of attire was intended to fool the theatre, and subsequently, you. You will have been told that nobody saw me leave the theatre that day, but you will not have enquired whether anybody saw Marianne leave. It cannot have entered your head to do so.'

'All true,' Ballantine admitted. 'And perhaps she avoided the possibility that anybody might prevent your departure, or think to watch where you went. The star of the play could not have simply walked out of the final rehearsal without encountering some opposition, not with the opening night so close at hand. But Marianne Daughtry might do as she pleased.'

Arabella inclined her head. 'A sensible suggestion.'

'I *was* told you had been seen leaving, however,' Ballantine said. 'I was informed that you had gone out for a time on the day of your performance, in the company of Lord Bedgberry.'

'I did no such thing.'

'No, I thought it an unlikely story at the time. I happen to be acquainted with Lord Bedgberry, who has denied it. And you cannot have been at Strangewayes that day, for you had already been killed.'

'But who told you that? Marianne?'

'No,' he said slowly. 'Robert Pile.'

Her brows went up. 'But he is her creature entirely.'

'Aye, so he is said to be. But I cannot fully make sense

of this aspect of the tale. On the face of it, it appears to be an attempt to throw the blame for your death on Lord Bedgberry, compounded by leaving your earthly remains at his lordship's house. But what was the purpose of any of that? If she had the power to mesmerise Charles Selwyn into committing murder for her, and she wished Lord Bedgberry to be blamed, why did she not simply mesmerise Lord Bedgberry? Why bother with Selwyn at all?'

'A fair question,' mused Arabella, frowning. 'I have no answer for you.'

'No, but perhaps we are all making an unfair assumption. Robert Pile is her creature entirely — unless he is not.'

'It did seem strange to me that he should have been slain,' Arabella agreed. 'I thought there must have been a falling-out, or maybe that Mr. Selwyn knew himself manipulated and took out his rage on Pile.'

'Perfectly plausible explanations, but we shall see whether they are correct. Let us work with the hypothesis that the charming Marianne's resentments were directed at Charles Selwyn, and perhaps his family. We require some other explanation for the targeting of the Werths.' Ballantine put the matter from his mind, for the moment; he had more pressing concerns. 'You do not have any idea where else I might find Mrs. Daughtry, I suppose?'

'I do not. I lingered here in hopes of finding just such a clue.'

'Without success?'

'Indeed.'

Ballantine regarded her in momentary irritation. 'A passing thought, ma'am, but upon remembering all these things, it did not occur to you to bring them to me?'

'It occurred to me.' She lifted her chin. 'But I did not, and do not, want to see Marianne Daughtry strung up for the benefit of some cheering crowd of onlookers, Mr. Ballantine.'

He might have applauded her compassion, save that he did not truly imagine that she felt any. Her gaze was as hard and cold as marble. 'What would you prefer to see, ma'am?'

'I would *prefer* to tear out her throat with my own teeth.'

She looked fully capable of it. Mr. Ballantine could not deny the justice of her feelings, but felt it incumbent upon him to say: 'There are consequences for taking justice into your own hands, of course.'

'And what is a fair magistrate likely to do to me, Mr. Ballantine? Kill me?'

He inclined his head. 'If you don't mind, I would prefer to see justice done in all due form. And with that in mind, I've to find out where she went this afternoon — after seeing Lord Maundevyle. Or perhaps *with* Lord Maundevyle.'

'Maundevyle?' Arabella blinked, arrested. 'What can he have wanted with her?'

'I am rather afraid that he had some similar ideas in mind to your own. After all, she has made unhappy work of his lordship's younger brother.'

Arabella's face twisted in a grimace. 'It is difficult to muster any sympathy for that gentleman,' she admitted. 'The last I saw of his face, he was on the point of tearing out my throat. It does leave rather an impression.'

'I imagine it would.'

'But I am bound to admit that he was not in possession of his senses at the time. He barely paused to register my presence, and there seemed little of the civilised gentleman about him. He was beyond his own control.'

'More like a wild beast than a gentleman, in fact, and I can well believe it, for I've seen him. He has yet to recover his wits, and that's a thing that is likely to enrage Lord Maundevyle.'

Arabella, oddly, smiled. 'My dear Marianne is in for an interesting day.'

'Aye, and it is likely to prove a short and messy one if I don't find her first. Your servant, ma'am.' He tipped his hat to the actress, and turned to go.

'Wait,' she said. 'If I undertake to leave her to the justice of Bow-Street, may I come with you?'

'Why would you wish to do that?' asked Ballantine, turning back.

'I might be of assistance.'

This was true, but for the deliberately obstructive actress to now turn helpful was too much to swallow. Ballantine waited.

'And if we should happen to be fortunate in our timing,' she went on, after a moment, 'I might bear witness to her quartering by the most notorious dragon in London.' She was smiling again. 'That will be almost as satisfying as ripping her apart myself.'

Mr. Ballantine decided not to cross so ruthless a woman. Besides, he had not time to argue. 'Very well,' he said, returning to the door. 'But if you should have any thoughts of getting in my way, madam, I shan't hesitate to take suitable action.'

'A reasonable stance.'

But Ballantine halted on the threshold, stopped by an appalling thought. 'A moment. I am forgetting that Lord Maundevyle has *already been here*. If he came with the intention of punishing Mrs. Daughtry's conduct, as seems probable, why hasn't he done it?' He whirled about, and surveyed once again the elegantly-furnished room: pristine. No signs of any struggle, or violence. 'He hasn't done anything to her.'

'A pity,' murmured Arabella.

'Why didn't he?' Ballantine thought fast. 'I can think of only two possibilities, and I don't like either of them.'

'If he had not met her before today, is he fully aware of what she can do?' asked Arabella. 'Maybe he imagines she can mend the damage she has inflicted, and has taken her to his brother. He may imagine himself less susceptible to her ways.'

'That is one possibility. And if that is the case, then they will have left here together. Most likely in Lord Maundevyle's carriage.'

'And if they did not…' Arabella shook her head. 'One would like to think that a dragon would be impervious to such manipulation as Marianne's.'

'Why, though? A dragon is fearsome enough, but Lord Maundevyle is still only a man. If he *didn't* know quite what she had done to his brother, or how powerful she seems to be, then he didn't know what she could do to him. And she has probably gone and done it.'

'Mesmerised him.'

'Aye. But to do what?'

Arabella's smile was twisted. 'Perhaps she has sent her new pet dragon after me.'

'I think you may have the right of it, and that's what worries me. For she cannot have known that you would come here. She will have sent Lord Maundevyle to the last place she knew you to be.'

'The Werth residence.'

'The Werth residence.' Ballantine was out the door at a near-run even as he spoke. 'And if Lord Maundevyle shows up at their front door, they will let him straight in.'

The butler had been as good as his word, to Ballantine's relief. While Ballantine had been talking with Arabella Everleigh, he had made his enquiries of the servants who kept up Lord Havely's carriage, and had information to offer.

It had been ordered, not long since, and the horses put-to for Marianne Daughtry's use. She had not been accompanied by any gentleman.

But there was no sign of the Maundevyle equipage anywhere on the street, which meant that they had left separately. Where Marianne Daughtry might have gone was anybody's guess; Lord Maundevyle was the more urgent danger.

SIXTEEN

Gussie, Clarissa, Ivo and Great-Aunt Honoria went all over the townhouse, room-by-room, just to be certain there was no Marianne Daughtry lurking anywhere within it, nor any incipient fires set by that enterprising lady. There wasn't. Nor was there any trace of Mrs. Everleigh, which puzzled Gussie, and cost her some little disquiet. Wherever that lady had gone, it was on no innocent business: the dead coldness of her eyes protested against her having any capacity for innocent business left.

Still, it was no concern of Gussie's, and she could do nothing about it. She dismissed the matter from her mind, and devoted herself instead to the defence of the house. 'We had better set up a watch,' she decided, once the search was complete, and the searchers had returned to gather in the hall.

'Stand guard against attack!' Great-Aunt Honoria agreed. 'And I was only saying to my dear Ivo last week, how *long* it is since I took part in anything so exciting as a pitched battle! You may count on me.'

'I hope it will not come to that,' Gussie said. 'A siege we may withstand, I believe, but there is to be no battling back-and-forth across the parlours and the drawing-room.

We must think of the furniture.'

A footman swept past even as she uttered this speech, and opened the front door with a flourish, for Lady Werth was returning. She came in, already removing her gloves, and regarded the assembly before her with some astonishment. 'I believe there is a marshal light shining in my niece's eye, and that is never a *good* sign,' she observed.

'We are preparing our defence against a summary burning,' Gussie informed her. 'Mrs. Daughtry bears the honours of villainess, we have decided, and may try to smoke her rival out of the house. But I see that you are tired, Aunt, and may prefer to retire to your room for a rest? Be assured that we have the matter well in hand.'

'If we are to be fending off invaders over Mrs. Everleigh's continued residence in this house, then I should prefer to draw it to a swift close,' Lady Werth replied. Suitably divested of her outer garments, she summoned Gabriel Footman as he was making his exit, and murmured to him: 'Pray ask cook to send up some refreshments to the drawing-room. Some cakes, and a little wine. And it seems we are plunged into the midst of a war, so a few cauldrons of boiling oil ought also to be prepared, and sent up to the roof.'

Gabriel Footman took these instructions without a word. He glanced sideways at Gussie and Clarissa, bowed to Lady Werth, and withdrew.

'Mrs. Everleigh isn't here, Lady Werth,' Clarissa offered. 'We have searched. But unless she has contrived to intercept the Daughtry woman somewhere — which is possible — then we do not suppose the murdering wretch to be aware of the fact.'

The air around Lady Werth palpably chilled, and frost crept over her hair. 'As fond as I am of the theatre, I cannot help but feel that the good folk of Strangeways have imposed upon us enough.'

'They have rather, haven't they?' Gussie agreed. 'And we do not, as yet, know why. Mrs. Daughtry's various dissatisfactions appear to be directed at Arabella and Charles Selwyn, after all. There must be some other explanation.'

'I have the greatest faith in Mr. Ballantine to discover what it is,' said Lady Werth crisply. 'You will excuse me, ladies, and Mr. Farthing. If I am needed in the war, then you may find me enjoying a brief respite in the drawing-room, but I would strongly advise you not to need me.' She swept up the stairs, leaving wisps of freezing fog in her wake.

'Far be it from me to criticise so august a personage as her ladyship,' announced Clarissa, 'but I call that poor-spirited.'

'It is better that she takes her rest,' Gussie said. 'She is coming over all icy, and if that goes on for very much longer we shall have an ice-statue on our hands again.' She added, brightening, 'But the boiling oil! A fine notion. Mr. Farthing, may we rely on you to man the cauldrons? The attic is your territory, rather.'

Ivo Farthing, wreathed in smiles, made his bow. 'Charmed,' he pronounced himself. 'Delighted,' and disappeared in a waft of ethereal smoke.

'Excellent. Great-Aunt Honoria, shall you pitch in with the flammable repellents, or should you prefer to occupy a more frontal position?'

'Oh, *pray* give me a firearm!' Honoria pleaded. 'It is an *age* since I had occasion to shoot anybody.'

'I should be delighted, only I am not perfectly certain we possess any.' Gussie racked her brain, but was blessed with no timely recollection of any pistol or shotgun that reposed anywhere in the house. They had used to have axes aplenty, of course, on account of the Books, but that was all over now.

'Are we so ill-supplied with weaponry?' said Great-Aunt Honoria, displeased. 'It could never have been so, in *my* day.'

'You are quite right, and we ought to have placed you

in charge of arming the household.' Gussie shook her head sadly. 'As it is, we will just have to make do. We might borrow a knife or two from cook, if she would be so good as to indulge us. Perhaps you might see what you can rustle up?'

This commission revived Honoria's flagging spirits, and she bustled away in search of every sharp, murderous object the house might be expected to harbour in its freshly-refurbished depths.

That left Gussie herself, and Clarissa. The two regarded each other in momentary silence.

'I suppose we ought to make fire defences, of some sort,' Gussie suggested, doubtfully. 'Buckets of water, and what-not.'

Clarissa did not appear overpowered with enthusiasm for the plan. 'How very... practical that would be,' she observed.

'Very,' Gussie agreed sadly. 'Truth be told, it is excessively dull only to sit here, and wait to be attacked by somebody.'

'Yes! And what if nobody ever comes? It will be a sadly wasted day.'

It was only at this moment, when divested of much else to occupy her attention, that Gussie noticed an absence. 'A moment,' she said, turning about. 'Where is Theo?'

Clarissa had given the matter no thought, it appeared, for she gave a careless answer. 'Wafted off somewhere, I suppose, in search of a book.'

But Gussie's instincts could not agree. For Theo to vanish at *this* moment, when all was cast into chaos, and enemies proliferated by the hour — no. For had they not searched the whole house, without running into Theo at any point? 'Did he come in with us?' she asked.

'Now that I think of it,' answered Clarissa, 'I cannot recall that he did.'

'Oh, dear. Here we are preparing for some manner of attack, and I begin to fear it has already come.' Gussie ran to the door, wrenched it open, and set off down the steps. She did not know what she expected to do, upon regaining the street; Theo's vanishment must have occurred more than half an hour ago. But she was a little reassured, upon pacing up and down the fog-ridden pavement, to find no Theo knocked senseless, and prostrate upon the stones. Or worse.

'He has gone somewhere,' she concluded, as Clarissa caught up. 'But whether from some whim of his own, or under *someone else's* direction, I cannot say.'

'By someone else, you mean Mrs. Daughtry.'

'Yes. Theo's focus was on Mr. Pile, rather, and I am not sure he was suitably persuaded by the probability of *her* guilt. If she found him here, and persuaded him to give her the benefit of the doubt—'

'Surely not,' Clarissa objected. 'Lord Bedgberry has never struck me as possessing the forgiving temperament.'

'But she needed only arrest his attention long enough to get a good look at him, or to touch him, or however it is that she works her marvellous mesmeric powers, and then what might he not do?'

'Well, but this is much better,' Clarissa said brightly. 'Now we have a mission. How shall we proceed?'

Gussie did not answer. The street had hitherto stood largely empty, only some one or two bundled-up pedestrians wandering past as she had searched the environs. But somebody else was emerging from the all-encompassing fog, a dark, hazy figure rapidly coming into focus. A tall gentleman, wrapped in a dark overcoat, his face obscured by the wide brim of his hat.

He was carrying a pistol. This last article she stood in no doubt of, for it was pointed directly at her own face.

'Oh, wonderful,' she smiled. 'Just such a firearm as Great-Aunt Honoria was in want of! How very obliging of you to deliver one, sir.'

'Don't move,' was the only reply she received, delivered in curt, if unmistakeably male, tones. This was not

Marianne Daughtry, nor was it Arabella Everleigh making some unlooked-for return.

Clarissa, blithely ignoring this command, drifted nearer to Gussie. 'Now, who is this?' she whispered. 'It is neither Theo nor Charles; and if I was expecting anyone outside of our own, dear families to arrive this afternoon, I would have said it would be the Daughtry woman.'

'Unless I am very much mistaken,' Gussie replied, beaming at her assailant, 'and, as we all know, I rarely am, then I believe we have the pleasure of addressing the elusive Mr. Pile.'

'A likely hypothesis. But what is he doing pointing a firearm at your face?'

'A fair question. Have I offended in some fashion, sir? If so, I am very sorry for it, I am sure.'

Since nothing in her manner could be less apologetic, it is doubtful whether this handsome admission would prove effective of much save riling her opponent — an outcome Gussie was perfectly prepared to tolerate.

Indeed, the pistol wavered; perhaps his hand shook. 'They say now as it might not have been Lord Bedgberry,' he growled.

'Do they? But this news can hardly come as a surprise to you, considering you planted the evidence against my cousin yourself. Now, did not you?'

'And it was working. But now Bow Street's got the wind up them, and that Runner—' He broke off, and tightened his grip on his pistol.

'Come, man, you won't find anyone more delighted to complain about "that Runner" than Gussie,' Clarissa encouraged. 'What has he done?'

'I hope he has gone after your darling Marianne,' Gussie put in. 'But I fail to see why that has you directing all this delicious ire at *me*.'

'If Lord Bedgberry don't hang,' said Robert Pile, 'then I've to find some other way.'

'To cause my household to suffer?' Gussie thought this

over. 'Killing Clarissa wouldn't do it, so I hope you will not be so discourteous as to try that. As for *me*, I am a mere insignificant Werth, of no importance at all. You had better make your attempt upon my aunt, perhaps, or even my uncle himself. That would certainly get everybody's attention.'

'No.' Robert Pile was shaking his head, and to Gussie's discomfort, he advanced upon her by a step. 'It was *you*, wasn't it? *You* ruined Will, you twisted him up, you made him—' He stopped again, to Gussie's chagrin, for things were at last turning interesting. 'I thought you would suffer, to watch your precious cousin hang. But it's you I should have done for in the first place. When I saw you at Strangewayes, I should have— done you in.'

Oh, dear. These were serious words, and if Gussie hoped to experience another minute as a living, breathing person (as opposed to a chilly waxwork, like Mrs. Everleigh), she ought now to make an attempt to preserve her life. She was considering the possibilities of lunging at the enraged person before her, and attempting, by some unspecific but heroic means, to wrest the gun from him, when her attention was critically distracted.

A loud *whump* sounded from somewhere disconcertingly nearby, and the day abruptly brightened.

She looked up. The fog was clearing away, blown or burned off by whatever was lighting up the sky, and moreover there was a vast and ominous shadow looming over Lord Werth's townhouse—

'Oh, there's Henry now,' Clarissa observed, and waved.

Whatever her faults may be, Gussie was not ordinarily cursed with slowness of wit. She promptly shelved the urgent, and *quite* interesting question of what the draconic Lord Maundevyle was doing pouring gouts of flame over the roof of her uncle's blameless establishment (or indeed the identity and fate of the aforementioned William) and dealt with the more immediately pressing of her two problems. She performed her lunge at the distracted

Robert Pile — with tolerable grace, what's more, and a pleasing efficiency — and succeeded in knocking the pistol from his hand. She followed up this success with a clumsy but effective blow to his averted face, and as Clarissa dove for the fallen pistol and came up with it in her hands, Gussie permitted herself the relief of a sharp kick to the man's shins.

'There, now, do stop moving,' Clarissa ordered Pile, holding the pistol like she knew exactly what she was doing with it. 'I will keep an eye on our friend here, Gussie. I think you had better go and talk to Henry, hm?'

More questions to consider later: why Clarissa might imagine Gussie would have greater success remonstrating with Henry than she, his own sister. Tempted as she was to enquire into this interesting point, her uncle's house was in danger of burning down.

'Right,' she agreed. 'Why don't you find out who this lamented William is, and what in the world *I* could be said to have done to him?' she suggested, and ran for the front door. Judging from the position of Lord Maundevyle's enormous bulk, she might be able to make herself heard from a higher vantage point: namely, the window in Ivo Farthing's favourite room.

Gussie ran for it.

SEVENTEEN

And what had become of Theo, in the midst of so many concurrent disasters? Was his life also endangered? Was he suffering intolerably from the predations and machinations of so heartless a villain as Marianne Daughtry?

Why, no. He was enjoying the cosiest of tête-à-têtes with this beguiling lady, and feeling really rather pleased with the progress of his day.

At first, he had been conscious of a little awkwardness. It has been mentioned before that (despite his wealth and elevated rank) Theo was not much in the habit of entertaining attractive ladies in private. Upon entering his own rooms with Mrs. Daughtry (wilting appealingly) on his arm, and the door then closing upon them, he had at first suffered an acute sense of being very much at sea. What did one *do* with an afflicted female, if such a being was abruptly thrust into one's care? His mother, cousins and aunts all being wrought from the sterner sort of stuff, he had never encountered one before.

But the lady did not appear at all at a loss. She sagged elegantly onto the handsome divan couch Hargreve had chosen (with, apparently, considerable foresight); smiled at him with palpable, if wan, courage; and declared herself *much better now, dear Lord Bedgberry.*

She seemed so thoroughly aware of his great kindness in rescuing her from her foe, in fact, and sheltering her stricken person, that Theo began to feel rather well-disposed towards himself. He had done rather a generous thing, had not he? And he was always being *told* that he ought to show a little more compassion for his fellow man (or, in this case, woman). Well, there. He was a reformed man.

What to do now?

'Um, may I get you anything?' he enquired. 'Perhaps that wound ought to be seen to.' He said this with a vague sense of helplessness, for he hadn't any staff; no Mrs. Gavell to summon, and leave everything in her capable hands.

Fortunately, Marianne was not cast into transports by either of these suggestions. In fact, she dismissed the extent of her injury by covering it up with a fold of her shawl, and smiling at him. 'No, I thank you. I shall be quite well, presently.'

Well, this was convenient, and nicely exonerated Theo from going to any particular effort. He always appreciated not having to go to any particular effort. He sat down in an adjacent chair, and attempted to look solicitous.

To his dismay, tears welled again in the lady's eyes. A distant thought, turning somewhere at the back of his mind, wondered at his own dismay; the lachrymose more usually irritated him, and why did this woman elicit so different a response? But it was a weak thought, fading by the moment, and soon there was nothing but his deep concern for her well-being.

'Oh, dear,' she said wretchedly. 'Do forgive me, Lord Bedgberry. It is only that I am so *shocked* by my dear Arabella's conduct. That she could fly at me like that! Me! And I only wanted to *help*.'

She did, of course she did. Her earnest desire to be of use or comfort to her friend shone in her beautiful eyes, and Theo felt stabbed to the heart by it. What a dastardly woman was Arabella Everleigh! Wickedly jealous of this vision of youthful beauty, whose star had risen as her own had faded. Theo said some of this.

She smiled at him through her tears, all heartfelt gratitude. 'I am sure no one could *wonder* at such feelings, could they? The poor lady.'

A moving compassion for her attacker; Theo was duly moved. He groped blindly for her hand, and held it, comfortingly, in his own. The delicate fingers closed around his.

'I do not know how I shall ever feel safe enough to leave this room,' she whispered, the tears beginning again. 'For I cannot become *less* her rival, can I? Everywhere I go, she is like to persecute me! It will end in my leaving the stage forever, I am sure of it.'

'No, no,' Theo assured her. 'It will not come to that. It cannot. I am sure something can be done — there is justice to be had, somehow.'

The tear-washed eyes gazed into his, twin pools of azuline blue for Theo to drown in. 'How?' she breathed.

Theo found himself with one or two ideas unfurling in his mind. There might be subtle, convoluted ways to protect the darling Marianne from further assault, yes; no doubt Gussie, so pleased with her own cleverness, would prefer some one or other of those.

For Theo's part, he preferred a more direct solution. Looking into those devastating eyes, he knew exactly how it should be done.

'You leave it to me,' he said, and, to his own astonishment, his reward came in the form of a lingering kiss.

To his even greater astonishment, he found that he enjoyed this effect of his chivalry immensely.

* * *

It ought to have entered Ballantine's head to consider a certain, crucial point. Once dispatched to wreak ruin upon the persecuted Mrs. Everleigh (and anybody else who might be so unfortunate as to be nearby at the time), Lord Maundevyle would not actually be obliged to enter by the front door. Or any door.

Not that it would have availed him much, if the idea had occurred to him; he could hardly get across London any faster, no matter the extent of the threat to the Werth household. Nonetheless, the reality of their unenviable situation burst upon him before he had got within a few hundred yards of the house. It could not be escaped, in fact, for the sight that greeted him consisted of a crimson, twenty-foot-long monster enjoying a reign of terror over the London skies. Gouts of bright flame lit up the heavens, slicing through the lingering ribbons of fog. Lord Maundevyle was already hard at work.

He had dispensed with all subtlety, then, and simply gone for the direct approach.

'I might have *known*,' Ballantine snarled, and began to run hard, leaving Mrs. Everleigh to follow as she could. Such a headlong dash through the winding streets had its own hazards, for down here the fog remained thick and impenetrable. The Runner dodged looming pedestrians as best he could; tripped and fell into the road; came up swearing, and ran on, heaping curses upon the name of Daughtry, the name of Maundevyle, and anybody else that came to mind.

As soon as he judged himself within hearing distance, he began to shout. 'Lord Maundevyle! *Henry Selwyn*! Devil take the man, he either can't hear me or won't listen—' He drew up outside the firmly closed front door of the Werth house, insensible to the presence of one or two persons arranged upon the step, and began to furiously pound upon it. There was no way to get within shouting distance of a stubborn, airborne dragon save by elevating oneself; expecting the dragon to come down was a waste of time.

He'd have to get all the way up the stairs, see if he could hang himself out of some window… was nobody going to answer the *door*?

Mrs. Everleigh drew level with him, by no means out of breath despite the scramble across the city. Well, she wouldn't be; she had left all such limitations behind when her heart ceased beating. 'Mr. Ballantine,' she said, laying a hand upon his arm.

He stopped, casting her an irritated look. 'I am a trifle occupied—'

'Shh,' she said.

Into the imposed silence came sounds; sounds Ballantine had not heard over his pounding upon the door. Gussie's voice. 'Henry, *really*!' she was shouting. 'To ignore a lady of your close acquaintance for weeks together, despite residing in the same city, is already a grave offence! To burn her house to the ground would be *the outside of enough*! I am almost tempted to think you do not care for me at *all*.'

Ballantine retreated several paces and looked up, bemused. There, he could just see her: a distant, feminine figure, hanging so far out of an upper-storey window as to put herself in danger of a sickening plummet down. She was showing herself to the dragon, he supposed, in hopes of catching his attention; whether by her words or by the sight of her familiar, human form.

It might work, he supposed, if anything would. Lord Maundevyle had obviously lost the use of his wits, thanks to the Daughtry woman's interference, but perhaps he could regain them. How long could her enthralling influence prove stronger than the nearer, and impossibly aggravating influence of Miss Augusta Werth?

The two persons whose presence he had overlooked now caught his eye. The incorrigible Miss Selwyn was one of them, whom somebody had unwisely *armed* — and the second, a man, shrouded in coat and hat, and held immobile by judicious use of the aforementioned weapon.

Curious.

Before he could intervene, however—

'I believe we are about to develop yet another complication,' said Mrs. Everleigh, her attention no longer upon Gussie. She was looking about herself, searching for something, he could not say what, among the gathered spectators to this catastrophe.

He ran a wary eye over those faces himself, and saw nothing to give him any alarm. 'Why do you say so, ma'am?'

'I am afraid I have not been entirely frank with you,' she said, without a trace of apology.

'*That* comes as no surprise.'

'My Wyrde, you see, is — well, the foresight at Strangewayes is not Marianne's, but mine. It is nothing very profound, and therefore not of the greatest use. But I am sometimes aware of approaching dangers, and there is one on the way.'

'More danger than *that*?' He jabbed an illustrative finger at the fire-breathing dragon.

'I am afraid so. It has been a merciless day, has not it? I shall be glad when it is over.'

Ballantine took hold of his temper, as best he could. Only then did he recall that he retained his ogreish form, enlightened to the fact by the appalled stares of those members of the crowd not too riveted by the dragon's progress. Fools, he thought savagely. To stand and spectate when there was a dragon on the loose — and some of them were calf-witted enough to be afraid of *him*, merely because he was a trifle larger and bulkier than the average man—

'What is the nature of this threat, ma'am?' he said, wresting his attention back to the vague predictions of Arabella Everleigh. 'Or perhaps you may know at what, or whom, it is directed?'

'I do not know, save that I suspect — oh, there it is.'

By *it* she presumably meant *he*, for shoving his way

through the over-excited spectators came Lord Bedgberry. Judging from the thunderous look upon his face, and the beeline he was making for Arabella, Ballantine guessed that his purpose was no happy one.

'The Devil fly away with that woman!' he growled, and advanced upon Theo. 'Not you as *well*.'

* * *

Henry really was a tiresome excuse for a gentleman, thought Gussie, precariously suspended from an attic window with her throat turning raw from shouting. Really, a great many men were tiresome in the extreme, from the simmeringly resentful Robert Pile to her own, dear, obnoxious cousin Theo. 'If we could all calm down and enjoy a nice cup of tea!' she yelled at the uncaring form of Lord Maundevyle. The roof had fairly caught by this time, she could hear the ominous crackle of flaring flame. Great-Aunt Honoria and Ivo Farthing were up there, hurling buckets of water everywhere; behind her, she could hear the intermittent thunder of footfalls as Mrs. Gavell and the servants ferried as much water as they could up into the eaves of the house.

It was a valiant effort, but insufficient to outmatch the determined efforts of a dragon. The rest would soon go if she did not stop him.

Shouting was not helping. She thought, once or twice, that he heard her; there came a fractional pause in his rampage, and the attention of the great beast turned, too briefly, her way. But it was never enough. Whatever hold Mrs. Daughtry had got over him could not be loosened by a few words hurled at him from a distance, however gravely she insulted his honour (and she *had*).

She would have to come up with something a bit more direct, then.

He was quite close, from her present vantage-point. Close enough that she could clearly see the wan glitter of winter sun on his blazing crimson scales; so close she could hear the roar of flame, feel the searing heat on her own skin. Once, her hair had almost caught on fire.

To run such risks merely for the pleasure of shouting at an oblivious male was not the behaviour of a sensible woman, Gussie thought. But she had more at her disposal than words.

She had boiling oil.

It was perfectly possible that her aunt's crisply-delivered instructions had not been intended seriously. She had likely spoken with a mixture of exasperation, weariness and withering jest as she had retreated up into the drawing-room and firmly shut the door. But if this was so, Gabriel Footman knew nothing of it, and neither did Mrs. Gavell. Their efficient and unthinking devotion to their mistress's every wish really did them credit, and Gussie reminded herself to mention it to her aunt. They ought to be commended for it.

Before she did that, however, she had a brimming copper pot full of boiling oil at her elbow, and a recalcitrant dragon to chuck it at.

Hefting the thing was no easy matter, despite the heavy gloves someone had thoughtfully supplied, and Gussie spilled a little over her arms. She hissed with the pain of it and cursed — she would suffer some little pain from those burns later, and Henry would be hearing about it. Still, she got it to the window-ledge, and prepared herself. Henry needed only to drift a little nearer, as he often did; dragons are not made to hover smoothly in mid-air, and there was a great deal of effort involved in the business of trying. Those great, swooping wings hauled him about, and it made for an unsteady flight.

Not quite near enough. She needed to get his attention for a clear five or six seconds, that ought to be enough. But as none of her praiseworthy efforts thus far had succeeded in producing this effect, it would have to be something truly outrageous.

Hm.

Gussie gathered herself for one last effort, promising her lacerated throat that there would be tea with honey in it soon.

She inhaled a vast breath.

'HENRY!' she bawled. 'While it may be of all things the *most improper* conduct in a lady, my feelings are grown too strong to be any longer concealed. I declare my hand, my heart, and all my earthly possessions are yours if you fancy them!'

He paused. He very definitely paused.

The great, crimson head turned sharply in her direction — and here came the enormous, lashing tail sweeping nearer and nearer—

Gussie was quick. She upended the copper pot. '*Look out below!*' she thought it polite to cry, and the stream of hot oil — probably not *quite* boiling anymore, it had been sitting for a little time, but still most uncomfortable — went splattering all over the end of Lord Maundevyle's tail.

He roared. The sound was loud enough to rattle the brick-work, and Gussie took a great deal of satisfaction in it.

Particularly since it tailed off at the end into a purely human scream, and the monster the size of a small barn abruptly vanished, taking his glittering crimson scales, his fires and his draconic rage with him.

The figure that went hurtling to the ground had two arms, two legs, a rather fashionable haircut and a good black coat.

'Oops,' said Gussie, watching his precipitate progress down into the garden with some small twinges of unease.

He landed inelegantly, but since this transformation had been effected at least halfway down, he did not appear to have met any especially messy end below. Nothing broken, she judged, or at least, nothing important.

Gussie permitted herself a smile of satisfaction.

'Excellent!' she declared, rather hoarsely; the word

emerged cracked and half in a whisper. She cleared her tortured throat, withdrawing herself, at last, from the window, and the freezing air beyond—

Mostly. For that was when she saw Theo — and Arabella Everleigh, upon whom he was advancing with no promising demeanour.

'Oh, for goodness' sake,' she gasped, and went pelting back downstairs.

* * *

Upon his return to the bosom of his noble parents, Theo's mood might best be described as *murderous.*

It had all been going charmingly. He had been cradled in the arms of a woman of surpassing beauty; kissed within an inch of his life; feeling all sorts of gentlemanly, not to say *manly,* impulses in the direction of her protection, which was unusual for him; and perhaps that was what had done it, in the end, the sheer incongruity of such feelings taking up space in Theo's breast — *Theo!* Of all people! He could palpably hear Gussie saying these very words, in tones of withering incredulity.

Whatever had done it, something had changed. Something had *snapped.* The parts of Theo's mind that had been lulled into complying docility by Mrs. Daughtry's strange and compelling arts had abruptly woken up.

And the desirable angel in his arms had promptly lost rather a lot of her gilded lustre.

The results had been — less attractive.

And now, *now,* when he had stalked across the city on foot, too irritated to get into a carriage; fought his way past pedestrians aplenty and through freezing fog; endured the intolerable discomfort of his bloodied shirt-front sticking to his heated flesh; well, he had been treated to the sight of Lord Maundevyle engaged in a spirited attempt to burn the inconvenient Mrs. Everleigh out of his father's townhouse after all, and getting along pretty well with it.

Not only that, but here were Ballantine and Mrs. Everleigh herself, looking at Theo as though they were mightily displeased with him.

And a ways beyond them, sitting on the front steps of the house, with a three-cornered hat on her head and a pistol in her hands, was Clarissa Selwyn. Her hostage had thought it politic to seat himself upon the cold pavement and keep himself very still, which seemed wise to Theo. Were he face-to-face with Miss Selwyn, armed, he might comport himself much the same.

'What in the *blazes* is going on?' said Theo.

'Oh, everything is as you see it,' answered Mr. Ballantine, eyeing Theo rather closely, for no reason Theo could determine. 'Lord Maundevyle has been ensorcelled into a dangerous fit of destructiveness, but I trust in your cousin's powers of persuasion — or at least, aggravation — to deal with that problem. Ah, yes. There.'

As the Runner spoke, the gouts of flame came to a sudden end, and the dragon vanished. Theo did not see what became of him, save that there was a bit of screaming going on.

'And *once* I had sufficient leisure to notice, I observed that his lordship's sister has one of our dastardly villains well in hand,' Ballantine continued. 'And now there is only the problem of Mrs. Daughtry to be considered — and, of course, you.'

'Me?'

Mrs. Everleigh, too, was subjecting him to a close and wary scrutiny. He attempted to pacify her with a smile, but this had not the effect he was hoping for. Perhaps it was the bloodied shirt-front that did it.

'Theo!' The voice was Gussie's, if lacking its usual strength and power. Here she came, striding out of the front door and shouldering her way past Clarissa-and-hostage as though their presence there were the most natural thing in the world. She appeared a little dishevelled, one arm streaked with livid red marks, and was that *oil* all over her skirts?

She, too, seemed unhappy with him, judging from her wrathful expression.

'Yes, what is it?' he said, with barely concealed impatience.

'Whose blood is that? Say it does not belong to some helpless innocent you happened to stride by in this pretty temper.'

'No,' said Theo.

He was standing quite near to Mrs. Everleigh, but unless he mistook the evidence of his eyes, that lady was bristling with wariness and attempting to distance herself from him. What's more, Gussie and Mr. Ballantine both had placed themselves where they could hurl themselves upon Theo at a moment's notice.

'Oh, I see,' he said. 'You imagine I am about to turn all *Charles Selwyn* and savage Mrs. Everleigh to death. Well, I won't.'

'Have you then savaged Mrs. Daughtry to death?' Gussie guessed. 'Bravo, Theo! I don't know when any news has pleased me more.'

'She may not be *dead*, entirely,' Theo answered, and shrugged up his shoulders.

'As long as she is safely insensible, at the least, then we may dispatch our good Mr. Ballantine to remove her,' said Gussie, with high good cheer. 'Whereabouts did you leave her possibly-lifeless corpse?'

'My rooms.'

Mrs. Everleigh was shaking her head. 'I really did think him on the point of doing something terrible,' she said with chagrin. 'My senses must be becoming disordered.'

Theo realised, belatedly, that she was referring to him.

'Oh, that is just Theo,' said Gussie. 'He is always on the point of doing something terrible.'

Mr. Ballantine, ogre-shaped, abruptly deflated into his human form. He adjusted his collar and the hang of his coat, regarding Theo with a mixture of exasperation and...

approval? 'It is not ordinarily my habit to applaud shows of violence among civilians,' he said. 'But in this case, I believe I am grateful to you, Lord Bedgberry.' He paused, and added, 'Though I should imagine it more convenient for everybody if she does not prove to be entirely exsanguinated. I shall have enough trouble over the matter of Charles Selwyn.'

'Poor Charles,' Clarissa put in. 'But he has had his revenge, I suppose. Hasn't he, Mr. Pile?' She smiled nicely at the man, whose aggression seemed to have dissipated into a simmering, and largely impotent, resentment. It fairly boiled off him.

All she received in response was a snarl.

'I had better see to poor Lord Maundevyle,' Gussie said. 'Everyone is likely to be rather wrath with him, unfortunately, but he will be all over bruises and in need of some attention.' She went back into the house, presumably to fish a slightly-battered Henry out of the garden.

Satisfied, now, that Theo posed no further threat, Mr. Ballantine turned his attention to Clarissa and Mr. Pile. 'Well, and what is to be done with you?' he mused, quickly taking charge of Pile. 'Thank you, Miss Selwyn, but I believe you may put the pistol away. And I should prefer it if you would,' he added, when Clarissa showed signs of incipient objection.

Clarissa sighed, and complied. 'I quite see why Gussie wants to become a Bow Street Runner,' she declared, shoving the pistol into a pocket of her red frock coat. 'It has all been rapturously exciting.'

'You're all monsters,' snarled Robert Pile. 'The lot of you.'

'Why, how kind,' simpered Clarissa. 'We do try.'

'Come, man, what have you been about?' said Ballantine, even as he secured Pile against all possibility of escape. 'It *was* you who abandoned Mrs. Everleigh at this house, was not it?'

He did not receive an especially coherent reply.

'Monsters,' he spat again, and for all his apparent docility of a moment before, he attempted to wrest himself from Ballantine's powerful grip. The target of all this wrath was — again, to his surprise — Theo.

'What on earth have *I* done?' said Theo, feeling rather injured. Really, all he did all day was *read,* and occasionally refresh himself with a little sustenance. Was that such an offence?

'Oh, we had a nice little chat while we waited for you,' offered Clarissa. 'It is all quite simple, really.'

'Do enlighten us, Miss Selwyn,' sighed Ballantine.

'Mr. Pile has a brother,' she said.

'And?'

'A soldiering brother.'

Gussie emerged from the house again, just in time to hear this disclosure. She had Lord Maundevyle with her. The man was indeed bruised, and he leaned rather heavily upon Gussie, but he appeared capable of largely independent movement. Not dead, then.

'A soldiering brother,' Gussie repeated. 'Is that the aforementioned William?'

Clarissa's smile was broad, and laced with a glittering satisfaction. 'None of us has met him, of course,' she said, silkily. 'Except for *you*, Gussie.'

'Now, how could I possibly have met Mr. Pile's broth— oh, dear.'

It took Theo a little longer to grasp Clarissa's meaning. Pile was of no high standing, so his brother could not be the sort of person Gussie would mix with in society. And if he was a soldier, then he wasn't in service, and— oh, dear.

'General Sir Robert Epworth?' said Gussie in a faint voice.

'General Sir Robert Epworth,' purred Clarissa. 'You did fine, thorough work, Gussie, and you are hardly to be blamed if not *everyone* is delighted with the results.'

It took Theo a moment to remember. Gussie had been

solicited by the aforementioned General to work her mysterious Wyrde upon a number of his men. Rather a large number, as it had turned out.

And, being Gussie, she had blithely done so, leaving a great many freshly-Wyrded soldiers and officers in her wake.

Gussie gave a short, irritated sigh. 'Why is it that people persist in believing that I have any control whatsoever over the nature of their own Wyrde?' I assure you, Mr. Pile, whatever Wyrde your brother manifested was the product of his own, latent capacities. I did not inflict it on him out of some pitiful desire to torment him. I have neither the inclination nor the power.'

'What did become of him?' asked Theo curiously.

'He and his brother share the same Wyrde,' Clarissa said, when Pile did not reply. 'Similar to Lord Bedgberry's, in fact. Only it seems William was not so accepting of it as our own, dear Theo appears to be.'

'He couldn't bear it,' put in Pile, unexpectedly. 'Said as I was filth. A *monster*. And how he were a monster, too, and he wouldn't have none of it.'

'He's gone, is he?' said Mr. Ballantine, gently enough.

Pile nodded, curtly. 'Buried him three weeks gone.'

There was silence following this pronouncement. Theo felt a stab of pity for the man and his unhappy brother, and even Gussie seemed to feel it, for she had nothing tart to say.

'And if you hadn't Wyrded him,' said Pile, 'you and your monstrous bloody family, he'd still be here. He weren't the one that was a monster. That's *you*.'

'Steady, now,' Theo objected, somewhat to his own surprise. 'Gussie only did as she was asked.'

'True,' Gussie said. 'But I did it in a thoughtless spirit and it did not enter my head that anyone might suffer for it. My apologies, Mr. Pile.'

He did not seem pacified. Perhaps his brother's words, and his fate, had rankled with him, though Theo could not altogether understand it. Just because someone else said you were a monster and you deserved to die, did that make you one? No. Did it mean you had to suffer and sigh, and torment yourself and others over it? No. Honestly, some people could blame others for *everything*.

'I had better apprehend Mrs. Daughtry,' said Mr. Ballantine, 'and convey her to gaol, or the morgue, as proves appropriate.'

'What about Pile?' said Gussie. 'After all, he has not actually killed anyone. Has he?'

'He has aided Mrs. Daughtry in her schemes,' said Ballantine. 'Though you paid for your activities with your life, didn't you, Mr. Pile? You went to the Selwyn house looking for evidence of Mrs. Everleigh's fate, evidence you could transplant to the Werth residence, and use to implicate *them*. Charles Selwyn caught you.'

'Ungrateful bitch,' growled Mr. Pile, ignoring the entire question of Charles Selwyn. 'I'd have done anything for her. Anything. But no sooner is my back turned than she's swanned off wi' some lord or another, and what of me? Off doing her bidding, like a fool.'

'Insupportable conduct,' said Gussie, nodding. 'Mr. Ballantine, if you should happen to find Mrs. Daughtry still alive, pray enquire with her about Mr. Pile. It is my belief Charles Selwyn would not have killed him, however disordered his wits, unless he had been instructed to do so by that lady.'

'You may be right, Miss Werth,' Ballantine allowed. 'Getting the truth out of her may be difficult, but life is full of these challenges.'

Pile appeared shocked at the idea, but Gussie was relentless. 'I am sorry, Mr. Pile, but it is best that you know. You were the only person who knew all her secrets, you see? Your very willingness to assist her meant that you were the only person who could betray her. When ensorcelled Charles Selwyn to kill Arabella Everleigh, she also compelled him to kill *you*. And it was probably she who dispatched you to the Selwyn house, too, even if you imagined it to be your own idea. She could not have known, then, about my uncle's Wyrde. She expected both of you to remain safely dead.'

Robert Pile had not time to make any further response; Ballantine, shaking his head, was hauling him away. 'You may be right, Miss Werth,' said the Runner again as he departed. 'Indeed, I hope so.'

So did Theo, a little. Charles Selwyn might be a horrible little man, but he did not deserve to hang for the crime of being susceptible to Mrs. Daughtry's unpleasant powers. Probably.

Lord Maundevyle had taken a seat upon the same steps lately vacated by Clarissa, and had not, until this moment, spoken. He looked sheepish and winded and in disrepair, but at Ballantine's parting words, his head came up. 'Charles would never go so far unless compelled,' he said. 'He may be a little wild sometimes, but he is no monster.'

'Neither are you,' said Gussie, soothingly.

'Even if I did very nearly burn down yet another of your houses?' His smile was faint, and crooked.

'All Mrs. Daughtry's doing,' Gussie said. 'And Theo has already taken his pound of flesh for it.'

Henry nodded. 'We have proved sadly susceptible to mesmerism, Charles and I. It is a little embarrassing.'

'Don't punish yourself,' said Theo. 'So did I.'

'Gosh, yes,' put in Gussie. 'I've never seen Theo fuss and flutter over a lady before. It was almost diverting.'

'Almost?' echoed Henry.

'It would have been the more diverting had it been less pathetic.'

'I wish I had mesmeric powers,' mused Clarissa. 'I would put them to far better use than Marianne Daughtry, too.'

'Heaven forbid,' said Henry, with a shudder.

Mrs. Everleigh spoke up. 'It could all be construed as my fault. If I had not decided to return to the stage,

Marianne might have gone on reigning over Strangewayes to her heart's content.'

Gussie shook her head. 'You should only blame yourself when it is absolutely unavoidable,' she said firmly. 'And even then, it is not very advisable.'

For once, Theo found himself in clear agreement with his cousin. 'The fault lies squarely at Mrs. Daughtry's feet. And Strangewayes will likely be the better for Marianne Daughtry's absence.'

'Shall you go on with your stage career, after all this?' asked Gussie.

Mrs. Everleigh did not need to give the matter any thought at all. 'Of a certainty. I shan't be prevented by such a little matter as murder.'

'That's the spirit,' Gussie approved.

'A question, Miss Werth, if I may,' said Henry.

'Yes, Lord Maundevyle?'

'Did you mean what you said?'

Gussie's only response to this was a roll of her eyes.

'Oh,' said Henry.

'It's my belief she meant every word,' offered Clarissa, with a wink as roguish as it was insinuating.

'What did she say?' asked Theo, who had either been too distracted or too out of distance to catch the words. 'And when?'

'No matter,' muttered Henry.

Gussie, to his annoyance and surprise, went off into a peal of laughter. And no matter how he asked or cajoled, she never would afterwards tell him what it had been.

EIGHTEEN

'I have been looking all over for you, Frosty, and here you still are. What have you been doing?'

It was Gussie who spoke, having sought her trusty companion at home to no avail, and having finally returned to the last place she had seen her: the home of the Maundevyles.

And there was Miss Frostell, and Great-Uncle Silvester, too. The pair were holed up in a suite of rooms a little secluded from the rest of the house; Gussie was conducted up by no less a person than Lady Maundevyle herself, in a markedly better humour than before.

'Your excellent governess remains with us, Miss Werth, together with your noble ancestor, and — as you will presently see! — they have been doing dear Charles a *great deal* of good. It is really so obliging of them. I have been uneasy about him, as you may imagine, and really, nothing could be more obliging than — yes, here we are, we will just knock upon the door before we go in; Charles does not bear surprises well at present, and we would not like to precipitate another unfortunate little event, would we?'

Gussie wondered at the sight of so proud and resentful a woman now politely rapping upon the door of her son's rooms before she entered, and all affability towards Gussie herself. Perhaps she was not entirely devoid of better feelings after all, or wholly lacking in affection for her children.

Or perhaps she had only resented the scandal of it all, and was pleased by any reduction in inconvenience. Gussie found her impossibly difficult to fathom.

'Charles!' carolled Lady Maundevyle, opening the door. 'Ah, Miss Frostell! Lord Silvester! Charming. I have brought you a visitor, as you see. And I shall have refreshments sent up immediately, for I am sure you must all be very hungry by this time.'

'That would be most welcome, your ladyship,' admitted Miss Frostell, looking up from a book she had apparently been reading from. Great-Uncle Silvester's gravelly voice continued to roll on in the background, pitched so low that Gussie could hear little of whatever he was saying.

The scene that unfolded before Gussie's wondering eyes was one of tranquil domesticity. The trio were gathered in a comfortable sitting-room, of no expansive proportions, but handsomely fitted-up. The decorative theme ran along crimson lines, brocade and polished teak and large sash windows overlooking the street two storeys below. A neat fire blazed in the hearth, before which sat Frosty in a deep armchair; Great-Uncle Silvester, perched upon the back of an antique couch; and slumped upon this handsome article was Charles Selwyn himself.

He was not nearly so well-groomed as Gussie had seen him before. In fact, he looked quite wild, at least in terms of his outer appearance: his hair had not known the attentions of a brush in some days, she judged, nor had he permitted himself to be shaved. He sat in shirt-sleeves and waistcoat, both of which were rumpled and a little stained, and he was restless, for his hands fidgeted endlessly with the fobs and seals with which his garments were adorned.

But there was an alteration in him, for he sat clear-eyed and quiet enough, restored to passable humanity and perfectly safe to approach. If he had temporarily lost himself to his lycanthropic side, little of the beast remained about him now.

'How good of you to come looking for me, my dear,' said Miss Frostell, smiling at Gussie. 'We have been keeping poor Mr. Selwyn company, Lord Silvester and I.'

'So I see, and to no inconsequential effect.' Gussie reposed herself upon a foot-stool near to the fire — she had got very cold today, what with all the dashing about in the fog — and subjected Mr. Selwyn to a considering stare.

He, surprisingly, smiled. 'Miss Werth. I don't suppose you would give up your governess to me entirely? She is a treasure.'

'She is not, in point of fact, my governess,' Gussie answered. 'She hasn't been for some years, and is at her own disposal.'

'I could not leave my dear Miss Werth, sir, but I shall be delighted to visit at any time you may care for another story.'

'Stories? Have you been regaling Mr. Selwyn with stories, Frosty?'

'Yes, my dear. It occurred to me — and your dear uncle, Lord Silvester — that poor Mr. Selwyn had perhaps got himself confused, and forgotten that he is a man, and not some wild creature. We did not immediately know what might be done about this, save to talk to him, and bear him company, and so we have.'

'The Whites never did have a modicum of sense between them,' Silvester put in.

Miss Frostell, oddly, blushed. 'I admit, we began less blamelessly. We have been talking to Mr. Selwyn about all his friends in London, and the great many interesting things they have been doing.'

'Gossip,' said Gussie, delighted. 'You retrieved Mr. Selwyn's wits with gossip! I am paralysed with admiration, Frosty.'

Miss Frostell, really far too good a character for the

household in which she found herself, did not like to view herself as a gossip. She flushed deeper, and went on, rather hurriedly, 'We ran out of news, of course, after a time, and it was your uncle's suggestion to take up a story-book instead. We have got one that is not too fanciful — not one of those with castles and villains and dark deeds, that is.'

'No, indeed. That might appeal to all the wrong instincts,' Gussie agreed. 'What have you been reading, instead?'

'It is called *Mansfield Park*,' said Miss Frostell, 'and I believe it was written by a lady. A very proper tale, about real people such as you and I.' Honesty compelled her to stop, and add, 'People such as I, that is. There do not seem to be any Wyrded people in it.'

'And you have been finding it enjoyable, have you, Mr. Selwyn?' asked Gussie.

'I believe I did not fully take in the earlier chapters,' he admitted. 'But subsequently I have been more absorbed than I might have expected.'

Quite the spectacle, for the last time Gussie had seen Charles Selwyn, he had been sulky, unpleasant and inclined to torment those about him for some private entertainment of his own. Now he was positively congenial. His recent experiences had achieved the impossible, and humbled him, though she did not particularly expect the effect to prove lasting.

Gussie beamed. 'Well, Frosty, you have been performing wonderful work. I am happy to tell you that, while you have been so blamelessly occupied, *we* have been very busy indeed. And now Mr. Ballantine has apprehended the villainess of our little story, and all is made safe.'

Mr. Selwyn's pleasant humour vanished. 'She ought to hang,' he said, darkly.

'In all likelihood, she will,' Gussie agreed. 'And I can set your mind at rest, sir. Mr. Ballantine is fully aware that you acted under that lady's undue influence, and not according to your own will.' She held his gaze as she spoke, aware that some small question remained as to the fate of Robert Pile. The theory she had herself put forward — that Mrs. Daughtry had preferred for the ensorcelled Mr. Selwyn to dispose of him for her — was plausible enough, but it might also be untrue.

She also felt, however, that if Selwyn had, in his disordered state, succumbed to a certain rage at the manner in which he had been treated by that miserable pair, and expressed it rather forcefully, he was not altogether to be blamed for it.

Charles Selwyn never blinked. 'I am pleased to hear it, Miss Werth.'

In all probability, the real truth would never be fully known. Gussie could not regret it.

She remained some little time longer with the cosy trio, availing herself of some of the cakes and tarts Lady Maundevyle had caused to be sent up, and regaling Frosty, Mr. Selwyn and Great-Uncle Silvester with a spirited account of her own, and Theo's, doings.

And when at last it came time to take her leave, she took Miss Frostell and her attendant grotesque with her — with a promise to return upon the morrow, for more of *Mansfield Park*.

'You would be most welcome to join us, my dear,' said Miss Frostell.

Gussie looked to Mr. Selwyn for permission. To her own surprise (and, perhaps, to his), this was granted.

'Thank you, Frosty,' she said. 'I believe I shall.'

But upon arriving home in the gathering dark, Gussie encountered not the serenity of restored peace, as she had expected, but some fresh hubbub, centred around her uncle's house.

Lord Werth's carriage had conveyed her to the

Maundevyle establishment, and now brought her back again, with Miss Frostell and Great-Uncle Silvester. When she had left in search of Frosty, Clarissa had been somewhere inside, tending to her brother Henry (after whatever fashion suited her; likely some mixture of real care for the injuries he had suffered, and a rousing mockery for the foolishness or susceptibility that had betrayed him into it). Neither had yet seemed disposed to return to their own home.

Lady Werth had not yet emerged from the drawing-room. Theo had collected six or seven books, and shut himself upstairs. Mrs. Everleigh had retired to her bedchamber, or possibly the garden, Gussie knew not which. Great-Aunt Honoria and Ivo Farthing had declared themselves exhausted after their fire-fighting efforts, as well they might be, and had vanished behind the firmly-shut door of their shared attic room.

As for Mr. Ballantine, he was probably restored to Bow Street, seeing to the dual problems posed by Robert Pile and Marianne Daughtry, and would not emerge for some time.

They ought, then, to have returned to a quiet street and a quieter house, but the pavement proved to be swarming with people. The carriage had to be halted a little way up the street, obliging Gussie and Miss Frostell to push their way through the crowd to reach their own front-door. Neither the darkness nor the thickening fog proved any deterrent whatsoever to the determined souls.

'What can be the meaning of this?' Gussie huffed, too weary herself to feel anything but annoyance at this development. Even her natural curiosity seemed all used up. 'Gracious, Frosty, some of these people seem to be—'

'Dead,' agreed Miss Frostell. 'Oh, dear.'

And so they were. Properly dead, conveyed in their coffins (in some cases), or on the shoulders of their living kin (in others). Gussie saw grief-stricken faces everywhere she looked, and began to understand. 'I have got out of touch with the newspapers, Frosty,' she said, abandoning her efforts to penetrate the mob, and retiring to the edges of it. 'Has there been something said about my uncle?'

'Aye,' came the answer, but it was Jem Coachman who spoke. 'Been a deal said about Mrs. Everleigh and that other actor, and how they isn't, rightly speaking, as dead as they oughta be, what with bein' murdered.'

'Yes, but that's been the case since last week.'

'And now sommat's been written about Lord Werth's part in it, Miss. Reckon it's all over London by this time.'

Oh, dear. This was a problem, indeed. If all of London was now informed as to the nature of Lord Werth's Wyrde, why, they would all be wanting their dead relatives revived.

Judging from the crowds of hopeful supplicants, near half of London did. And more were arriving all the time.

'Where is my uncle, Jem? Do you know?' Lord Werth had returned in the mid-afternoon, and upon hearing of the damage to the roof, had retired immediately into his book-room. An understandable response, Gussie thought, on the whole.

'Last I knew he was shut up in his library, Miss. He won't be pleased to hear of this, not one bit.'

He wouldn't, indeed. It was too late to take it up with whichever irresponsible paper had advertised his capabilities, either; they might be successfully forced to pay for the damage they had done, but nothing could undo it.

'I had not known Lord Werth's Wyrde to be so very rare as all that,' Miss Frostell commented. 'To look at all these poor folk, you'd think they had never heard of it before.'

'I never heard of any such thing, to be sure,' said Jem. 'Here, reckon as we'd best get you in another way. Round the back. Come on.'

Gussie had never gone in by the back door before, but under Jem Coachman's care — and with the judicious use of his elbows, and an occasional fist — they were successfully restored to the house, and Jem left to oversee the return of Lord Werth's carriage and horses into their proper places.

That left the problem of what to do about the mob. Gussie, never usually short on ideas, found herself at a loss. It had been all too exciting a week, and far too exciting a day; she was quite weary.

Inside, the house was so quiet there might have been some enchantment upon it, that had sent all its inhabitants into slumber. Gussie steeled herself, and went towards the book-room.

'Uncle?' she said, having tapped upon the door, and tentatively opened it. 'I am sorry to disturb you with another problem, but you had perhaps better look out of one of the front windows.'

Judging from Lord Werth's expression, he had been wishing that whatever errand had kept him away from the house all day had gone on rather longer. His brows snapped together, but any irascible response he might have made dissipated in a sigh. 'Some fresh disaster?' he said, rising from his comfortable chair before the fire.

'Come upstairs,' was all that Gussie said by way of answer.

Shortly afterwards, gathered together at a window overlooking the street, Gussie and her uncle spent some several minutes half-hidden behind the heavy drapes as they observed the tumultuous scene. 'The work of some newspaperman, apparently,' said she. 'Not only is London informed as to the *fact* of Mrs. Everleigh's return to life, they are now also informed as to the *method* of it.'

'I cannot *give* life to them, Gussie,' said Lord Werth. 'Only some semblance of it, and it is not the same thing at all.'

'No, but to them it must seem to be close enough.'

He sighed. 'It is not that I am without sympathy for them, but I cannot haul every deceased and lamented Londoner out of the grave. They must see that, surely.'

They palpably did not. Silence reigned at the window, neither Gussie nor Lord Werth being blessed with any helpful ideas as to how to proceed.

More people were arriving, some carting corpses, some without. The importunate crowd, Gussie foresaw, would be there forever, growing ever larger. They would never be able to safely leave the premises again. Even Mr. Ballantine must be stymied by this situation.

She traced an idle shape upon the cold, half-frosted window, watching as yet another new individual added himself to the melee. Though this person, it seemed, possessed some better capacity than the rest, for managing crowds; he did not linger upon the edges of the mob, but by some mysterious means threaded his way seamlessly through it, pausing occasionally to speak to some of those he passed. To Gussie's surprise, one or two of these turned away, and left. Then several more.

By the time the newcomer had worked his way to the doorstep, the mob was thinned to half its former size, and still decreasing.

Gussie exchanged an astonished look with her uncle.

'We should find out who it is,' she said, when a loud knock resounded upon the front door.

Gabriel Footman was already moving to open it, when Gussie got into the hall. On the other side stood the mysterious newcomer, neatly dressed in a dark overcoat and hat. He in no way looked as though he had just fought his way through so desperate a clamour as had recently occupied the street outside. There was not a mark on him.

'Lord Werth?' he said, espying Gussie and her uncle in the hallway. 'Miss Werth? Excellent. How good of you to come to welcome me in person.'

He made a movement, as though he would come in, but Gabriel Footman held up a hand. 'Not likely, sir. Who might you be?'

'Cornelius Goodspeed,' came the answer, and Mr. Goodspeed doffed his hat. He proved to be an elderly man, his hair quite white, and his face as wrinkled as crumpled paper. But his grey eyes were bright and keen, and there had been no hint of infirmity or failing vigour in his step. 'I am here to take up the position of butler,' he added.

'Oh, have we secured one at last?' said Gussie, interested.

'No,' said Lord Werth.

Mr. Goodspeed smiled. 'But you must have done so before long, for I perceive you to be in great need of one.'

'How did you disperse the crowd?' asked Lord Werth.

'I can be persuasive.' Mr. Goodspeed said nothing more, nor did he need to. The effects of his persuasive nature had just been ably demonstrated.

'Gabriel,' said Lord Werth. 'Please take Mr. Goodspeed to Mrs. Gavell, with instructions to get him settled in. Lady Werth will see you in the morning, Mr. Goodspeed. At present, she is a little indisposed.'

Mr. Goodspeed bowed. 'Very good, my lord.'

And so it came about that the household at the house of Werth was augmented by one, very capable butler. And he lost no time ingratiating himself with either Lady Werth or Mrs. Gavell, for among his many talents was one of particular aptness to the circumstances: he proved curiously adept at removing old bloodstains from fine carpets, and Lady Werth's favourite parlour was, by this means, saved.

And while, for some weeks longer, supplicants for Lord Werth's estimable powers continued to arrive at the door, a word or two from Mr. Goodspeed proved amply sufficient to turn them away again.

More From
Charlotte E. English

House of Werth:

Wyrde and Wayward
Wyrde and Wicked
Wyrde and Wild

Modern Magick:

The Road to Farringale
Toil and Trouble
The Striding Spire
The Fifth Britain
...and more!

www.charlotteenglish.com

Made in United States
North Haven, CT
25 November 2022

27195107R00131